C000065154

Born and raised in Stockport, J.D. Welch has always loved reading, puzzles and music. After graduating in Chemistry from Oxford, she had a variety of management roles before becoming a sales and marketing director.

Since having children, she has focused on caring for her family, writing, coding and continuing to recommend great reads.

Dear Fellow Reader,

Thank you so much for choosing this book, the third and final part of my first trilogy, which began with *The Einstein Code* and continued with *The Darwin Code*. I so hope you enjoy it.

If you also enjoy puzzles, you might have fun with the codes and ciphers within the books and also on my coding website:

www.juniorcodecrackers.com

On it you will find lots of other ciphers and codes to try, plus tips and hints on setting and cracking codes. You could even be JCC Champion of the Month and join lots of other superb code crackers in being named on the site.

You never can tell who might see your name…

Warmest wishes,

J.D. Welch

To Laura, Emma and Neil, with love.

J.D. Welch

THE QUANTUM CODE

AUSTIN MACAULEY PUBLISHERS™

LONDON • CAMBRIDGE • NEW YORK • SHARJAH

Copyright © J.D. Welch (2018)

The right of J.D. Welch to be identified as author of this work has been asserted by her in accordance with section 77 and 78 of the Copyright, Designs and Patents Act 1988.

All rights reserved. No part of this publication may be reproduced, stored in a retrieval system, or transmitted in any form or by any means, electronic, mechanical, photocopying, recording, or otherwise, without the prior permission of the publishers.

Any person who commits any unauthorised act in relation to this publication may be liable to criminal prosecution and civil claims for damages.

A CIP catalogue record for this title is available from the British Library.

ISBN 9781528911566 (Paperback)
ISBN 9781528911573 (E-Book)

www.austinmacauley.com

First Published (2018)
Austin Macauley Publishers Ltd™
25 Canada Square
Canary Wharf
London
E14 5LQ

My warmest thanks to all of you who have read, enjoyed and reviewed my books; and to all the lovely people who have invited me into schools, libraries, societies and to festivals to discuss code cracking and writing. It means so much to me.

Thank you to all my fellow writers at SCBWI, who have supported me with feedback, encouragement and friendship, especially Alison, Dale, George, Andy, Kathryn, Anne, Deborah, Susan and Cath; and also to Marion and Catherine for all the work you have put into organising our northwest branch.

Special thanks to Neil and Emma for reading the entire book and giving valuable feedback on it, to Laura and Emma for artistic input, and to my family and friends for the fun, laughter and companionship we all enjoy so much.

Chapter 1

The Critical Test

Life was about to change forever – on the basis of a yellow stick? Amazing that those six swabs would reveal the answer to a life-long mystery Ben hadn't even realised existed until yesterday. But before he could unwrap it, a nurse opened the door, banging Freddie's back.

'Ow!' he complained, glaring at her, as if not having X-ray vision was her fault.

'Sorry.' Her eyebrows rose as she saw Ben's visitors. 'It should only be two to a bed.'

'I'm taking care of my niece and nephew until my sister gets back,' Mum explained, gesturing towards Jess and Freddie. 'With all that's happened, I can't let them out of my sight. She shouldn't be long.'

'Let's hope so. Else matron will have my guts for garters.' The nurse squeezed past Jess and Mum to get to Ben's side, her kind face radiating concern. 'How are you?'

'Fine, thanks,' Ben assured her, determined to get back home.

She didn't seem to believe him, because she checked his blood pressure for perhaps the fortieth time that afternoon – or so it seemed.

But this time she smiled. 'It's fine now. You can leave if you want.'

'Yes!' Ben punched the air triumphantly. 'We'll be home for my birthday!'

'Traffic permitting. Where are they?' Mum complained again, checking her watch. Aunt Miriam and Uncle Henry had returned to the hotel to pick up their bags and Mum's car, but had been absent for ages. Until then, Ben was confined to bed, since he didn't have any clothes, apart from the flimsy hospital gown. The police had taken everything he had been wearing in the pool for evidence.

The nurse left to get the doctor to sign him out.

'Can't wait to get home.'

'We need to get this done first,' Marcus said, handing Mum her swab.

'I'm pink and you're blue? That's so sexist!' she complained.

'Exactly!' Jess agreed.

Marcus shared a smile with Ben. 'I'd gladly take the pink swabs, but it would probably confuse them.'

'Yeah, they'd get a Y-tail where they were looking for an X,' Ben said.

'That's right!' Freddie cried. With his eyebrows raised and his bulging eyes, he looked insultingly astonished.

'I'm not stupid, you know! Dads have an X and a Y, and mums have two X chromosomes.'

'At last,' Freddie muttered.

Ben flashed him the glare he deserved.

'Ben's a bright boy, just like his mum,' Marcus said.

Appreciating the support, Ben smiled at him, a little shy now that their new relationship was beginning. Never having had a father, Ben was unsure how it would feel. It was strange to think Marcus was just as much a part of him as Mum.

He was paying for the twenty-four-hour turnaround too. What an amazing birthday present it would be to have a dad as brave, generous and good as Marcus. His fourteenth birthday was going to be his best birthday ever.

'Do you think we might try simultaneous swabbing?' Marcus asked, raising an eyebrow at Mum, as if flirting. Ben shot him a look. His blue eyes were twinkling.

'I think we might risk it,' Mum replied, deadpan.

'So we swab one cheek for thirty seconds, right?' Ben checked, desperate not to muck this up, the most important test of his life.

'I'll time you,' Jess volunteered, looking at her watch. They waited. 'Right, go! Isn't it exciting?'

'Hn,' Ben agreed, rubbing the swab against the inside of his left cheek.

'One swab would be perfectly adequate, but I suppose the other is in case some idiot gets hold of the wrong end,' Freddie said.

'I' is 'e righ' en',' Ben retorted, knowing that when Freddie said, 'idiot', he generally meant him.

'Time's up!' Jess said.

Ben leaned over and inserted the yellow swab into the stand on his bedside table.

'Careful it doesn't touch mine,' Marcus warned as he and Mum inserted theirs. 'We don't want to cross-contaminate.'

'No. This test has got to be right,' Mum replied.

'Yes. Belt and braces. I don't want Rufus messing things up,' Marcus said, displaying the animosity towards his elder brother which Ben could well understand.

Mum had shocked them all yesterday by revealing that his father was not an IVF donor, (a life-long lie he'd completely swallowed) but either Marcus or his brother. Apparently, she'd had a brief fling with Rufus, in an attempt to get over her breakup with Marcus, and later realised she was pregnant. But whereas Marcus had been delighted, once the shock had dissipated, Rufus's determination not to be Ben's dad had been deeply offensive and hurtful.

'You're wasting your time. Marcus is definitely your dad,' Freddie said again, as all three of them swabbed their other cheeks. 'My paternity test was scientifically sound.'

Mum removed her swab. 'As far as we know. The earwax studies are small and limited.'

'Yes, but in the absence of new studies, and unless a mutation has occurred at that particular site, which is extremely unlikely, it *was* scientifically sound.'

'I know, Freddie. And thank you. But this tests multiple sites, and is therefore safer,' Mum said, depositing her second swab into the stand. Ben added his with a pleasant ripple of excitement, followed by Marcus, who grinned at him.

'What next?' Mum asked.

Marcus flicked through the instructions and looked up, grimacing. 'You don't happen to have your passports with you?'

'I've got mine in my bag, but not Ben's,' Mum said.

'Do you have a photo of him?'

'I always carry Ben's photo. Will this do?' Mum showed it to everyone. There he stood, gawky, gap-toothed and grinning gormlessly.

'I was about five!' Ben complained.

'Six.'

'You haven't changed much. Apart from the teeth,' Marcus teased.

'Thanks,' Ben said, sarcastically.

'That's not recent enough, is it?' Jess said.

'It's the only one I have with me while the police have my phone.'

'I'll take one now,' Marcus offered.

'Not wearing this,' Ben protested, meaning the hospital gown.

Marcus shrugged. 'Take it off then.'

'No way. I'd be naked.'

Jess giggled, blushing. With two brothers (Robert, 17, was at home in Didsbury), Ben would have thought she was well used to male bodies by now, but approaching 13, she was probably prey to the hormones that made teenage life so exciting – and occasionally embarrassing. Or maybe it wasn't just hormones. He was prey to treacherous blushes too. It might be yet another physical trait he and his favourite cousin shared, as well as their blue eyes and blond hair. Which Marcus had too, but not Rufus. As far as Ben was concerned, he didn't need the paternity test. Marcus was definitely his dad. But Mum was a scientist and Mum wanted to be sure.

'If I can have your phone, I'll take a selfie,' Ben said.

Marcus passed over his phone. 'Remember, don't smile.'

'Marcus, if you're Ben's dad then you'll be my uncle, won't you?' Jess said.

'Not unless I'm Sue's husband, no, sadly not,' he replied.

Mum span around. '*What*?'

Marcus raised his hands in feigned innocence. 'I was just pointing out that I'm not genetically related to Jess, just as Henry is only Ben's uncle by being married to Miriam. Otherwise he'd be no relation.'

'You had your chance to be my husband fourteen years ago,' Mum retorted, with such vehemence that Ben gawped. 'You left me.'

'The most stupid thing I've ever done. Ah well, young men sometimes are stupid.'

'Young women too. To think I allowed myself to be consoled by Rufus.' Mum frowned.

'Yes. Pity that. Else we'd know for sure Ben was mine.'

'We *do*. I told you. It's a single gene.' Freddie was glaring at Mum, as if that would make her give way.

'Which could have mutated,' Mum pointed out, for about the fiftieth time.

Freddie flapped his hands, as if her argument was an annoying fly. 'A one in a billion chance.'

'If those chances didn't sometimes occur, then we wouldn't have evolved,' Mum said.

Freddie glared at her. 'I *know*! But Ben is Marcus's son, or I'm an onion.'

Jess laughed. 'I almost hope you're an onion.'

But that would mean... '*Jess*!'

'Sorry, Ben. No, of course I'm hoping Marcus is your father.'

'I'll be thrilled if I am,' Marcus said beaming, then clapped his hands. 'Right, action. I'll go and get this printed off somewhere.'

'Where?' Jess asked, never one to miss the chance of asking a question, even one as obvious as that.

'There'll be plenty of printers in the hospital.'

'They're just for hospital use, aren't they?'

'Marcus has a way with nurses,' Mum said.

'Ouch.' Marcus winced.

Why? Ben waited for him to leave before demanding an explanation.

'Marcus took someone with him on his travels after he dumped me,' Mum replied. 'A nurse he'd met.'

'Oh.'

'So you're not keen on nurses, then?' Jess asked.

'On the contrary, I think they're incredible. They've saved my son. It wasn't her fault, anyway. Marcus had broken up with me. He was a free agent.'

'He still is.'

'Apparently so, but I'm not. I've got the only man I need,' she said, smiling at Ben. He smiled back, enjoying the promotion to man. 'Can't wait to get you home,' Mum added.

'Can't wait to *get* home.'

'Where *are* Miriam and Henry?' Mum fretted, checking her watch again. 'They're taking an age.'

Where indeed? Marcus was back before they were, carrying papers.

'I've got a copy of all the documents we need. I need you to sign this, Sue, to state this is a good likeness of Ben. Ben, you need to sign this consent form, please,' he said, handing them both papers and a biro, 'then if you could pass the form on to your mum and me, we'll do the same. Then we just need to wait for our DNA to dry.'

'Another thirty minutes,' Jess said, checking her watch.

Marcus grimaced. 'Why does time go so slowly when you're desperate for something to happen?'

'Time's relative. I told you,' Freddie crowed.

'I think the credit goes to Einstein, don't you?' Mum said.

Before Freddie could reply the door opened, so Ben expected another nurse. But it was Aunt Miriam – at last! And she was carrying Ben's bag. But not Mum's.

'Oh, hello Marcus, are you still here?' she said, smiling at him.

'Mm.' Marcus smiled briefly, intent on his phone. He looked worried.

'Bad news?' Ben asked, knowing it could be from the Chief.

'Nothing for you to worry about,' Marcus replied, which could mean anything.

'Are you all right, Miriam? You seem a little distracted,' Mum asked.

Aunt Miriam was frowning. 'They wouldn't let me have your bag. Or your car.'

'Who? The hotel?'

'No. The police. They need them for evidence.'

'*No*!' Mum looked horrified.

'How will we get home?' Ben said, equally dismayed.

Mum looked at Aunt Miriam. 'Will it take long?'

'I've no idea. Sorry. Here you are, Ben,' Aunt Miriam said, handing him the bag.

'Thanks.' He started to rummage through it. It was terrible timing. The police should have inspected the car yesterday.

'Although I'm not as desperate as Ben for clothes, that's a pain too,' Mum said. 'Those clothes in the hotel are irrelevant. I wasn't wearing them when I was kidnapped. They're all new.'

'Sorry,' Aunt Miriam said.

'It's not your fault, Mimi,' Mum said, using her childhood nickname for her big sister (who was now much smaller than her, and as dark as Mum was fair). 'I'm annoyed with the police.'

'You can, of course, come home with us,' Aunt Miriam offered. 'If you want to leave your car.'

'Oh, I don't know what to do,' Mum replied. 'It all depends on how long the police want it for.'

'We can't stay in Oxford!' Ben protested.

'It might be easier.'

'*What*?'

'I'll be here,' Marcus said.

'Yeah, but I want to be home. You'll be back at work soon, won't you?' Ben asked, since SPC Agrochemicals, where Mum and Marcus worked, was based in Wilmslow, twenty minutes from Stockport on a clear run.

'Hopefully,' Marcus said, looking grim. He was probably thinking of the Chief, Ben assumed.

'Where's Henry?' Mum asked her sister.

'He's trying to find a parking place. He's a bit grumpy.'

Ben rolled his eyes. His uncle was usually grumpy.

'Come home with us,' Aunt Miriam urged.

'He won't want us crowding your car.'

'You won't be crowding our car. You're not missing Ben's birthday.'

Tomorrow. Fourteen. '*Please*, Mum.'

'Okay. I'll come back for my car later in the week,' she decided.

'*Yes*!' He resumed his search of the bag, but it wasn't there.

'Are you all right, Ben?'

'Has anyone got my phone?' If the police had taken it, he'd be in terrible trouble for not revealing the Chief's texts.

'I stayed to clear up whilst you and Jess went down to the pool. I've got it,' Freddie said.

Ben was staggered that Freddie had been considerate towards him, but mightily relieved.

'Thanks, Freddie.'

'It's okay,' he said, handing it over.

Ben switched it on, wondering if the Chief would have been in touch again. He checked his Inbox, but there was nothing new. Maybe the police had already arrested him?

'Marcus, is Nixon still free?' Jess asked, a clever question, Ben thought. Nixon was working for the Chief, so both dangerous and horrid. It would be fantastic if the police had arrested him too.

'I think so,' he replied.

'Stop thinking about them,' Mum said. 'They are vile, despicable nonentities. They must *not* infect our minds. Think happy thoughts,' she urged, smiling at him now. 'It's your birthday tomorrow. We're going home.'

'Yeah. I'll need you all to leave, please, to get dressed.'

But before they could, the door flew open. Ben expected to see Uncle Henry, but Inspector Walker strode in, looking so serious that Ben was worried. Her colleague, who followed her in, wasn't smiling either.

'Sue Baxter, we are here to arrest you,' Inspector Walker said. 'You do not have to say anything. But it may harm your defence if you do not mention when questioned something which you later rely on in court. Anything you do or say may be given in evidence.'

Ben's jaw dropped.

'Why?' demanded Mum, looking equally stunned – and scared.

'In connection with mass murder, attempted murder, kidnapping and extortion.'

No! The horror on Mum's face was heart-breaking.

'It's not me,' she said, shaking her head. 'I'm not the Chief.'

'Are you going to come quietly, or do I have to cuff you?'

'It's not me!'

'It's *obscene* to suggest that of Sue,' Aunt Miriam protested. 'She would never kill anyone.'

'Come on,' Inspector Walker commanded, clipping a handcuff onto Mum's wrist.

Ben couldn't speak. He was stunned.

'No!' Jess howled.

But unheeding, they started to walk Mum away. She turned her head to look at him. Looking apologetic.

'It's not me. Honestly.'

'I *know*.' Barely able to stifle the urge to drag Mum out of their grasp, Ben was forced to watch them leading her away. Powerless. Incredulous. And utterly, utterly terrified.

Chapter 2

The Aftershock

Ben was dressed. Numb, but dressed. He went to the door and opened it.

'Okay,' he called. Marcus was on the phone, so focused on his conversation that he didn't even react, but the Winterburns trooped in. They too looked stunned.

'They think she's the Chief,' Ben said, but it didn't help. It was just as unbelievable when he said it out loud. How could the police possibly think that of her? Mum wasn't a murderer; she was a pacifist, against killing anyone, let alone children.

'They've set her up. They kidnapped her, half-murdered her son in front of her and now they've framed her. They are evil beyond belief,' Aunt Miriam fumed.

'She's just an easy scapegoat,' Uncle Henry said.

Aunt Miriam whipped round. '*Why*? *Why* is Sue the scapegoat? How on earth could anyone be so *stupid* as to imagine that she would harm *anyone*?'

He raised his hands defensively. 'They must have evidence.'

'*Fabricated* evidence!' Aunt Miriam seemed as furious as Ben was numb. 'That's all they can have. Sue would never harm any child – but endanger *Ben*? That's just ludicrous. And deeply, deeply, offensive.'

'That man, Kashani, must have lied,' Uncle Henry said, referring to the ice-cream poisoner, Goatee Man's mate, who had been arrested.

'A murderer is hardly to be trusted, Henry! They *surely* must have more than that.'

'But *what*?' Ben said.

'That text about the cyanide was strange, Jess said. 'Have you still got it, Mum?'

'What text?' Ben asked.

'I'll get it,' Aunt Miriam said. She found her phone in her bag and shared it with them.

It's cyanide not 993. Tell medics.

It was from Mum's mobile, but…

'That's not from Mum. No way.'

'I know it's odd. She usually ends with a kiss,' Aunt Miriam replied.

'She was in a hurry,' Uncle Henry said.

'Exactly. That's why it's so strange,' Jess said. 'Aunt Sue was in a hurry to save Ben's life. She'd phone you. It's faster.'

'That's right,' Ben realised. 'Let's tell the police.'

'Yet it's from her mobile.' Aunt Miriam looked doubtful.

'Mum didn't send it. No way.'

'Okay. But then who did?'

'I'll bet *he* sneaked it from her bag.' Ben loathed Ballantyne, Mum's repellent boss (and very likely, the Chief), so much that he didn't even want to speak his name. But they all knew who he meant.

'He accused her at the Warden's party,' Jess said. 'He must have got the idea there.'

'Or someone did,' Freddie said. 'The Board were all there. It could be any of them.'

'Lord Charles and Sir John would never do anything like that!' Uncle Henry said, naming SPC's two top men.

'A title doesn't make you a saint,' Aunt Miriam snapped.

'Of course not. But they are men of standing.'

'I agree with Dad,' Jess said. 'I don't think either of them could have done it. It's like in lessons, where everyone looks at the teacher, everyone would be looking at them, wouldn't they?'

'Not necessarily,' Aunt Miriam said, but Ben thought Jess had made a very intelligent point.

'We can debate this at home. We'd better get going,' Uncle Henry said.

Ben stared at him in disbelief. 'You can. I'm not.'

'*Going*? Going where?' Aunt Miriam said.

'Home!' Uncle Henry was wide-eyed with indignation.

'We're not going home while Sue is here,' Aunt Miriam said, spacing out the words as if explaining to an idiot. Well she was. Academically, Uncle Henry was phenomenally intelligent, but he could be as stupid as anyone at times.

'We can't afford The Beaumont!' Uncle Henry cried, referring to Oxford's swishest hotel. (Though he'd loved staying there for free).

'We don't need to stay anywhere. We're not going to sleep. We're not going to eat. We're not going to waste time on anything until Sue is free,' Aunt Miriam declared, fizzing with fury.

Whilst Uncle Henry blustered that *he* needed sleep and *he* needed to eat, the door opened. Ben gasped, scared now, half-expecting Ballantyne, or Goatee Man.

But it was just Marcus.

'Andrew Masterton, the best solicitor in Oxford, is on his way to the station,' he said.

'Oh, that's wonderful, Marcus, thank you. How did you manage that?' Aunt Miriam asked.

'He's an old family friend. He'll give Sue all the support she needs over the next day or two.'

'Day or two?' Ben echoed, horrified. They could keep Mum *all night?*

'Sorry, Ben. They have to charge your mum or release her within twenty-four hours. But in serious cases like murder they can apply for a twelve-hour extension.'

'Wednesday morning?' Jess looked as horrified as him. 'When can we see her?'

'We can't, sorry.'

'*What*?'

'I'm so sorry, Ben,' Marcus said. 'Not whilst the police are questioning her.'

'But that's not fair!' Jess protested.

It was more than unfair, it was unbelievable, impossible… Ben couldn't convey the torrent of emotions whirling about inside him. He wanted to scream, to shout, to smash things, but it would be useless against the gargantuan powers of the police. He clenched his fists and squeezed.

A nurse entered. 'Is everything all right?'

Ben wondered if she'd noticed Mum being led away. Of course she would have, he realised. Everyone in the hospital would have seen Mum in handcuffs. He cringed with embarrassment, whilst reflecting how absolutely awful Mum must have felt. How humiliating. How horrible. She just didn't deserve the kicking life was giving her. No, not life. *Him,* Ballantyne. Repellent, evil and frighteningly clever, he had won again. He had kidnapped them, he had murdered children and now he'd had Mum arrested.

The nurse noticed Ben's agitation. 'I might get the doctor to look at you again.'

'No don't. I'm fine, just upset.'

'We're all upset,' Aunt Miriam said. 'It's so unjust.'

'I'm afraid I need the room for someone else,' the nurse said.

Ben headed for the door.

'Hang on, Ben! Your test,' Jess cried.

'Sorry,' Ben apologised to Marcus. He couldn't believe he'd forgotten the paternity test. Mum's arrest had been as terrifying and brutal as a tidal wave, obliterating everything in its path.

'I'll sort that out.'

'Thanks, Marcus. I do want you to be my dad,' Ben said, feeling he should reassure him.

'I know. Me too.'

'They can't find her guilty, can they?'

'No, Ben. No way. She'll be back in a few hours. They can't possibly think it's her.'

But they clearly did.

They emerged from the hospital into bright sunshine, which felt wrong at such a calamitous time.

Whilst Uncle Henry, Aunt Miriam and Freddie argued about staying the night, Marcus made some phone calls.

Jess and Ben walked away from the argument.

'Did you say anything about Mum to the police?' Ben asked. Following the poisoned pool nightmare, his cousins had apparently been questioned in the police station whilst Ben was unconscious.

'No,' Jess replied. 'We were just talking about the pool.'

'Did your dad? Freddie? Any of you?'

'I don't know, I wasn't with them, but I doubt it. They don't suspect your mum, Ben. None of us do.'

'But I can't work out why the police do.'

'It's a good thing we're out of the hospital.'

'Why?'

'At least we can get on with finding the Chief. And he can't find you. Hopefully.'

Yeah,' Ben replied, with a shiver travelling down his spine. Ballantyne had tentacles that stretched across the city. Ben had the feeling that wherever they were, he would find them.

Marcus rang off and beckoned them over.

'My Ma would be delighted if the three of you would stay with her. You can have the top floor.'

'Really? How kind of her,' Aunt Miriam replied, glaring at Uncle Henry.

'It's only for a night or two, if that. It won't take Andrew long to get Sue free. What evidence can they possibly have?'

'This might be part of it,' said Aunt Miriam, showing Marcus Mum's text.

He shook his head. 'That means nothing. They could have cloned that phone easily, they had it for over a week.'

'How does cloning a mobile work?' Jess asked.

Unbelievable. Though his cousins were smart in every other respect, they had as little grasp of modern technology as the average caveman.

'They can send texts that appear to be from you. They can access all your contacts. But the police must surely know how easy cloning is. They must have other evidence,' Marcus said.

'They can't have!'

'I know, Miriam, I know. Andrew Masterton will force them to reveal what they do have. Then we can prove it's all lies. Here's the number of a decent guest house,' Marcus said, handing them one of his cards, on the back of which he'd written it. 'It's good value, Henry.'

'Blow value,' Aunt Miriam said. Uncle Henry opened his mouth, doubtless to protest, but didn't get the chance, because she quickly added, 'Thank you, Marcus.'

'We've got to get going. I'll drop the kids at Ma's on my way to the lab.'

'Where is it?'

'Norham Gardens. You know it?'

'Oh yes,' Uncle Henry said. 'Very nice.'

'It's home,' Marcus said, shrugging. 'That's all.'

Watching Jess and Aunt Miriam hugging goodbye, Ben felt such an intense longing for his mum that he almost broke down. He took a few deep breaths, blinking back the treacherous tears.

'Once we've got a room, we'll come and see you and decide on a plan,' Aunt Miriam said.

What plan? Ben had no confidence in Aunt Miriam and Uncle Henry to come up with a plan, despite their undoubtedly brilliant brains. They were dealing with a different kind of cleverness: cunning, evil and dangerous. They were all way out of their league. Even Marcus, who had infiltrated the 993 gang, had still not managed to prove that Ballantyne was the Chief.

He put a hand round Ben's shoulder. 'Come on. We need to go.'

'We're parked miles away,' Aunt Miriam glared at her husband.

'It's not far! I didn't have change!' Uncle Henry protested. He never did, the skinflint.

Marcus led them to his navy blue Jaguar. As he unlocked it, he asked Ben to hold the padded envelope that held the key to his parentage.

'Sit next to me in the front,' he added. Freddie, who usually nabbed the front on grounds of seniority, looked miffed, but what did that matter now?

Ben sank into the soft leather seat feeling as if all the stuffing had been knocked out of him. His head was spacy. He wanted to cry.

But Marcus looked at him with such a curious expression on his face that Ben was alarmed.

'I need you to do something for me. But you mustn't tell anyone else, understand?' Marcus said.

''Course not. What?'

'Nixon left his phone at the basins in the Gents.' By the time he'd realised, I'd checked his Inbox and copied a text out. It's in code, so it's presumably from the Chief.'

'That's a clue!' Jess enthused. 'Our first genuine clue!'

'I used to get every text he did,' Marcus said. 'Nixon used to text me too. But now they've all dried up.'

'Since you saved us?' Ben said, feeling guilty.

'You saved your mum,' Marcus replied, omitting to add that he had saved Ben's life. 'Yes, it's since then. I'm worried it could be about an attack, else I wouldn't ask.'

'Hope not. But that text would get them arrested,' Jess said.

'Hopefully,' Marcus said. 'If not, we could thwart the attack at least. But we need to solve it. And I haven't time. Not right now.'

'We'll do it. Won't we?' Ben asked his clever cousins, knowing it would be them that would solve it, not him.

'Oh yes,' Jess said.

'Sure,' Freddie said, looking casual. But he loved proving how clever he was. He would probably crack it in five seconds.

At the next red light, Marcus found the code and passed the paper over to Ben.

QGSCQGSCUGSLSWDPQKZWPFZYQWCZLCTBN

As Ben looked at it, his hopes deflated faster than a punctured balloon. No spaces. One long word, or lots of short words of unknown length?

'It's way too hard for us.'

'I've not had chance to look at it properly. It did seem a stinker.'

'Can we have a look, Ben?' Jess asked.

He passed the sheet back, desperately hoping they could make sense of it. It was a clue. But it was far too hard for him.

'Why can't we prove it's Ballantyne?' he said to Marcus.

'Could be Knox,' Freddie said, referring to SPC's Chief Executive, Sir John Knox.

Marcus bit his lower lip. 'It could be either of them, that's the trouble. I need more evidence. Until we have that, we can't prove who it is. Or that it's not your mum.'

'It's certainly not easy, this code,' Freddie said. 'A, E, O and I must stand for rare letters, because they don't appear.'

'Not if it's Playfair, it doesn't work like that,' Marcus said.

'Playfair?' Jess echoed, sounding excited. Ben turned to her, hopeful suddenly. 'I've read a whole chapter on how to solve Playfair Ciphers! In *Have His Carcase*!' She clapped her hand to her mouth, looking horrified.

'What's up?' Ben asked, worried.

'I forgot to give it back to The Beaumont. I've still got it.' Jess couldn't have looked more stricken if she'd accidentally burned down the famous hotel, but it was just an old paperback.

'That's brilliant, Jess,' Marcus said. 'I read it as a boy. Dorothy L. Sayers explains exactly how to crack Playfair through Peter and Harriet doing so.'

Jess got the book out of her bag. Ben watched her searching for the right chapter.

'Oh fiddlesticks!' she declared, about as violent a curse as Jess ever used. 'Theirs is separated into words.'

'That's so that readers of average intelligence can solve it. This isn't supposed to be easy to solve,' Freddie said.

As if they didn't know. Ben rolled his eyes.

'It might help if you split it into pairs,' Marcus suggested.

'Why?' Ben asked.

'Playfair is always in digraphs. Groups of two letters,' he added.

'Okay.' Ben wondered why they weren't just called pairs then.

After a minute or two of driving through countryside, mainly green and golden fields with a tree or two, Jess said, 'Nothing springs out at me. Let me check in the book whilst you have a look, Freddie.'

Marcus braked behind a slower car, but soon managed to nip into a gap and overtake it. As they accelerated away, Ben turned to his cleverest cousin. 'Any joy?'

'Not yet, no. See what you think.' Freddie passed the paper back. But if Freddie couldn't crack it, Ben had no chance.

QG SC QG SC UG SL SW DP QK ZW PF ZY QW CZ LC TC BN

'There's a lot of Qs,' he noticed.

'Good spot, but that doesn't really help in Playfair, unfortunately,' Marcus said.

'Oh no!' Jess cried, alarming Ben again.

He spun round. 'What?'

'They had a date at the start and it had to be in June. That was their way in.'

'The Chief's texts never start with dates,' Marcus said.

'No. That would be far too easy,' Freddie said.

'But it can't be that hard for Nixon, can it?' Ben asked.

'He'll know the key, so he'll know the code,' Marcus said. 'Unfortunately, I don't.'

'What's the key?'

'Say your key was MAGIC. You write it at the top of your grid, then continue from the start of the alphabet, omitting repeated letters. Then take opposite diagonals or go down or across.'

'Which?' Ben asked, thinking it sounded horribly complex.

'Jess will know from the book. But the problem is, this cipher is very short. They had a long letter, if I remember correctly. It may be too short to crack. Sorry, guys. It may be impossible.'

'If we can't crack it, it's not a clue,' Jess said.

'Then we will. We've got to crack it. Somehow,' Ben said.

'But first, say hello to Ma,' Marcus said, pulling into a long drive. 'And don't tell her about this code. Or anyone. If they find out I've got it, the Chief will not be pleased.'

Ben looked at him, alarmed. He knew exactly what Marcus meant. The Chief would kill him. He turned to his cousins.

'Don't tell anyone, *please*. Not your mum, not your dad, not anyone.'

'We won't,' Jess said.

''Course not,' Freddie agreed.

But Ben knew them far too well to believe them. Marcus might just have made the biggest mistake of his life.

Chapter 3

The House in Norham Gardens

Daphne's house was large, double-fronted, and Victorian. And even better, apparently, might have appeared in a book.

'Is this *it*?' Jess asked, as they approached the front door. '*The House in Norham Gardens*?'

'I don't know which house Penelope Lively based it on, but ours is one of the few with turrets,' Marcus replied.

Ben looked up. He was right. Weird!

Jess looked delighted. 'I loved that book!'

'Ma knew the author when she lived in Oxford. She has a signed copy, I think. You can re-read it if you like,' Marcus said, ringing the bell.

'Not until we've got Aunt Sue back. I'll be too busy for reading until then.'

'Wow, Jess!' Ben declared, impressed. He had never known her not to read.

'Her arrest is the biggest travesty of justice I have ever known, apart from perhaps Nelson Mandela. I am determined to prove that to the police,' Jess said, chin out, looking so determined that Ben would back her against almost any enemy. Except Ballantyne and the police. But he appreciated her commitment and knew he would value her clever brain, so he thanked her.

'No more,' Marcus warned as the door opened and Ben's brand new grandma, a tall, elegant woman, beamed at them. 'Hello, Ma. Thanks so much for helping out.'

'My absolute pleasure. Come in, all of you,' she said, smiling warmly and stepping back.

Used to Aunt Miriam and Uncle Henry's large Victorian house in Didsbury, Ben expected a similarly dark, forbidding and gaudily-tiled hall. But Daphne's hall was wooden floored, spacious and light, with a large walnut bureau to their left.

'Do you mind if I go? I've got to get this into the lab before six-thirty,' Marcus said, brandishing the paternity test envelope, 'and then I've got a meeting, but I'll be back before eight, I hope.'

'Of course not,' Daphne replied. 'I've made up your old bed for you, if you'd like to stay here.'

'Oh, Ma, that's wonderful. I'd much rather be here with all of you than at the hotel with those fossils,' he joked, meaning the SPC Agrochemicals Board. 'Great. Right. I'll see you later.' With a brief kiss on his mum's cheek, he fled and left them alone with her.

'It's not Mum. She would never hurt anyone,' Ben said.

'I know that, Ben,' Daphne replied. 'Of course, I do. And the two of you have been through so much. It's dreadful. But I'm sure it's some terrible mistake and that Andrew will have her out in two shakes of a lamb's tail.'

'Yeah,' Ben agreed, her confidence inspiring a flicker of hope.

'Would you prefer to go straight to your rooms, or have a drink first?'

Keen to get to the code, Ben declined Daphne's offer, but Freddie didn't, so they were led down the hall, past photos of Marcus and Rufus – and Geoffrey, the grandad he'd never met, Ben presumed. He had a nice smile, and was tall and blond, like Marcus and Ben.

'What a terrible shock. Totally ridiculous. I can't imagine what the police are thinking,' Daphne said, leading them into a surprisingly modern kitchen, with wooden worktops and units. It was very bright, due to the expanse of glass overlooking the spacious garden.

'It's lovely. Are these handmade?' Jess asked, her hand on a worktop.

'They have to be, to fit these houses. They're years old, but you wouldn't know it, would you?'

'No.'

On the central table, where Daphne invited them to sit, there was a glistening blueberry pie, dusted with icing-sugar.

'Did you make it?' Jess asked.

'Oh no. I bought it from the coffee shop. I was hoping I'd see you again before you left, Ben. But not in such awful circumstances, of course.'

A worm of worry gnawed at him, urging him to get to work, to waste not a single second, but still he recognised, and appreciated, her thoughtfulness.

Just yesterday (incredible to Ben, because it seemed several days distant) he'd chosen a blueberry pie in the upmarket coffee-shop where Daphne had delivered her bombshell that she was convinced she was Ben's grandma, and Mum had dropped the even bigger bombshell that his IVF donor dad was a lifelong lie.

Now Ben was very glad indeed he'd not had the chance to explode at Mum (as he might well have done had the shocking truth slipped out at home, rather than in company).

'Ben, what did you want to drink?'

'Sorry.' Seeing his cousins' drinks – coffee for Freddie and milk for Jess – he requested water.

'That's easy then,' Daphne said, turning on the tap and filling a tumbler. 'I've got a big meeting tonight, unfortunately, that I can't wriggle out of. It's awful timing, but I'm afraid I will have to leave you soon. Will you be all right alone?'

'Definitely,' they assured her, exchanging glances.

'Code,' Jess mouthed at him. Ben nodded. Did she think the cyanide had affected his brain permanently? The hospital had explained that it causes oxygen deprivation, which had made Ben so light-headed that he'd passed out, but the hospital's treatment of him had been wonderful.

Daphne brought four plates to the table alongside Ben's water, and then got them all spoons. Next, she added a jug of cream (Ben was impressed – it was straight from the carton at home) and then sat down to join them. She cut a generous slice of the pie for each of them.

They all tucked in. The pastry was golden, buttery and meltingly comforting, the blueberries warm, rich and delicious, making purple swirls in the cream.

'This is sumptuous,' Jess said, which Ben assumed meant tasty.

'I've never tasted better,' he agreed.

'Not even in Stockport?' Freddie scoffed. He loved sneering at Ben's home.

'Not even in Didsbury,' Ben retaliated.

The doorbell rang. *Mum?* But as quickly as the thought had appeared, it dissipated like a wisp of smoke. Mum wouldn't know they were here.

'I wonder who it is?' Daphne said, standing up.

'I hope it's not Mum and Dad. *We need to get cracking that cipher*,' Jess whispered, as Daphne disappeared into the hall.

What else did she think he was planning to do? Learn the bagpipes?

'They're in here,' Daphne was saying, her voice so loud they must be just outside – so they had very little warning of the visitor's approach.

When he followed Daphne into the kitchen, Ben gasped. But Ballantyne smiled, as if relishing his discomfort. However, his eyes were as icy as ever. Tanned, with snow-white hair, but looking fit and toned, he radiated menace.

'Hello, Ben,' he said, in his creepy voice. 'Since I am still your mother's manager, I wanted to check you had accommodation tonight?'

'Yeah,' Ben said, wondering how he had tracked them down. It wasn't just clever, it was spooky.

'Why?' Jess asked, as she so often did.

'I am acting in *loco parentis*.'

Jess's jaw dropped and she looked aghast.

'I beg your pardon?' Daphne snapped, looking deeply offended.

Ben wondered why? He wished he could have understood the foreign phrase.

'Well, Sue can't do it. She's been arrested,' Ballantyne said, feigning disgust. But it was his fault. Ben glared at him.

'That's a silly mistake, that's all,' Daphne said, dismissively. 'Ben doesn't need you in loco parentis.'

'What does it even mean?' Ben cried, his growing frustration at not understanding their conversation overwhelming his reluctance to appear in any way vulnerable in front of Ballantyne, though he knew it was like putting your hand into a hungry lion's mouth.

'It's Latin for in place of a parent,' Jess said.

'*What*?' Ben was absolutely horrified. Ballantyne thought he could take the place of Mum? But while he reeled, Jess addressed Ballantyne.

'My mum is delighted we're staying here, and if anyone's acting in loco parentis, it's her, Ben's aunt.'

Ballantyne noticed Ben's outrage and his lips twitched with amusement. 'It's very unusual. Protective parents like yours letting you stay with a virtual stranger? Mrs Wright is merely the mother of one of your mother's colleagues. Would your mother be happy that you were staying here?'

As if he cared what Mum thought. Ben was speechless. The man's nerve was astounding.

'There's nothing unusual about it. I have a very large house which is empty, except for me, so Marcus knew there was plenty of space,' Daphne said.

'Oh, *he* arranged it, did he?'

'Yes, with Ben's Aunt Miriam. Now, I have to go out shortly, so…' Daphne looked at the door, but Ballantyne didn't budge.

'Are you leaving them alone?' he asked, wide-eyed with apparent outrage. But inside he must be delighted.

This is why you've come. This is what you wanted, Ben realised. To get us alone, and at your mercy.

Don't tell him, he silently urged Daphne.

'They're hardly children,' she replied. 'Freddie's fifteen, aren't you?'

'Yes.'

'And it's only for a couple of hours until Marcus gets back.'

'Not that long,' Ben said quickly. 'He'll be back any minute now.'

'My parents will be too,' Jess said, as if she was as alarmed as Ben. He flashed her a grateful glance.

'How did you know we'd be here?' Freddie asked.

'Yes, how did you know my address?' Daphne said.

'I interviewed Marcus on the milk round, when he was a callow undergraduate. Despite being completely ignorant of the business, he was full of confidence even then,' Ballantyne sneered.

'He may well have been, but that doesn't answer my question, Mr Ballantyne. How did you know where I live? I'm ex-directory,' Daphne said.

'I had your address on his application form.'

'You've remembered that from fifteen years back?' Daphne sounded astonished, but Ben didn't even raise an eyebrow. Mum had complained of Ballantyne's astounding memory many times.

'Fourteen, actually. I never forget anything,' he boasted.

'But how did you know I hadn't moved?' Daphne said.

'Who would want to leave such a delightful house?'

'I must ask *you* to leave, please. I have a meeting to get to,' she said, ushering him out.

Watching him leave, Ben's scalp was prickling, as if crawling with Ballantyne's bugs. Jess looked equally uncomfortable, but Freddie didn't seem bothered. They sat in silence until Daphne returned.

'What an unpleasant man!' she exclaimed.

'He is. Mum hates him,' Ben said.

'I don't blame her. I'm so sorry, could I leave you the clearing up? Just put it in the dishwasher,' Daphne said, opening it up. She bustled around the kitchen, picking things up and opening drawers, getting things out. 'Sorry I've got to dash. It's a big night for Oxford Humanists. We have Sir Christopher Cockerell speaking.'

'Really? We met him,' Freddie said. Sir Christopher was St Saviour's Warden, the college's overall boss, but he had been surprisingly normal and nice.

Daphne smiled. 'He's lovely, isn't he? Right, I'll lock up. These are the front door keys if you want to let your aunt and uncle in.' She handed them to Ben. Freddie looked hurt, whilst Ben felt honoured. He thanked her. 'Here's some money for dinner,' she added, getting a bundle of notes from a cupboard, which she also handed to Ben.

He tried to hand some back. 'That's far too much.'

'You can give me the change. Shockingly, I have some takeaway menus in the middle drawer there. I recommend the Chinese.'

'Thanks. That's really kind of you. Mum will pay you back.'

Daphne stopped and looked at him. 'Ben, there's no need. You're my grandson. You're family now.'

'Thank you,' he said, feeling embarrassed. Though pleased she was his grandma, Daphne still felt more like a stranger than a relative. 'Will the solicitor phone here if there's any news on Mum?'

'Yes, he will. Feel free to answer the phone. There's one on the dresser and one in my study, at the other end of the hall. There's paper there, if you want to take a message, or draw to pass the time.'

'Thanks,' Ben said, really touched she had remembered that he liked drawing – and the paper would be ideal for code cracking.

So as soon as she shut the front door, he and Jess went to get some pens and paper from the study – bigger, tidier and lighter than Aunt Miriam's and Uncle Henry's studies, though it only contained a double bookshelf, whereas theirs would put many public libraries to shame.

They took them back to the kitchen, where Freddie was waiting.

'Don't you think it's funny Marcus suddenly getting this code?' Freddie said, before they had even sat down.

'No. It's great,' Ben said.

'It's downright weird, that's what it is. I mean, he's been working with Nixon for months, who's as careless as anyone could be, yet it's only now he's got this code. And he's given it to you.'

'What are you on about?'

Freddie swung round to face him, his face alight with passion. 'The swimming pool changed everything! That text about the cyanide. It was meant to save you.'

'It's not Mum! Don't you dare say that!'

'I'm not. Back off,' he said, stepping back, hands uplifted defensively. Ben took a few deep breaths, trying to calm down, whilst Freddie continued. 'I'm not talking about your mum. It isn't her, is it? Think about the Chief. *Think*, Ben. He texts you, he draws you in, but he doesn't want you to get hurt.'

'Ben nearly died in that swimming pool!' Jess protested.

Freddie whipped round to face her. 'But the Chief saved him. The Chief texted Mum to say it was cyanide.'

'That was to incriminate Aunt Sue.'

'What if it wasn't? What if the Chief wanted to make *sure* Ben didn't die?'

'He got me into the pool!' Ben cried. 'Ballantyne got me into the pool.'

'It's not *Ballantyne*!' Freddie's eyes were wide, he was yelling. 'Can't you see? He keeps upping the stakes. First, it's attempted murder, and you get drugged. Then it *is* murder, but you get saved. Now he's having fun, handing you the codes rather than texting them.'

'*What*? What the hell are you saying?' The tension was like steel bands squeezing Ben's skull.

'He'll kill any teenager he can, but he doesn't want *you* dead. He *knows* you'll play the hero, and he *wants* you to play the hero. It's your dad. He's showing you off. It's Marcus!'

Ben stared at him, feeling the blood draining from his face.

Chapter 4

The Impossible Code

'It can't be him, Freddie!' Jess protested, but Ben felt sick. Freddie's conviction that Ben's dad was a murderer made the incredible seem possible.

'Who else would want to make Ben a hero? Besides his mum? And it's not her,' Freddie said.

Ben couldn't argue. It was a very good point.

But Jess could. 'It's not Marcus. It's not in his nature to kill.'

'How do you know what's in his nature? You didn't even know him a fortnight ago,' Freddie argued.

'No, but Aunt Sue did. And she didn't suspect him, did she?'

'Look where it's landed her. In jail.'

'He wouldn't do that to Mum,' Ben protested. 'He likes her.'

'Maybe not. He's a brilliant actor,' Freddie replied. 'Remember how he conned us all last week?'

'Yeah,' Ben admitted, recalling his astonishment when he first heard Marcus telling the Chief's four "investors" (creeps) about planning to execute him and Mum. Which led him straight to another objection to Freddie's argument. 'But he saved us! Nixon didn't. He did.'

Freddie's face was alight with passion. 'Of course, he did. That's my point. He wants to save you.'

'But he saved Aunt Sue too,' Jess said.

'Then. But now she's in prison. He's probably angry she lied to him.'

Biting his lip, Ben reflected that Freddie could well be right. He'd felt angry with Mum (and Rufus had been furious), when she had revealed that one of the two brothers was Ben's father. Maybe Marcus was still angry about it.

'He's not that mean. He wouldn't switch the blame onto Aunt Sue,' Jess said.

'Not that mean? He's poisoned children!' Freddie cried.

'He's *not* the Chief!' Jess protested. 'We've got to know him recently. He's kind, loyal and brave.'

Freddie looked at her as if she was insane. 'What's he done that's *brave*?'

'He stood up to the Chief.'

'He's not standing up to anyone if he is the Chief, is he?'

For a second, Jess was stumped. But she soon recovered. 'So why would he have had Ben kidnapped?'

'Nixon would have done that. Goatee Man and Kashani work for him, not Marcus. Then Marcus had to think of a way to save him,' Freddie said.

Though Ben's stomach churned at the prospect, though it absolutely sickened him to consider Marcus as the Chief, Freddie was making more sense to him than Jess was.

'Ballantyne hates Aunt Sue. Ballantyne hates Ben. It's Ballantyne,' Jess argued.

'So – why – did – he – save – him?' Freddie demanded, spacing out every word.

'That's true,' Ben admitted, his head in his hands. The swimming pool had changed everything. He almost felt like weeping. He took a deep breath and looked at them. 'I don't want it to be true, of course I don't, but everything you've said makes sense, Freddie.'

'I know.'

'But he's not like that, Ben,' Jess argued. 'Murderers are cold and clinical. Or charming with huge egos. Oh!' As she clapped her hand to her mouth, wide-eyed and horrified, Ben realised that Freddie had convinced her too.

'Charming, egotistical and a complete and utter liar, but so convincing that they start to believe themselves, that's psychopaths. That's Marcus,' Freddie said.

'I hope it's not. I hope you're wrong,' Ben said, with shivers coursing through him.

'Of course you do,' Freddie replied. 'He's your dad.'

If Freddie was right, then they were awaiting the Chief's return in his childhood home. Ben felt responsible for his cousins and guilty, as if it was in some way his fault.

'I've got to get you away from here,' he said.

'You've got to get us nowhere!' Freddie cried. 'What will he think if we run away from him? He'll know we suspect him. He can't know that.'

'That's true, Ben. If Freddie *is* right, and I'm afraid he is now, sorry…' Jess trailed off, looking almost as devastated as Ben felt.

'It's okay. Me too,' he assured her.

'Then we can't let Marcus know. Freddie's right. We have to get the evidence to convince the police.'

'What evidence?' Ben asked, despairing. They had no evidence. If they had, they could have given it to the police and freed Mum.

'That code, maybe?' Freddie said.

'Why would he have given it us then?' Ben asked. 'If he is the Chief?'

'Because of his ego. He thinks we won't crack it. So we've got to.'

'I don't like it,' Ben said, checking his watch. 'How long do you think he'll be?'

'An hour at least,' Jess said. Ben nodded. It would take him closer to two hours to get the DNA dropped off at the lab and then return to central Oxford for a meeting. 'In a weird way, do you kind of hope your dad's Rufus now?' she asked timidly.

Ben briefly wondered if it might be easier. But he didn't like Rufus.

'No, not really. Anyway, he won't be. Freddie's test showed that.'

'It did. Marcus is your dad. Where's that code?' Freddie asked.

With absolutely no enthusiasm for cracking it, Ben retrieved it from the pocket of his jeans. He felt terrible – full of guilt, sick with worry, and very, very scared. But Freddie was a hundred times more intelligent than him, so it was best to go along with his thinking, because Ben's brain felt as incapable of thought as a lump of lead.

He blankly looked at Jess's neat letter pairs.

QG SC QG SC UG SL SW DP QK ZW PF ZY QW CZ LC TC BN

There was no way to know how long the words were. It was way out of his league.

'Do you think he said it was in digraphs to put us off the scent?' Freddie asked.

'If it's not in pairs, we don't stand a chance. Not quickly,' Jess said.

'It's too short for frequency analysis to help. He might even be telling the truth about it being a Playfair Cipher. It's probably impossible to crack, being so short,' Freddie said. 'He's probably teasing us, like the Chief does.'

'But we have this,' Jess said, getting *Have His Carcase* out of her bag. Her belief in books was impressive, but insane. How could an ancient book help them outwit the Chief?

Ben felt terrible. His mum was in prison and his dad might be a murderer. Not directly, he hadn't put the cyanide in the pool, he'd been in the meeting with Mum whilst someone (Goatee Man?) did that. So he could easily have sent the cyanide text to Aunt Miriam, Ben realised.

He had tried to save Ben – but not the other teenagers and children they had poisoned. Some of them had died, but Ben had lived. If only he could have got more of them out of the pool. If only...

'Try and help us crack this, Ben. Please,' Jess said. 'Worrying makes it worse.'

Ben nodded, realising she was right. 'Okay.' He tried to tune in to their conversation, without any confidence he'd understand. It was often like trying to catch a racing greyhound once they got going.

'The most common digraphs are TH and HE probably, since THE is the most common word in written English,' Freddie said.

Ben recalled Marcus explaining that digraphs were two-letter pairs, helping him. Why had he helped? He knew what Freddie would say: you're his son.

Freddie's argument made chilling, terrifying sense.

'Ben, could you draw something for us?' asked Jess, seemingly determined to rope him in. 'A five by five square is what we need. Then, say the key is NORHAM, it would be entered at the top.'

She would do it equally well, but Ben realised she was trying to stop him worrying, so he drew a square.

N	O	R	H	A
M				

'Like this?'

'That's right. Then you fill it with the rest of the alphabet, omitting duplicates.'

'From B or P?' Freddie asked.

'What?' Ben asked him.

'From the start of the alphabet or continuing. Omitting the letters in the key, obviously.' Freddie glared at him.

Ben shook his head, wondering how Freddie would feel if his mum was in jail and his dad a murderer? But empathy wasn't Freddie's strength. Intelligence was his forte. If any of them could crack this code, it would be him.

Jess looked up from her book. 'Next is B, according to DLS.'

Ben started to fill in the grid.

'No H. You've got one in the key,' Freddie said.

'No J. Because there are only 25 spaces, you combine I and J,' Jess said.

'Huh?'

'I stands for both I and J. Or J does.'

'Why?'

'Five fives are twenty-five. The alphabet contains how many letters?' Freddie said, as if speaking to a four-year-old.

'Stuff off! I get it, okay?' Ben snapped, continuing with the alphabet, being careful to omit M, N and R. He pushed the finished grid across the table towards his cousins.

N	O	R	H	A
M	B	C	D	E
F	G	I/J	K	L
P	Q	S	T	U
V	W	X	Y	Z

'Well done, Ben,' Jess said.

'That's rubbish!' Freddie cried.

'What?' Ben was hurt. He'd done exactly what Jess had said.

'The end of the alphabet is always at the bottom. That's a weakness, a way in. Unless the key is *syzygy*.'

'*What*?'

'Alignment of the Sun and the Moon and the Earth, or another planet,' Freddie replied. Ben stared at him in disbelief, but he looked serious.

'It won't be that, Freddie,' Jess said.

'Even a half-wit could do this,' Freddie snapped.

'This one can't,' Ben said.

Freddie's stomach grumbled. 'Why don't you ring for a takeaway then?'

'We can't have a takeaway. There's no time.' Ben checked his watch. It was just past six. Marcus was probably stuck in traffic.

'And we're what? Running away?' Freddie said in the taunting tone Ben hated. Ben's jaw clenched.

'We can't run, Ben,' Jess said. 'It's a panicked reaction, not a clever one. And if he is the Chief, we've got to be even cleverer than he is.'

'And none of us has had lunch, have we?' Freddie complained, rolling his eyes at Ben, as if he'd volunteered to be poisoned.

Ben buried his face in his hands. 'I can't think of food when *he* might be the Chief!'

'He might *not* be, Ben,' Jess said. 'I still think Ballantyne's more likely, on behaviour. But that may just be because Marcus is a very successful psychopath.'

'God, I hope not.'

'Stop praying to non-existent gods and get us some food!' Freddie snapped.

'Okay. What do you want?' Ben asked, because Freddie was the pickiest eater he knew. He remembered Daphne recommending the Chinese takeaway and fished the menu out of the middle drawer. Freddie looked at it for a while before deciding.

'Chicken and pineapple and *plain* boiled rice.'

'Okay. Jess?'

'Chicken and cashew nuts please. I love cashew nuts.'

Ben needed to get away from his cousins, so he took it to Daphne's study, which was at the far end of the hall.

He switched on the computer whilst dialling the takeaway, but she had chosen a clever password, so he couldn't log in. He did manage to place the order though, and the woman promised to be quick.

Ben's mind was churning. Freddie and Jess might be right about not running away from Marcus, but they could be equally wrong. Though highly intelligent, they were about as streetwise as babies.

Ben started pacing around. Was it Marcus? Was it Ballantyne? The idea of his dad being a murderer was so revolting that he desperately hoped that it was Ballantyne. But hoping wasn't the same as knowing.

The one person he longed to consult was Mum. But she was locked up for something she would never do, because of Ballantyne accusing her of being the Chief. Ben punched his hand, because he couldn't punch the slimy man himself.

He had no way of knowing. Either Ballantyne was the Chief or Marcus was. And they both knew they would be here alone this evening.

So they were in terrible danger. Not just Ben, but his cousins too. He couldn't stand that.

Ben opened the door.

'Okay, Ben?' Jess called down the hall.

'Yeah, fine,' he responded. 'I've ordered the food. Just need the loo.'

He tiptoed to the front door, checked he had his phone and Daphne's keys, then opened it. He paused, listening. There was a bird singing outside, but inside his cousins were quiet, probably immersed in the code.

He left, gently pulling the door shut behind him. Ben had noticed Marcus forking right at the top of Parks Road to get to Norham Gardens, so he knew if he followed that route he would come to St Saviour's, where Ballantyne would probably be, and so would Marcus later. Or perhaps Ballantyne was at his hotel right now. Where would he be staying? The St Saviour's porters would probably know.

The evening was getting chilly. The clouds were gathering and a wind was whipping up. Running was a satisfying release of energy, after so much sitting around.

Past the park, past the Pitt Rivers Museum, Ben soon reached the science park. At the crossing the pedestrian lights were on red, so he paused.

He heard an engine revving up on the left. As the lights changed to green, he stepped on to the road, but a peripheral movement made him turn his head. A car was accelerating towards him, a white Mercedes with tinted windows.

Ben stared at the car, stunned. The car's bonnet gleamed in the sunshine, the engine roared like a lion, yet he couldn't move. Mesmerized, he watched it speeding towards him, trying to understand.

It wasn't going to stop. They didn't want to stop. They meant to hit him.

Ten feet, nine, eight, seven... It was them! Jolted to his senses, Ben threw himself forwards, fearing it was too late.

Chapter 5

Too Close for Comfort

He crashed onto the pavement, amazed it had missed him. Stunned and delighted to be alive. He had gashed one elbow but was otherwise unscathed. As the car sped off down Parks Road, towards St Saviour's, he sat reeling.

They had very nearly killed him, as the people rushing towards him were keen to point out.

'They nearly hit you!'

'They only just missed you.'

'They were inches away. You could have died.'

Ben nodded, thinking I was meant to die.

A woman crouched down beside him. She had a purple bob, and an eyebrow piercing. He supposed she was a student.

'Oh my god, are you okay?'

'Yeah,' he lied.

She put her arm around him as if to comfort him, but the only person that could comfort him now was Mum.

Needing her, wanting her, missing her, hot tears threatened to fall. He wiped his burning eyes and shrugged the concerned student off.

'Thanks.' Still shaky, he got up.

A mobile was pressed into his hand by an older woman, who reminded Ben of a teacher.

'Talk to the police. They need your details.'

Ben was horrified. The police were his enemy. But she looked so astonished at his hesitation that he put the handset to his ear.

A policeman asked him for his name and address.

'We don't live here. We're from Stockport.' Ben turned away from the crowd and lowered his voice. 'It's not her, can't you see? It's not her. They tried to kill me. She loves me. It's not her.'

'Calm down, son. Is this Ben Baxter?'

'How the hell do you expect me to calm down? You've got my mum!'

The policeman cleared his throat. 'Where are you, Ben?'

'By the science park on Parks Road.'

'So you were crossing South Parks Road?'

'Yeah, I guess so.'

'Where are you staying? Are you still at The Beaumont?'

'No! We were going home until you arrested her.'

'So you're in Oxford tonight then? Where?'

'In Norham Gardens.'

'What number?'

As Ben looked up, trying to remember, he noticed everyone was staring at him. Deeply uncomfortable, he walked further away from them to say, 'I can't remember. Daphne Wright's house.'

'We'll find it. We'll be along to talk to you.'

'Never mind me. It's not *her*.'

But, unheeding, the policeman rang off. As Ben returned the mobile to its owner, she was looking at him as if he were mad. But some other people were staring at him.

'Are you *that* Ben Baxter? The ice-cream guy?' one asked.

She could have chucked a bucket of ice over him and had a lesser effect. They might have heard him complaining about Mum being arrested. They knew him, so they'd easily find her name. They would surely tell the media. Someone would be tempted by the cash, or the fame. Mum's face would be everywhere, on the news, in the press, online. Everyone would think she was a murderer.

He had been so stupid, an awful, terrible son. She had warned him repeatedly that once you lost your temper, you lost the battle. You lost control of what you were saying and what you were doing. He'd blown it, big time. Not for him, but for her, which was far, far worse.

And they were all staring at him, expecting him to say – what?

'I'm not Ben, I'm Dan,' he said, borrowing the name of one of his best friends. 'I don't even know what you're talking about.'

He started walking away from them, ignoring their questions. He started running to escape them. He accelerated to shake them off. Fortunately it worked. As he ran, he kept glancing at the road, looking for the Mercedes, so he was glad of the trees that screened the pavement from the road. Though there was no sign of the dreaded car, he was also grateful that there was no need to cross another road until he finally reached Norham Gardens.

It was reassuringly quiet. He was delighted that there were no cars on Daphne's drive, for he couldn't face Ballantyne, or even Marcus right now.

His hands were shaky. Even unlocking the door was hard. He was a hopeless, stupid mess.

Jess entered the hall and saw him.

'It's Ben!' She looked at him accusingly. 'Where've you been?'

He told her.

She clung to him.

'We could have lost you forever.' Jess squeezed his waist even tighter. Looking down at the top of her golden hair, Ben realised she would have been devastated if the car had hit him. As would Mum. As would Aunt Miriam.

'You were an idiot,' Freddie said. He was eyeing them uncertainly. Gently, Ben pulled away from the hug.

'The police are coming. The press might be too,' he added, trying to suppress the guilty pang.

'*What*?'

He had to tell them. They'd know soon enough. So, thoroughly ashamed of himself, he did.

'Maybe none of them will say anything,' Jess said.

'They will, Jess. Someone will talk.'

'Maybe they didn't hear.'

'Maybe I'm a unicorn,' he retorted – both stupidly and unkindly, he rapidly realised. 'Sorry, Jess.'

She looked at him so kindly that he knew she'd forgiven him immediately. 'It's fine. You're shaken up. I understand.'

'You've been a complete and utter cretin,' Freddie said. Brutal, but true. He'd been worse than a cretin, he'd betrayed his mum. 'But on the plus side, it makes it far less likely that your father's the Chief.'

Stunned, Ben frowned. 'What?'

'Well, it contradicts the cyanide text completely, doesn't it? Why was that trying to save you, when the car was trying to kill you? Marcus wouldn't want to kill you. He's delighted about being your dad.'

'Yes, it can't be Marcus, Ben,' Jess agreed. 'It must be Ballantyne.'

As if he'd heard, the doorbell rang.

Not now, Ben thought, not now, please.

They approached the door together. The figure through the glass was a short, fat man – not Marcus or Ballantyne, not Goatee Man and not Nixon. The police?

Ben clicked the security chain into place before opening the door.

'Takeaway,' the stranger said, proffering white bags. Ben released the chain to get the food, surprised it had taken so long to arrive. They took the bags through to the kitchen and found crockery and cutlery.

Before he could eat, Ben gulped a large glass of water and refilled it before joining his cousins at the table, which was covered with papers.

'It can't be Marcus,' Ben repeated, feeling better as they started eating the food (which was as tasty as Daphne had promised).

'*Probably* not. Unless that was Goatee Man going rogue,' Freddie said.

'Huh?' Ben questioned, his mouth too full to say any more.

'Like he did with the knife,' Jess said.

'What knife?' Freddie asked, narrowing his eyes.

Ben wished Jess was better at keeping secrets from her family.

'He tried to kidnap Ben on Friday evening,' she revealed.

Freddie looked at Ben as if he'd lost his mind. 'Why on *earth* didn't you tell the police?'

'They've got Mum!'

'They hadn't then, had they?' Freddie said.

Trust him to remember.

'Ben didn't want to scare Aunt Sue. They'd almost been murdered that morning, remember?' Jess said.

'They weren't though, were they?' Freddie replied, sounding far from pleased.

'Thanks,' Ben huffed.

Freddie frowned at him, looking puzzled.

'Maybe now they'll release her. They will know she wouldn't want to hurt you,' Jess said.

'Yeah, maybe,' Ben agreed, but he wasn't convinced. 'Wish I could have got to Ballantyne.'

'What would you have done with him if you'd got him?' Jess asked.

'I don't know. I just hate the fact that he knows where we are.'

'So does Marcus,' Freddie said. 'And it might be him. If Goatee Man was taking you to the Chief, Goatee Man knows how to find the Chief. How come Marcus doesn't?'

'No, Freddie, that's wrong. Goatee Man would have had to ask Nixon.'

'So he knows who the Chief is, but Marcus doesn't? Pull the other one,' he said, eyeing his sister with such scorn that Ben rushed to her defence – even though he thought that Freddie was probably right.

'He was either taking me to the Chief, or Nixon. Either way, he wanted money. That's what he said. Not me dead. Or he'd have knifed me there and then.'

'In the Covered Market? No way.' Freddie shook his head. 'Too many witnesses. That's probably what stopped him killing you just now,' he said, showing no emotion whatsoever. Both Ben and Jess gawped at him as he continued, 'Anyway, forget that. We need to solve this.' Freddie jabbed at their papers.

Ben was amazed that his clever cousins hadn't already solved the code, and doubted that he could contribute, but he picked up a sheet of their workings.

*QG SC QG SC UG SL SW DP QK ZW PF ZY QW CZ LC
TC BN*

He asked Jess to explain a square of letters she'd drawn.

Q	T
H	G

'We were hoping the message might start with THE or
THAT, so that *QG* is code for TH. That would mean Q is in
the same column as H and the same row as T,' she said.

'Okay,' Ben said, baffled. 'What next?'

'Well, the next digraph, *SC*, is probably E something,
because of THE.'

She had drawn another square:

S	E
?	C

'It's hard, isn't it?' Ben said.

'We understand it. We just need a breakthrough.'

'If you can't get it, I won't.'

'Maybe you will. Look at the beginning. It repeats. So it's
a repeated word, or group of letters.'

'Could it be THAT? Oh no, it couldn't,' Ben realised.

But even though Ben had admitted his mistake, Freddie
still sneered, 'THAT THAT? THAT THATCHED ROOF?
Do you think it's a landmark? Or that the Chief has a stutter
in texts?'

Ben made a point of ignoring him and instead stared at the
code.

*QG SC QG SC UG SL SW DP QK ZW PF ZY QW CZ LC
TC BN*

As he spooned more rice onto his plate, he had an idea,
but got scared and stopped.

'Are you okay, Ben?'

'Sure.' Before scaring Jess too, he rested the spoon on his bowl and looked at the code again. Yes, it could be. Hoping Freddie or Jess would point out his mistake, he tested it aloud. 'Could it be 993 in letters?'

'Oh gosh!' exclaimed Jess, looking so frightened that he knew that at least he wasn't being an idiot.

Seemingly calm, Freddie considered the code. 'Could be. Yes. That could be it.'

993, the fungicide which SPC had had to scrap because it was far too toxic to enter the food chain, was the poison with which the Chief apparently planned to murder millions of children and teenagers. It was the poison which Ben had begun to hope was just a hoax, since the attacks so far had been with other poisons, to which there were antidotes. But there was no antidote to 993.

Meanwhile, Jess was busy writing.

'It looks possible, doesn't it?' she asked, showing them a new square.

Q	N
I	G

'So, this means Q and N would be in the same row?' Ben.

Jess nodded. 'You go to the opposite corners of the square or rectangle they make.'

He checked the Norham grid to try and understand.

N	O	R	H	A
M	B	C	D	E
F	G	I/J	K	L
P	Q	S	T	U
V	W	X	Y	Z

'So *QN* would be PO in this?'

'Exactly. We'd draw this, see?' Jess replied.

Q	P
O	N

'Oh,' Ben said, suddenly understanding. 'So those squares don't tell us what order the letters are in, but it does give you the row and column.'

Jess beamed. 'Exactly! Q is in the same row as P and same column as O.'

'That's brilliant, Jess.'

'I didn't think of it. Dorothy L. Sayers did.'

'She'd have nicked it off military intelligence,' Freddie said, as if he'd know. 'If spies really did use it.'

'They must have. Peter Wimsey was supposed to be a secret agent. She was a very clever lady. She wouldn't have lied,' Jess replied.

Incredulous, Ben looked at her. But Jess looked serious. Wasn't the whole of fiction a lie? Stories were created and imagined, not the truth. (Though he recalled Mum arguing that they often showed more truth than reality.)

Freddie snatched the page out of his hand, surprising him.

'Forget the Norham grid. That grid doesn't matter. Every key leads to a different grid.'

'Q and N are three letters apart in the alphabet.' Jess said. 'Neither is in the key, then. They're in the same row.'

'G and I would be on the third row then, and Q and N on the fourth. They're not in the key either,' Freddie said, secretly impressing Ben, but he wasn't going to say so, not after the way Freddie had been behaving.

Meanwhile, Jess was writing again.

S	N
E	C

'So S is with N and Q on the fourth row. That means at least one of O, P and R is in the key,' Freddie realised, fast as a flash. 'Probably O.'

'Then we can probably sketch out the last two rows,' Jess said. 'At least.'

'How?' Ben asked. His clever cousins were way ahead of him. He watched, deeply impressed, as Jess sketched out a grid. She first realised that N and S were five letters apart, so probably occupied the fourth row. Then G went above N, and I above Q, meaning two rows of the table were almost fixed.

G	H	I	K/L	L/M
N	P	Q	R	S

'Wow!' Ben grinned at her.

'It was your insight into 993 that gave us this,' Jess said.

'And it could easily be wrong. In which case, this is a waste of time,' Freddie pointed out, making Ben feel guilty. But at the speed his cousins' minds were working, it was at least not much time.

'So either K, L or M must be in the key,' Jess said.

'Probably L?' Ben surmised.

'That would mean two of the last few letters are in the key. Probably T and something,' Freddie said.

Meanwhile, Jess was saying, 'This means T and U must begin the last row. T's not in the key. U's below H.'

U	T
H	G

'So V, W, X, Y or Z is in the key?' Ben said.

'Two of them are. W and Y probably,' Freddie replied.

'Those squares are amazing, Jess,' Ben congratulated her.

'It's all thanks to Dorothy L. Sayers. I couldn't have done it otherwise,' she replied, for about the fiftieth time.

'If this is right,' Freddie said, making it seem as likely as a dragon suddenly appearing.

'If it is right, I'll write to Dorothy L. Sayers and thank her,' Ben vowed.

'You'd struggle,' Freddie sneered. 'She's been dead for years.'

'But it's really nice of you to say so,' Jess added, glaring at her brother. 'If so, C is in the same column as N. Meaning the key's very short, or C is the first letter.'

'Then E's above S,' Ben noticed, from the second letter square Jess had drawn.

'It's probably in the key too, then,' Jess said, writing it in.

C				E
G	H	I	K/L	L/M
N	P	Q	R	S
T	U			

Ben looked at what Jess had written below the cipher.

QG SC QG SC UG SL SW   DP QK ZW   PF ZY QW   CZ LC TC BN
ni   ne   ni   ne   th   re   qe

Ben frowned. 'There's no Q in three.'

'You insert Q or X or Z between repeated letters in Playfair, Ben.'

'She told us that ages ago,' Freddie snapped.

Ben glared at Freddie. 'Something must have wiped it from my mind. I don't know. Maybe the car coming straight at me?'

'That's your own fault for going out there.'

'Stop it, you two. I think Ben is right about L,' Jess said.

'It probably contains O, W and Y too, so it could very well be COWLEY,' Freddie said.

'Could be.' Jess flashed him a meaningful look.

'Why?' Ben recognised the name because Mum had often mentioned Cowley Street, where in her student days she had shared a rented house with Aunt Miriam and two friends of theirs.

'It's part of Oxford. We might have the key,' Jess said. 'If so, we can solve the cipher.'

'That's amazing! Well done, you two.'

'And you. We'd never have got it without you spotting 993,' Jess said.

'It's hardly surprising.' They'd only heard of 993 a couple of weeks ago. Since it was a potential business breakthrough for Mum, he'd known of it for years.

'No. But it was still a fantastic insight,' Jess said.

'Stop congratulating yourselves. It's probably wrong,' Freddie snapped.

'It stacks up with the cipher so far.' Jess was filling up the grid.

'Funny that Marcus didn't think of it then, isn't it? He's been involved with 993 a lot longer than we have,' Freddie said.

'He had a lot on his mind,' Jess said.

'Maybe more than we know,' Freddie replied, darkly.

Suddenly Ben suspected Marcus again. Maybe Freddie was right. Maybe Goatee Man had been going rogue. Or maybe Jess was right. Maybe Marcus had been too busy to think about the code and was on their side.

But which was true?

While he wondered, Jess completed the grid.

C	O	W	L	E
Y	A	B	D	F
G	H	I/J	K	M
N	P	Q	R	S
T	U	V	X	Z

And as they cracked the cipher – working together, because Playfair was complicated at first, but the diagonals quickly became easy to spot – they realised that their workings so far had been right and that they were cracking the code. They were worried, frightened and mightily puzzled by the deciphered message:

993 arrives at five twenty

Ben checked his watch. Six forty-five. It had already arrived.

'Why is the Chief telling Nixon that? He's supposed to be making the 993,' Jess worried.

'Why would Marcus tell us? It's probably a lie,' Freddie said.

'He's not telling us anything. He didn't think we'd crack the code.' Jess seemed to suspect Marcus again, Ben noticed.

'You'd think he'd have thought of 993. He's been aware of this plot for a long time. 993 should be at the front of his mind,' Freddie said.

'Do you think it means 993 arrived today?' Jess asked.

'Yes. It must mean today, or else it would give a date,' Freddie said.

Jess stood up. 'We've got to warn the police.'

Ben remembered Marcus's warning to tell no one. 'We can't! They'd know Marcus had pinched the text. It would get him killed.'

'He *will* know about the text, if he's the Chief,' Freddie said.

'If he is, why would he give us this then?' Ben said, jabbing his finger at it, exasperated by Freddie's obstinacy.

'Because he thought we wouldn't solve it,' Freddie said in a sing-song voice, like a young child taunting a rival.

'Maybe it's to distract us from stopping the attack,' Jess said, distracting Ben from retaliating. 'Maybe it's happening right now. We should definitely tell the police.'

'We can't!' Ben cried. 'We need to text him and tell him what it says.'

'We've got to tell the police. Not about him, but about the attack,' Jess said.

'No!' Freddie glared at her. 'Tell them nothing. Tell him nothing. We don't know for sure who the Chief is yet. But we're close, very close. It's one of three now, Ballantyne or Knox or him.'

'We *must* tell them,' Jess insisted.

Ben stared at them, torn.

Chapter 6

The Police Interview

The doorbell rang. The cousins eyed each other uncertainly.

'It could be a friend of Daphne's,' Jess said, as convincingly as a teacher insisting that there really is a Tooth Fairy.

'Or a Jehovah's Witness. You go. I need to think,' Freddie said.

'You're the teenager, not her,' Ben said, disappointed in Freddie, but not surprised. He was a coward.

The doorbell rang again, and the caller started banging on the door. He advanced down the hall, reminding himself the door was locked, solid and partly see-through. Through the stained-glass Ben saw a slender figure of about his own height (about 1.85 m when he'd last been measured).

Goatee Man was about his height, but broader.

'Who is it?'

'Police.'

'Ask for his warrant card, Ben. Put it on the chain,' Jess advised, as he unlocked the door. He did so, thankful for her wisdom.

'You're right to be cautious,' said the caller, who was Detective Inspector Liam Cunningham, according to the ID card. 'Can I come in?'

'Sure.' Ben released the chain and let him in. He had short brown hair and a narrow face.

They led him into the kitchen, where Freddie had turned over the papers, but left all the food cartons sitting where they were. Jess glared at him. He deserved it.

DI Cunningham leant back against the worktop, his white shirt and black trousers reminiscent of school uniform, Ben thought. He folded his arms. 'Tell me about your near miss with the car. What happened?'

'It tried to hit me on the crossing. A white Merc, like theirs. It just missed me.'

'The pedestrian crossing on South Parks Road?'

'Yeah.'

'And your signal was green, so theirs must have been red?'

'Yeah.'

'It was parked,' Jess said. 'When it saw Ben, it started up and headed for him.'

'Were you there?' the policeman asked.

'No. Ben told me.'

'Then let him tell me, if you don't mind. What did the driver look like?'

'It had blacked-out windows. Tinted glass. Like theirs does.'

'Who are *they*?'

'Kashani and Goatee Man. We don't know his name.'

'I've seen the photo-fit of Goatee Man,' DI Cunningham said. 'But we've got Kashani. So it was him driving, that Goatee Man?'

'Maybe. But that car's still in Manchester. I think,' Ben added.

The DI frowned. 'Why?'

'They switched from a white Merc to a black one when they kidnapped me.'

'Which was last Thursday?' he said, showing he'd researched the case.

'Yeah. That's right.'

'Leaving it where?'

'The Didsbury Road car park near home. Stockport,' Ben added.

'But they drugged you,' Freddie said. 'They could have switched back to the white car.'

'They'd have had to carry me. I went out like a light,' Ben added.

'Or both of them could have driven a car down?' DI Cunningham suggested.

'Yeah. I guess so. If Goatee Man can drive.'

'Whether he's passed his test I don't know, but I bet he does.'

'I bet it was him then,' Ben said.

'But regrettably you can't prove it. The plates were stolen,' the policeman said.

'Were they? I didn't have time to notice.'

'No, but the woman who called us did.'

'That was good of her,' Ben said, feeling guilty he'd not thanked her.

'Would you like a drink?' Jess offered.

'No thanks. I've no time. I heard your mum was arrested.'

'Yeah. Have you seen her?' Ben asked, desperate for news. How soon would she be released? Why hadn't she been released already?

'No I haven't, sorry,' Inspector Cunningham replied, seeming to understand Ben's urgency. 'But it's strange her attacking you. Because you nearly died, didn't you? From the cyanide?'

'Mum wouldn't have wanted me attacked. She'd never hurt me. Or anyone. She's good. She's kind. She's nice. She is *not* the Chief.'

'But my colleague, who is questioning her right now, seems convinced that she is. Do you happen to know why?'

'She's mad!' Ben declared, flaring up.

'No, Ben, she's not,' Jess said. 'She had a good reason to suspect your mum. The text.' Jess explained it to DI Cunningham. 'But it wasn't Aunt Sue who sent it,' she added. 'She would have phoned my mum, not typed out a text in a hurry.'

'They must have cloned her phone when they kidnapped her,' Freddie said, as if it was his idea, not Marcus's.

DI Cunningham nodded. 'I presume you told Inspector Walker this?'

'We didn't know about the text then. But Mum would have,' Jess said.

'She might not have thought of cloning then,' Ben said, absolutely positive that it wouldn't have occurred to Aunt

Miriam, but not wanting to give the misleading impression that she was stupid.

'I'll make sure she knows. Thanks for your help.' He took some papers out of his bag and started scribbling. He detached a sheet and gave it to Ben. It told him to contact St Aldate's Police Station if he had any concerns.

Ben had one concern that dwarfed every other.

'Are you going to free my mum?'

'It's not my case. It's Inspector Walker's. But I'm certainly going to ask a few questions.'

'Thanks,' Ben said, trusting that he would.

He smiled, his eyes crinkling. 'No problem.'

Ben escorted him to the door feeling much more positive about the police, or some of them at least. DI Cunningham was on his side, he felt. And so did Jess, he discovered, when he returned to the kitchen.

But, as so often happened, Freddie disagreed with them both.

'He's not on your side any more than Inspector Walker. Anyway, the Playfair Cipher's more important. Why do they need to tell Nixon it's arriving here tonight?' Freddie said.

'We need to ask Marcus,' Ben said. 'He'll know.'

'No! If he's the Chief, he'll realise we're getting too close,' Freddie said.

'Oh gosh, it's difficult, isn't it?' Jess said, burying her face in her hands.

It was. It was mightily difficult. And before Ben had decided upon the right course of action, the doorbell rang again.

Behind the glass was a slender figure of medium height with brown shoulder-length hair.

'It's Debs,' Ben told Jess, who was with him.

He opened the door. Her usually friendly face was full of distress. She was wearing work clothes; a brown suit and a green patterned blouse.

'What the hell has happened, Benbo?' she asked, using the nickname she'd bestowed on Ben ever since they'd watched *The Hobbit* together, on account of his supposed resemblance to Elijah Wood. (It was the blue eyes, apparently.

But she had probably been desperate for a nickname for him. She had nicknames for everyone).

'Come in, Debs. This is Daphne's house,' Ben said, realising as he did so how stupid he sounded. Debs knew his house as well as anyone, being Mum's closest colleague and also her closest friend.

'I know,' Debs replied, stepping inside. 'Marcus told me where you'd be. Hi, Jess.'

'Hi, Debs.'

'Mum's been arrested.'

'I know, Benbo. It's nuts! Crazy! The police have lost their minds.'

'Did you see it online?'

'No, Marcus told me. There's been nothing in the media, thankfully,' Debs responded. Ben gave a sigh of relief. 'The police have gone stark staring raving mad.'

'They think she's the Chief.'

'That's plain daft,' Debs said, her Yorkshire accent giving emphasis to the phrase. 'Anyone with an ounce of sense would know she'd never hurt a fly, let alone children. She's still in custody?'

'Guess so. She'd have phoned me if she was free.'

'I know she would. Sorry, Benbo. And what about you? You've been in the wars.'

Ben was horrified. '*What*? Is that on the news?'

'Not you so much as the children who died,' she replied. Realising she meant the swimming pool, and not the hit and run, Ben breathed again. She would definitely have mentioned the attack on him tonight, if she'd heard about it. 'But what about you? Are you fully recovered?'

'Oh yeah, fine now, thanks.'

But others weren't, Ben thought, bowing his head as he recalled the horrors of the pool. It was too hard to take it in, even now, that they had deliberately laced the pool with cyanide, that they had poisoned innocent teenagers having fun at a party. But with 993 in the pool, many more of them would have died.

Debs and Jess had been chatting.

'What if they use 993?' Jess said, as if she'd been reading Ben's mind. 'There aren't any antidotes if they do use it, are there?'

'None at all. Never ever dive in any pool that you have even the slightest smidgen of suspicion might contain 993, Benbo. If it had been 993, you'd be dead. Every single one of those swimmers would be dead. Even some of the rescuers might be, depending on how much they'd got on their skin.'

Ben knew 993 was absorbed through skin, but had hoped shutting his mouth and closing his eyes as much as possible would allow him a few minutes' grace in the pool. Evidently not. He had been stupid again. And again, nearly died.

Uncle Henry was right to call him reckless. He had been so unfair to the people who loved him, especially Mum.

He had put her through so much suffering recently. He was a terrible, thoughtless son.

He would never dive into danger again, he vowed.

'Alright, Benbo?' Debs asked.

'Yeah. I'm fine thanks. But Mum isn't. We've got to get her free.'

'I can't understand why she isn't.'

'Me neither,' Jess said.

They hadn't even moved off the doormat before the doorbell rang again. Through the glass he easily recognised the tall thin man and short stout woman, so he opened it immediately.

Uncle Henry and Aunt Miriam joined them in the hall. As soon as he heard his father's voice, Freddie emerged from the kitchen.

There was a quick conversation about the lack of news on Mum, the absurdity of the charges and the guest house they had found. Apparently, Debs had been en route to Heathrow.

'It's very kind of you to return for Sue,' said Aunt Miriam.

'I can't go anywhere while Sue's in prison. They'd ask about her. What would I say?'

Whilst the adults chatted about Debs' changed plans, he checked his phone. He had a new message from an unknown number. A code.

'All right, Ben?' Aunt Miriam asked.

'Yeah, fine,' he lied, but he wasn't. This wasn't from Marcus. It was from Nixon, or the Chief.

'We haven't eaten yet. Have you?' Uncle Henry said.

'Yes. We had a takeaway, thanks, Dad,' Jess replied. 'Daphne had to go to a meeting.'

'Oxford Humanists. Sir Christopher Cockerell is speaking,' added Freddie.

'Is he?' Uncle Henry looked interested, as he always did at the mention of a titled person, and especially a titled scientist.

'Never mind him. What about Sue?' Debs said.

Ben nodded his approval.

'I've got a good mind to go to that police station and demand they release her,' Aunt Miriam declared.

'Yeah!' Ben agreed, all set to join them in the car – but then remembered the code. Meanwhile, Uncle Henry was arguing that it was no use going to the police station.

'P'raps not, but it'll make us feel better and it might just work,' Debs said.

'I'd rather you three stayed together, here. Would you mind, Ben?' Aunt Miriam said, as if apologising, but it furnished him with the perfect get-out.

''Course not!'

'We can get something to eat in town,' Uncle Henry said, showing where his priorities lay.

'Afterwards,' Debs insisted, glaring at Uncle Henry. He huffed and made a point of checking his watch, but didn't argue.

'Good luck. If you see Mum, tell her I love her.'

'You can tell her yourself, Benbo. We'll be bringing her back with us,' said Debs, and as he watched them getting into her car, he had a faint hope that, with DI Cunningham's support, they might just succeed.

Chapter 7

Saint or Psycho?

They returned to the kitchen, where Ben showed the code to his cousins. Jess offered to write it out, and since she had the neatest handwriting and avoided the careless slips he would often make, Ben accepted.

As she started writing, she said, 'You're very low on charge, did you notice?'

'Stuff it!' Though this was a blow, Ben always tried to avoid swearing in front of Jess. He had never heard her swear, and he suspected that at her posh girls' school, swear words were as shockingly offensive as boys.

'You're lucky I remembered your mobile,' Freddie said, as if Ben was blaming him for forgetting the charger.

'I know. Thanks. Once you've copied it out, switch it off, Jess, please.'

Soon the code was copied out in Jess's neat writing. And she had already spotted a pattern.

'The ends of the lines are the same, as if it rhymes,' she said.

'So it's probably from the Chief. Nixon wouldn't bother with rhymes,' Freddie replied.

And as Ben viewed the code, he agreed.

XKS CHTU PSNC DJNOUBDAGU PUGR AUGDUR

QK UTUJ BOUHI QCHQ XKS NHJ NHQNC QCU NCDUR

RKO HP VUOJUO CUDPUJAUOY KJNU BDB PCKV

QCU CHOBUO XKS GKKF QCU GUPP XKS NHJ FJKV

ASQ DGG YDTU XKS H PQHOQ

DGG CUGL XKS HGKJY

DR XKS QCDJF DQP CHJASOX

QCUJ XRSOU QCDJFDJY VOKJY

'It's very long,' he said, checking his watch.

'But that makes it easier to crack,' Freddie said.

'But a bit longer to decipher, once you've cracked it,' Jess said, worrying Ben. If it was a warning of an attack again, they had to act fast.

'There's both *J* and *I* so it's not Playfair. Looks like a simple substitution cipher.'

Simple for Freddie, maybe. Ben rolled his eyes. 'Why do you bother saying cipher, not code?'

'Because they're different. Codes have symbols standing for whole words, or parts of words.'

'Like emojis,' Jess interjected.

'Oh, right,' Ben said, understanding now.

'But in a cipher, one symbol or letter stands for another,' Freddie said. 'So this is a cipher, Playfair are ciphers and all the Chief's codes so far have, in fact, been ciphers.'

'Okay. It's a cipher. I get it. So what does it say?'

'*QCU*'s probably THE,' Freddie said, pointing to the fourth line.

'It's on the last line too,' Jess said. 'So *J* is probably N.'

'And *H* must be A, mustn't it?' ventured Ben, noticing *QCHQ*.

'Yes, must be. It's on its own too. There may be a key,' Freddie added, 'like in Playfair, but in substitution ciphers you continue alphabetically.'

'Huh?'

'A–B–C – you know.'

'Of course I know that!' Ben snapped. 'What do you *mean*?'

'If your key ends in *S*, the next letter is *T* – unless *T* is in your key.'

'Good.' Ben was relieved to have a seemingly easy code that Freddie understood. Jess was busy writing out an alphabet.

'Do it in lower case, Jess. That's coding convention,' Freddie said. 'Codes are written in capitals, and the uncoded message is called the plaintext.'

Ben rolled his eyes, irritated by Freddie's constant need to show off. He was clever. They got it.

'Why are you even bothering?' he murmured to Jess, who had scrapped the alphabet she had begun.

She shrugged. 'I suppose it helps to avoid mistakes.'

a	b	c	d	e	f	g	h	i	j	k	l	m
H				U			C					
n	o	p	q	r	s	t	u	v	w	x	y	z
J						Q						

'So the top row is the alphabet?' Ben asked, confused.

'It's the plaintext!' Freddie snapped, as if Ben had insulted him.

'That means the message in English, before you translate it into your cipher,' Jess explained.

'So *Q* in the code – '

'Cipher!'

Ben glared at Freddie. 'Cipher, stands for T in the alphabet. I mean the plaintext,' he quickly added before Freddie snapped at him again.

Jess was now inserting the letters that they thought they had identified underneath the code, making guessing the words much easier. But it was a little more confusing, because she couldn't fit it on the page, so she was splitting each line into two.

'Couldn't you just write tiny?' Ben asked her.

Jess grimaced. 'Not really, sorry. It needs to be spaced out so that we don't get confused.'

'Okay,' Ben said, not really meaning it. But as he watched her filling in letters, he began see what she meant.

X K S   C H T U   P S N C
       H A   E   H
D J N O U B D A G U   P U G R   A U G D U R
  N   E   E   E   E   E

Q K   U T U J   B O U H I   Q C H Q   X K S
T   E   E   E A   T H A T
N H J   N H Q N C   Q C U   N C D U R
  A N   A T   H   T H E   H   E

R K O   H P   V U O J U O   C U D P U J A —
       A   E   N E   E   E N
U O Y   K J N U   B D B   P C K V
E   N   E

Q C U   C H O B U O   X K S   G K K F
T H E   H A   E
Q C U   G U P P   X K S   N H J   F J K V
T H E   E   A N   N

Their deductions came thick and fast after she had finished.

'*T* stands for V and *P* for S, I think,' Jess said.

'*N* stands for C – can and catch, look!' Ben said, pointing to the bottom row of the second section.

'That's the Chief at the end,' Jess added.

'*XKS* is you,' Freddie spotted.

Jess added this to her table, and it was clear that lots of the cipher was alphabetical.

a	b	c	d	e	f	g	h	i	j	k	l	m
H		N		U	R		C	D		F		I

n	o	p	q	r	s	t	u	v	w	x	y	z
J	K			P			T			X		

'It's a substitution cipher with a key, and the best bet for the key is HANBURY,' Freddie declared, sitting back, arms folded.

'I think you're right, Freddie. It's not got E in – you can see the alphabet – C, D, E, F, G – then leave out H. Then comes I, J, K, L, M, then leave out either N or O. So N is in the key! It probably is Hanbury. I can't think of another word that would fit.'

Jess was practically a dictionary on legs, so that convinced Ben – and worried him.

'Hanbury? That's so weird. Does that mean he sent it?' Ben asked. 'Why would he tell me that?'

'He's playing with you, Ben. It's Ballantyne,' Jess said. Ben nodded. That fitted his taunting, nasty personality. Except…

'Why would he make it so easy to crack then?'

'We need to see what it says.'

'You start with the key, then continue the alphabet. So after Y comes Z.'

After writing in a few letters, Jess stopped. 'That's wrong.'

'What's up?' Ben asked, looking at it.

a	b	c	d	e	f	g	h	i	j	k	l	m
H	A	N	B	U	R	Y	Z	C				

'C's under i, not h.'

'What if C comes after Hanbury?' Ben said.

'That's not a proper substitution cipher. Well it is, because it's one letter representing another, but it's not how you're meant to do them,' Freddie said. 'You're meant to start with the next letter of the alphabet after the key.'

'But Ballantyne wants to confuse us. He'd twist it. It's Ballantyne who's written this,' Ben said, suddenly convinced.

'Marcus might want to confuse us,' Freddie said.

'Or it could be Nixon, getting it wrong,' Jess said, creating another code. 'That seems to fit so far.' She finished the grid.

a	b	c	d	e	f	g	h	i	j	k	l	m
H	A	N	B	U	R	Y	C	D	E	F	G	I
n	o	p	q	r	s	t	u	v	w	x	y	z
J	K	L	M	O	P	Q	S	T	V	W	X	Z

'XKS is you,' Freddie said. 'I think that's right.'

Ben left them to crack it and marched around, thinking of Ballantyne. He'd got Mum arrested and he'd tried to get Ben to go with him earlier. He was much more likely to be the Chief, than Marcus – except why would he want to save him?

'Oh my giddy aunt!' Jess exclaimed.

Ben shot over to read what she'd written.

You have such incredible self-belief
To even dream that you can catch the Chief,
For as Werner Heisenberg once did show,
The harder you look, the less you can know.
But I'll give you a start,
I'll help you along.
If you think it's Hanbury,
Then you're thinking wrong.

'What the hell does that mean?' Ben said.

'I think they mean that the Chief isn't Hanbury,' Jess replied.

'We didn't think he was,' Freddie said.

'But maybe they're lying. Maybe this means the Chief *is* Hanbury,' Jess said.

'He'd never call himself Hanbury! He's a Lord!' Freddie protested, and given what little he knew of Hanbury, Ben believed him.

'Whoever wrote this has very little respect for him.'

'Good spot, Jess.'

'*Heisenberg* is interesting,' Freddie said.

'What exactly *is* Heisenberg?' asked Ben.

'A scientist. One of the principal architects of quantum theory,' Freddie replied.

'Huh?'

'It's *Heisenberg's Uncertainty Principle* they mean. The more you try to pin an electron down, the more uncertain its position and momentum become!' Jess said, beaming.

'That's nuts.'

'But it's true. It's been tested lots and lots of times.'

'The whole of quantum mechanics seems nuts to an unscientific mind,' Freddie said, digging at him, Ben thought, 'which is why I'm convinced Nixon couldn't have written this. But Marcus could. He would know about Heisenberg. It's very famous.'

'It's not famous and it's not Marcus!'

Freddie smirked. 'Who are you trying to convince? Me or yourself?'

Himself. But he'd rather pull a fingernail out than tell his maddening cousin that he was right. So Ben said nothing.

'Everything is uncertain, down to the tiniest particles. That's the key to creation. That's the wonder of the universe,' Freddie said, waving his arms about, just like his dad did when excited about physics.

'I could do with a lot less uncertainty right now,' Ben said.

There was a key in the door. Who was it? Daphne, back much earlier than she'd said? Or Marcus? And why did that make him so nervous?

'It's only me,' called Marcus.

'Don't tell him we've cracked the Playfair,' whispered Freddie.

'Why?'

'It's a test.'

Ben looked at him, but Freddie's wide-eyed insistence convinced him to comply for now. Marcus was either a saint, or a psycho, he reminded himself, as his heart started thudding and his stomach churning.

Hearing his footsteps advance down the hall, Ben attempted to look relaxed, despite his inner turmoil. Marcus entered the kitchen, the power of his muscular body evident beneath his tight white shirt. Ben recalled those arms holding him captive and being unable to escape. But Marcus wasn't looking menacing now, he was grinning broadly.

'I made the lab just in time. By tomorrow night, we'll know for sure.' He looked genuinely delighted. But, as Jess had pointed out, psychopaths could be charming. 'Any luck with that code?'

'Not yet,' Freddie said. He was good at lying, but Ben wasn't. It often made him blush.

'Let's see if I can help. I've got ten minutes before the Board meeting.' He smiled again, as seemingly friendly as a golden Labrador – and so unlike Ballantyne, who always made Ben feel as edgy as if he was infested with poisonous ants.

Yet someone had saved him, twice. It wouldn't be Nixon. It couldn't be Ballantyne. It must surely be Marcus.

But to save him from the pool, he must have known about the poison, Ben suddenly realised. He had lied!

'I must pick up the spare keys,' Marcus said.

Ben gulped. If he'd lied about the murders, he had lied about everything. So he must be the Chief and spare keys could admit him to the house at any time – even when they were all asleep and at their most vulnerable.

'Here's your cipher,' Jess said. She somehow retrieved the right sheet and showed it to him.

QG SC QG SC UG SL SW DP QK ZW PF ZY QW CZ LC TC BN

'So you think it is Playfair, do you?' he asked. 'Not a substitution cipher?'

Ben exchanged a quick glance with Freddie. Was that a hint that he'd sent the Hanbury Cipher?

'Maybe. But without the key, it's impossible,' claimed Jess.

'I'm not surprised,' Marcus seemed to sympathise – or was he secretly delighted? 'It's far too short. Long codes are easier to crack. Something this short could mean anything.'

'The repeat at the beginning is the way in,' Freddie said.

Ben glared at him. He was practically telling Marcus they had cracked it! He just couldn't resist showing off.

'The repeat at the beginning is interesting, I agree,' Marcus said. 'It could be our way in. But it could also be their convention, to lock and padlock it.'

'What does that mean?' Jess asked.

Ben, too, was baffled, but Freddie looked as if he understood. (Though even if he didn't, nothing would persuade him to admit it.)

'If they always begin messages with the same phrase, then if a message arrives that doesn't begin with it, it's suspicious,' Marcus explained. Or lied.

'Oh I see. So that might not be a clue at all?' Jess said, as if duped.

'Sadly, no.'

But that was rubbish. Marcus must know that. Was he putting them off the scent deliberately? So why had he given them the code?

'Sorry, guys. I can't make any headway with the code. I might have sent you on a wild goose chase.' He turned to Ben. 'I came to tell you about the test and that I won't be back as early as I'd hoped. I'm going out for supper with the Board. Will you be okay on your own?'

'Sure.'

'What about food?'

'Your mum gave us money for a takeaway. We've eaten, thanks,' Ben replied.

'Good old Ma. That's great.' He checked his watch. 'Right, I'd better get cracking.' He checked his mobile. 'There's something even more devious than I suspected going on. I'm determined to get to the bottom of it. If you can make any headway on that code, let me know. But if you do, I'll be amazed.'

'If we do, we'll be amazed,' Jess responded.

'Stay safe. Don't go out. You're safe here,' Marcus said, his sky-blue eyes utterly genuine.

He might well care for him, if he was his dad. But why had he killed those other teenagers? Or allowed those other teenagers to be killed? Please don't let him be the Chief, Ben begged a silent, uncaring, impotent universe, as Marcus pointed out that he was panting again.

'You're not well. You should still be in hospital,' he said, seemingly thoughtful and caring and genuine. The opposite of the Chief.

Confused, Ben followed Marcus out to the hall, where he took some spare keys from the drawer in the walnut dresser.

'See you later. Tomorrow will be a very big day for all of us,' he said, meaning the paternity test results, Ben assumed. Or could it be another threat?

'As long as we've got Aunt Sue back,' Jess said.

'We will have. By then we must have. I'll bet she'll be back before I am tonight.'

'I hope so,' Ben said.

But are you the Chief? The blue eyes, the wide smile and the open expression seemed to beam out compassion and goodness and honesty. But were they hiding a devil inside?

Chapter 8

Not Exactly Alan Turing

Ten minutes after Marcus had left, they were still arguing.

'He wouldn't have attacked us in his mum's house, would he? He'd be the obvious suspect,' Freddie said.

'So you're still convinced it's him?' Ben asked.

'Obviously.'

'But I'm not,' Jess said, smiling at him. 'Have you locked the door?'

''Course. But he's got keys.'

Freddie darted him a worried glance. Ben felt that he had to apologise for his dad and hated doing so.

'I can't help it. It's his mum's house. He lived here.'

'He's not going to hurt us here! Marcus would be the prime suspect, as you said, Freddie,' Jess said.

'Marcus doesn't want to kill Ben. He wants to save Ben. It's his vanity. Ben is his son, so he's half of Marcus,' Freddie added, needlessly. He'd already said so, countless times.

'I hate the fact that he saved me, but wasn't bothered about the other people dying,' Ben said, thoroughly miserable now.

'Maybe not. Maybe he genuinely had no idea,' Jess said. 'If they know he saved you, maybe they don't trust him anymore.'

'That's a good point,' Ben said, relieved. Then they wouldn't have told him about the attack beforehand, or the ice cream attack, in case he stopped them. That could explain everything. His gut said Marcus was innocent. Maybe he was right. He shared his thoughts with his cousins.

'So why haven't they killed him then?' Freddie asked.

'Because then the police would arrest them,' Jess said.

Ben didn't buy that argument. 'They've killed *children*, Jess. They've not arrested them. They've arrested Mum.'

'But who sent that text?' Jess asked. 'It can't have been Marcus, if he's innocent. But I can't see Nixon or Ballantyne sending it either. Maybe we're wrong about Ballantyne. Maybe the Chief is Knox.'

'But then why would he kill children and want to save Ben? It's Marcus I tell you,' Freddie insisted.

Ben's text alert bleeped. There were two new messages, both from Marcus. The first was in their usual cipher, followed by another string of capitals. He showed his cousins the texts, noticing the battery life was now very low indeed. 'We'd better get them written out before my phone dies.'

'I'll do it,' Jess offered, so Ben handed her his phone. 'These prove he's on our side, don't they?'

'I don't trust him,' Freddie said, shaking his head.

'I know. I think I do,' Ben said.

'You don't trust him. If you *think* you do, you don't. If you did, you'd have said you trust him. So you don't.'

'Yeah, all right, I don't. Not completely. My gut says I should, but my brain says be careful. I just can't think of anyone else that would want to save me,' Ben said, feeling treacherous again. 'Could it be anyone else? Are we missing anything?'

'Well, we know it's someone who knew about 993. That means an SPC insider,' Freddie said, narrowing it down to about 20,000 people worldwide.

'It's got to be someone from the HQ and senior to Mum and Debs. Products are pretty secret until they're launched,' Ben said.

'So that means: Ballantyne, Marcus, Nixon, Curtis, Hazel, Knox and Hanbury.'

'Yes, but Curtis and Hazel don't really get involved in products. Certainly not Hazel. She's HR.'

'What?'

'Human Resources,' Ben replied. 'They look after people, not products. And Curtis is an accountant. He wouldn't be so involved.'

'He wouldn't have the vision to launch this scheme,' Freddie said.

Though Ben didn't like him crediting the Chief with vision, he agreed that Curtis wasn't a serious candidate. Nixon would never take orders from him. No one would.

'So we're down to Knox, Hanbury, Marcus, Nixon and Ballantyne,' Jess said.

'Nixon can't be the Chief. Nor can Marcus. They were talking about the Chief in that meeting. The Chief wasn't there.'

'Unless Marcus was fooling Nixon,' Freddie said.

'Or Nixon was fooling Marcus. But I don't think either of them was.'

'But that text saved your life. Which of them would want to do that, other than Marcus?'

'I can't think of anyone.'

'Neither can I.'

'Unless it's to incriminate Mum, like Jess said,' Ben said.

'Either Nixon or Ballantyne would love to do that. Or Marcus if he's a psychopath.'

'He's not a psychopath!'

'A lot of senior business people are. They are ruthless, feel no guilt about lying, and usually highly intelligent. Like Marcus,' Freddie said.

Ben lapsed into silence. Marcus was very good at lying, and he hadn't seemed guilty about it. But that had been to protect Ben. Mum had believed him. But had she been conned by him too? Had they all been?

'Could you translate this, guys, whilst I copy out the other?' Jess asked.

Ben went over to get it. She handed him her numbered cipher, Puck's closing speech from *A Midsummer Night's Dream*, which was their book cipher. Book ciphers were easy to use and read, because they just involved taking the first letter of the numbered word.

1	2	3		4	5	
If	*we*	*shadows*		*have*	*offended,*	
6	7	8	9	10	11	12
Think	*but*	*this,*	*and*	*all*	*is*	*mended,*
13	14	15		16	17	18
That	*you*	*have*		*but*	*slumbered*	*here*
19	20	21		22	23	
While	*these*	*visions*		*did*	*appear,*	
24	25	26		27	28	29
And	*this*	*weak*		*and*	*idle*	*theme*
30	31	32		33	34	35
No	*more*	*yielding*		*but*	*a*	*dream,*
36	37	38		39		
Gentles,	*do*	*not*		*reprehend;*		
40	41	42		43	44	45
If	*you*	*pardon,*		*we*	*will*	*mend:*
46	47	48	49	50	51	52
And,	*as*	*I*	*am*	*an*	*honest*	*Puck,*
53	54	55		56	57	
If	*we*	*have*		*unearned*	*luck,*	
58	59	60		61	62	63
Now	*to*	*'scape*		*the*	*serpent's*	*tongue,*
64	65	66		67	68	69
We	*will*	*make*		*amends*	*ere*	*long;*
70	71	72		73	74	75
Else	*the*	*Puck*		*a*	*liar*	*call;*
76	77	78		79	80	81
So,	*good*	*night*		*unto*	*you*	*all.*
82	83	84	85	86	87	88	89
Give	*me*	*your*	*hands,*	*if*	*we*	*be*	*friends,*
90	91	92		93	94	
And	*Robin*	*shall*		*restore*	*amends.*	

It didn't take long to decode the cipher.

46	57	92	5		89	39	5	45		52	58
A	L	S	O		F	R	O	M		P	N

Somehow Marcus had managed to sneak another look at Nixon's phone, which seemed incredible, as Freddie pointed out.

'Why is he even bothering to send it to us when he thinks we're so stupid we can't spot it's 993?' he added.

Ben forbore to retort that his cousins hadn't spotted 993 either.

'Your phone is almost out of charge now, Ben, so I've switched it off. At least I finished first,' Jess said, handing him the phone and the code.

GZ NW CG CQ PB YD HF KZ OU TN HN YS HJ RP UR UM DE HK QD UR RM LH JW TV UZ NL RM NW PR LC HK QJ GT

'You've put it into pairs. Digraphs,' Ben added quickly, seeing Freddie's mouth open.

'There's a J, but no I's and no spaces. It's probably Playfair, I think,' Jess replied.

'They've changed the key,' Freddie said.

'*What*? Isn't it COWLEY?'

'Not unless their message begins MTQC.'

Ben looked at the grid and realised he was right. 'Stuff it!'

They all stared at the string of letters. *UR UM* struck Ben as faintly comical and then he noticed another *UR*. He pointed it out.

'*RM* repeats as well,' Jess said, drawing a letter square.

R	T
H	M

'So does *NW*,' Freddie said. 'And one of those is after *RM*. I'll bet *RM* is TH and *NW* is E blank.'

Ben was dubious about his insistence that every short text must contain TH. But Jess was trying it out so, unable to think of a better suggestion, he watched her.

N	E
?	W

'Say R and M aren't in the key and T and H aren't too, how would that grid look?' Ben asked.

'You might as well ask how any grid would look,' Freddie scoffed, but Jess understood what he'd meant and drew it out. She filled in the bottom row, then started filling in the rows above.

H I	H I K	L M	M N	N O
O P	P Q R	R S	S T	T U
V	W	X	Y	Z

'I think Heisenberg applies here, but maybe not to the bottom row,' she said, unsettlingly.

'How do you mean, Heisenberg?' Ben said.

'Uncertainty. I just meant I think we are safer making assumptions about the bottom row than the others. Most words don't contain V, W, X, Y or Z.'

'Oh right.' So why hadn't she just said so, instead of spooking Ben out about the Hanbury cipher?

'If I was setting a key, I'd always include a letter from the bottom row,' Freddie said. 'Else it's too hackable.'

'But they might be complacent. They might believe changing their mobiles and using difficult ciphers is enough,' Jess said.

'If you're right, I'm a banana,' Freddie scoffed.

'It might be right.' Ben hoped it was, so that he could prove his most exasperating cousin wrong.

'If I were choosing a key, I'd use rare letters,' Jess said, apologetically. 'But if this *is* right, P must be in the key, not Q, because U isn't, unless the key is qadi.'

'Yeah, but cardi's got an R in,' Ben said, meaning the abbreviation for cardigan.

'No, I mean Q–A–D–I, an Islamic judge. It's a great Scrabble word when you haven't got A or U. So are qat and qi, but they would be very short keys.'

'Cat?'

'Q–A–T, an Asian plant, also spelled K–H–A–T.'

'Oh. Right,' Ben replied, feeling as stupid as he so often did in the presence of his cousins.

'T and M share a column – the fourth, probably – and R and H do too, meaning S and U aren't in the key. And nor is K,' Freddie said, 'based on letter frequency. So in the unlikely event that this is right, the key contains two of N, O and P. Plus L and I.'

'E too, I think,' Ben said.

Freddie's head snapped round to look at him. 'How come?'

'It's got to be in the same column as W, hasn't it?' he said. 'If this is right.'

'*If,*' Freddie scoffed.

But Jess looked delighted. 'Good spot, Ben! So it's the second or seventh letter of the key!'

'Can we try E second?' Ben suggested.

'Sure.'

'There are more assumptions here than idiots on a reality show,' Freddie snapped.

Ignoring Freddie, (who had surely never seen a reality show in his life) Ben looked at the grid. It seemed okay, so far, to him.

	E			
	H	K	M	N O P
Q	R	S	T	U
V	W	X	Y	Z

'Working backwards – do you mind?' he said, picking up the pen.

'Why not? You've probably screwed it up already,' Freddie grumbled.

He filled in a few more boxes.

	E			
			D	F
G	H	K	M	N O P
Q	R	S	T	U
V	W	X	Y	Z

He hesitated. 'Do we have any pairs in the code to check it against?'

'Do you mean digraphs?' Freddie asked, with more sarcasm in his voice than cheese on a pizza.

Ben and Jess checked the code against the grid.

GZ NW CG CQ PB YD HF KZ OU TN HN YS HJ RP UR UM DE HK QD UR RM LH JW TV UZ NL RM NW PR LC HK QJ GT

'*GZ* must be OV, not NV,' he said.

'Envy, envious – there are lots of words containing NV!' objected Freddie.

'But not starting with them. Is there?' he checked with Jess, wondering if there was another useful Scrabble word (nvadi?) which would prove him wrong.

'Not that I know. It's probably OVER,' she said.

Ben grabbed the pen and drew:

G	O
V	Z

'So O is above Z and N and P are the two in the key!' Ben realised.

'Then *KZ* is OX. It's Oxford, I bet,' Freddie, sounding excited now. '*OU* is FO, which is right, and *TN* is RD, telling us N is below E in the key. This grid might be right.' He made it sound as unlikely as County winning the FA Cup. Ben felt he was being unfair. But Jess didn't seem to mind.

'Brilliant!' she enthused, beaming.

Whilst Freddie muttered to himself, they made a few stabs at guessing the key: LEAPING, PEALING, and even PEARLIER.

'Maybe we're wrong about the L and it's PETREAN,' Jess said.

'What?' Ben asked.

'Alluding to rock. It could be a pun on Nixon's first name,' she explained.

'Marcus wouldn't do that,' Freddie said.

'No, but Ballantyne might.'

Ben agreed with Jess. But then he spotted a flaw.

'Oh no! It must be wrong. Rats!' He hit the table.

Freddie jumped. 'Will you stop doing that? What's up?'

'It ends with MQ. Look. *GT* is MQ.'

Freddie rolled his eyes. Had he been stupid again?

'Q is probably the spacer, Ben,' Jess said. 'If the message contains an odd number of letters, they add the spacer to maintain the digraphs. They did it last time, remember?'

'No. I didn't. But I'm glad you did. Any ideas on the key?'

Freddie was now looking unbearably smug. 'Seven letter word, containing P, L, I and two of A and C, it must be *PELICAN*.'

'Or *PENICILLIN* taking out duplicates,' Jess spotted, very cleverly, Ben thought.

But Freddie didn't agree. 'Idiot! N isn't below E then.'

'Oh yes.' Poor Jess looked shamefaced.

'I think you were amazing. I think you were too, Freddie. I think we all were, to have cracked it so quickly, when it's spy level.'

'It can't be. You're not exactly Alan Turing,' Freddie said, glaring at Ben.

You're not exactly Alan Turing either, thought Ben, but didn't say so.

With Freddie maintaining that the assumptions they had made meant this grid could well be worthless, Jess and Ben divided up the cipher and started decoding it.

P	E	L	I	C
A	N	B	D	F
G	H	K	M	O
Q	R	S	T	U
V	W	X	Y	Z

GZ NW CG CQ PB YD HF KZ OU TN HN YS HJ RP UR
UM DE HK QD UR RM LH JW TV UZ NL RM NW PR LC
HK QJ GT

'Oh, it's Dad's old group!' Jess exclaimed. She had started at the beginning. Ben looked across at her workings. OV ER PO PU LA TI ON OX FO RD.

'Over Population Oxford is that environmental group Rufus belongs to, isn't it?'

'Yes.'

'So we've cracked the code,' Ben said, grinning at her. His section began TATQTHEK, which was less promising. But as he continued, he realised that the message did make sense, especially when they combined their decryptions and crossed out the Qs.

OVER POPULATION OXFORD NEXT MEQET Q TONIGHT AT Q THE KEY Q YOU BE THERE Q EIGHT PM Q

It was already 20:30.

'It's a shame we've missed it. We could probably see them coming out of the meeting, but we'd have to go there,' Jess said.

'*Where*? Where are they? Where's the key?' Ben asked.

'I think they'll mean the pelican,' Jess replied, referring to a pub, Ben assumed. He'd seen The Eagle and Child and The Lamb and Flag – though many of them would get laughed out of town in Stockport, no pub name would surprise him in Oxford.

'Where is it?'

'In Corpus's front quad,' Freddie responded.

'*What*?'

'Corpus Christi, the college.'

Convinced he'd misunderstood, Ben persisted. 'They have a pub in their front quad?'

'No!' Freddie said, looking at him as if he'd finally flipped. 'It's a pelican.'

'A *pelican*?'

'Yes. Not a real one. A stone one.'

Ben shook his head. Oxford was insane – but there was no time to question it. He checked his watch again.

'We could be there in half an hour,' Jess said. She clearly wanted to go, but sounded as worried as he was.

He got up.

Jess looked aghast. 'Not *you*, Ben. Us! We're not the Chief's targets, you are.'

Ben tried to look confident. The thought of going out again with the white Mercedes about made him very nervous, but he couldn't possibly let Jess go out into the dark night, with just Freddie to protect her. He was about as protective as a lettuce leaf.

'I'm coming with you.'

'That's stupid,' Freddie said. 'It could be a trap.'

'Only if Marcus is the Chief. And if he is, he doesn't want to hurt Ben,' Jess said.

'It won't be a trap. Marcus is on our side, not *his*. Going there will prove it,' Ben realised suddenly. 'Nothing will stop me proving that.'

Freddie looked at him sideways. 'Let's hope not.'

Chapter 9

Ballantyne Bites

Ben locked the door and turned towards the road, wary, listening and watching. In the evening shadows, everything looked sinister. It was cool. Freddie suggested returning for their jackets.

'There's no time!' Ben cried, determined to establish Marcus's innocence.

'This could be our big chance!' Jess looked so excited – and so young. He was right to accompany her. In her books, the goodies always won. But against the Chief, there was no way to win, unless they could prove it and catch him. (Or preferably, leave it to the police to do so, but the chances of that were falling every single second they continued to believe Mum was the Chief).

'It could be a trap. Maybe Marcus wants to get us there,' Freddie said, wrapping his arms round his body and rubbing his arms.

Maybe he did. But Ben hoped not. He so, so hoped not. As Norham Gardens joined Parks Road, cars started to pass them. Even though there was a grass verge and lots of trees between them and the traffic, Ben was nervous.

'What are you looking for?' asked Freddie.

'*Them.*'

Freddie smirked.

'Ben is right to be cautious,' Jess said. 'They could come from any direction. They could be skulking in the Parks.'

Ben turned his head towards the Parks (which was just one, as far as he could make out). The thick shrubbery behind the railings could hide anyone. Or anything.

'Hurry up!' he urged Freddie, who was loitering. 'We don't want to miss them.'

'I am hurrying!' Freddie claimed, but he sped up, nevertheless.

They passed the Pitt Rivers and the science buildings. The unease in Ben's stomach increased with every step.

'South Parks Road coming up,' Jess announced, as if he didn't know.

A car swung around the corner in front of them, blaring music. He froze. The car screeched to a stop, a showy but impressive Audi convertible.

Ben exhaled, relieved to see Hazel Finch, SPC's HR Director, emerge. Mid-height, slim, with immaculately groomed shoulder-length auburn hair, she was as sharply dressed as usual. She hurried towards them, leaving the music playing.

'Sorry about that. I had to see you. I've been trying to call you.'

'Oh, sorry, my mobile's nearly out of charge. What's up?'

'What's happened?'

'About what?' Ben was confused.

'Your mum. Something has, I know it, but no one's telling me anything. Sir John and Sir Charles have been in a meeting with the two Peters.'

'Who?'

'Ballantyne and Nixon,' she replied. Ben still thought of Ballantyne as Richard. 'Marcus is too busy to blink, never mind answer his phone, and Debs is away.'

'She's just back. Mum's been arrested,' Ben admitted.

She looked stunned. Her green eyes were as round as plates. '*Arrested*? Why?'

'They think she's the Chief.'

'Sorry?'

'The mastermind behind the murders,' Jess explained.

'More like the scumbag,' Ben added.

'That's disgusting! How could they? She's no more a murderer than I am!'

'I know. But sorry, Hazel, we've got to go,' Ben said, checking his watch.

'Hang on, Ben, this is important. Has she got a lawyer?'

'Yeah. The best in Oxford, apparently. Marcus is paying for him.'

'That's crazy. We should be. It's disgusting when you think of the years of commitment she's given us. We are very lucky to have her working with us.' She folded her arms decisively, as if Ben had been arguing. But, of course, he agreed with every word she had said. 'I'll do everything I can to change that, Ben.'

'Thanks, Hazel.'

'My pleasure. Where are you staying?'

'With Marcus's mum. My new grandma,' Ben added, feeling a bit self-conscious about it.

'In Norham Gardens,' Freddie said, as if boasting.

'What number?'

'No idea, sorry,' Ben replied.

'If there's any news, how can I contact you if you haven't got a mobile?'

'Use mine?' Jess suggested.

'That's a good idea. What's your number?' Hazel asked, pulling her mobile out of her bag. They exchanged numbers, whilst Ben checked the time again: 20:53. The meeting would be finishing soon.

'We've really got to go, Hazel. Sorry.'

Hazel raised her eyebrows. 'Where are you off to in such a hurry?'

'To meet my parents,' Jess lied, impressively quickly.

'Oh. Stick together then. Take care.'

'We will. Thanks.'

Ben was glad of Hazel's car blocking South Parks Road, meaning any other cars had to slow down. His cousins didn't seem to notice his relief as they reached the opposite side.

'Aren't the women in SPC nice?' Jess said. 'Aunt Sue, Debs, Hazel – they're totally different from the men.'

'Lord Charles and Sir John are nice,' Freddie said, clearly as blinded by titles as his father.

'I hope we're not late.' Ben accelerated and hoping Freddie would too.

'Marcus paying for Aunt Sue sort of proves that he's on her side,' Jess said.

'Rubbish! He's just doing that to *look* as if he's on our side. To please Ben. He wants Ben to like him. That's obvious.'

'Well, he does. Don't you, Ben?'

'Yeah, but can you just hurry up?' Ben urged Freddie.

'What if he's on Marcus's side, not hers?' Freddie said.

'Who?'

'Andrew Masterton.'

'Don't be silly, Freddie. That can't be the case,' Jess said.

'Can't it? How do you know?'

'The police would notice, wouldn't they?' Ben asked, really not sure.

'Not if he's subtle.' Infuriatingly, Freddie stopped. 'There's every reason for him to fund your mum's defence. But there's no good reason for anyone else to save you other than him.'

'I know. I get it. But unless we hurry up, we might miss them.'

'I don't think it's Marcus. He's on our side, I'm sure,' Jess said. 'What if that text wasn't meant to protect Ben, but just to entrap Aunt Sue? That could easily mean Ballantyne…'

'Ballantyne *what*?' someone demanded behind them.

Horrified, Ben wheeled round. It was Ballantyne, right behind them, his eyes flashing fire. How much had he heard? Had they just landed Marcus in terrible trouble? Deadly trouble?

'I was just about to say that maybe you told the police what you said to Aunt Sue,' Jess said.

'And what particular thing would that be?' Ballantyne demanded in his sneering tone.

Terrified they'd betrayed Marcus, Ben's mouth was as dry as a dust bowl. He swallowed, trying to generate some moisture.

But Jess remained defiant, looking Ballantyne in the eye, though physically he dwarfed her. 'That she was the Chief.'

'Ah, you remember the Warden's party,' Ballantyne said, a smile playing on his thin lips.

'Yes, of course. And what you accused Aunt Sue of doing,' Jess said. Ben was impressed. Standing up to an adult with authority was always hard, but standing up to Ballantyne took more guts than that. He was proud of Jess. He'd admire her even if she wasn't his cousin, but he was delighted that she was.

'Well once again, I was right, wasn't I? Whilst many teenagers died earlier today, Ben is heading into town, both hale and hearty.'

'I was lucky.' Ben bowed his head, feeling terribly guilty again.

'Yes, remarkably lucky,' he sneered. '*Again*. No wonder the police are interested in your mother. She managed 993 for SPC, but it looks as if she is managing it in quite another sense now. A criminal sense. A deadly sense. Yes, unless any other evidence comes to light, it seems your mother is this Chief you keep mentioning.'

'Or you are,' Ben retorted.

His nostrils flared and his eyes narrowed. 'That won't work. That won't work for a second. Why would I want *you* to look good? Why would I care two hoots about saving you?' He seemed genuinely angry – and worse, he seemed to be repeating their argument.

'To make Aunt Sue look guilty,' Jess said.

'Why would I need to *bother*? She's done that so magnificently herself.'

'She is *not* the Chief!' Ben raged.

'You show a touching, but utterly deluded, loyalty to your mother.' He waved at someone behind Ben. 'Well, good night,' he called in a cheery tone, as if they had been enjoying a pleasant chat.

Ben looked round and saw Hanbury emerging from St Saviour's. Ballantyne was heading towards him.

'Come on!' He strode away towards the Sheldonian, looking back as he walked. The two men were standing outside St Saviour's, deep in conversation. 'It's weird, those two talking. As if they're planning something.'

'Haven't they got a big deal going on? It could be SPC stuff,' Jess said. 'But then again… how much do you think B heard?'

'Nothing important,' Freddie replied.

'Are you sure?' Ben asked. 'He said what you say.'

'He didn't have to hear me. He would make those points anyway. He's a bright man who thinks logically. Like me,' Freddie added, in case they had missed his point, which had been as subtle as a scream.

'He might have been trying to stop us getting there. He might know,' Ben said, checking his watch. It was just past nine.

'If it's Marcus, this could be a trap,' Freddie said.

'What did Jess say about names?'

'I'm saying *who* he is, not *what* he is, aren't I?'

'It's not him.'

'Why *now*? Why does he get those now off N's phone? Why not before?'

For that Ben had no answer. It was a lucky breakthrough, or (*please, no*) Freddie was right. Try as he might, Ben couldn't quite suppress the memory of Marcus's power in that horrific murder attempt, nor of the way he had fooled them about Mum during the seeming eternity of her kidnap.

Jess too agreed that the sudden access to Nixon's phone was suspicious.

'As if N were letting him, or maybe – and I really hope not, Ben – that M thinks we're getting close to the C and he's trying to put us off.'

'How do these ciphers put us off?'

'They take up time. And stop us thinking about anything else. *If 993 has arrived,*' she added in a whisper, '*then they might be close to a big attack.*'

'Which could be there!' Ben realised suddenly. 'Where is Corpus?'

'Not far.'

'*Where*?' Ben demanded, furious with her for wasting seconds. Seconds that could save lives. Seconds that could make all the difference.

'Behind High Street,' Freddie said.

Ben sped off, ignoring their entreaties to wait.

Chapter 10

Treachery

He tore past the Bridge of Sighs and the dome of the Radcliffe Camera. Ben had got used to these Oxford landmarks over the weekend and knew he would emerge onto High Street. Uncertain which way to turn, he paused there and waited for Jess, a few paces behind.

'Where now?'

'We need to cross,' she said, but the traffic was too heavy to risk it.

'Come on!' Ben urged the lights. People could be about to die – but if they plunged in front of a bus, doubtless they would too.

Waiting for a gap in the constant stream of buses, taxis and bikes allowed Freddie to catch up. Suddenly a bus stopped, and a gap appeared, so they raced across the road, dodging a few cyclists. Freddie turned left and headed into a very narrow, very dark passage. Ben pulled him back. Most toddlers were more streetwise.

'Isn't there another way?' he asked.

'Not as direct,' Jess said.

So this was the best route. But the passage was so narrow that Freddie was blocking the entrance.

'Let me past, Freddie. I'm biggest,' Ben said.

'There's no one else here,' he argued.

'Someone could turn into it.'

'They could turn in behind us as well as in front of us.'

'Well you go at the back then,' Ben snapped, ready to thump his infuriatingly logical cousin.

'Why don't you...' Freddie began.

Ben clenched his fists, but finally Freddie got the message and stepped aside.

Ben raced down the spooky passage, trying to ignore the burgeoning fear. Thankfully, it soon widened, with a few cars parked on the pavement and road, but still no people. Ben rounded the car barrier and emerged into a large, open area.

'Oriel Square. They're very good rowers,' Freddie said.

'I don't give a stuff! Where's Corpus?'

'Just around the corner,' Jess said. There was only one turn, on the left. University buildings were ahead and to the right. 'It's Merton Street.'

Merton Street was pure Oxford, dimly lit and flanked by ancient stone colleges towering above them. Ben could imagine medieval monks passing by – but it was currently deserted. The absence of people worried him.

Jess told him that the huge wooden arch was the entrance to Corpus.

'Where is everybody?'

'I'll check with the porters,' Freddie offered. He marched through the small doorway cut into the original arch. Or was that original too? Ben had no idea.

He and Jess waited outside, worrying. The street lights (like old lanterns) had been selected for style rather than illumination, but the front of Corpus was sufficiently well lit for Ben to see the pelican badge, amongst many other symbols, above it. Freddie had been right about the pelican, it seemed. His Oxford knowledge was awesome, though hardly surprising given the frequency of the Winterburns' visits here.

He soon emerged, looking smug. 'There's no college supper tonight.'

Ben presumed Freddie's nonchalance meant everything was fine, but with Freddie, it was always better to check.

'So no one is poisoned?'

'No. But OPO are here. The students are down for Easter.'

'Down where?' Ben asked.

'Up means Oxford. Down means going home. Or anywhere else.'

So everywhere else was inferior to Oxford? Rubbish!

'They'll all come out through this gate, unless they're residing in the college,' Jess said.

'Shouldn't we tell Marcus?' Ben was feeling guilty again.

'No. The less we tell him the better,' Freddie maintained.

'That's not true,' Jess protested. 'We've got to trust him until we know for certain that we can't.'

'We can't tell him. We mustn't.'

'We should. We've got to play along with him until we know for certain.'

'You don't play along with the Chief!' Freddie snapped.

The siblings stared at each other, both highly intelligent, both utterly convinced they were right. Ben took a deep breath. This mattered. It really mattered. Think!

If Marcus was the Chief, it was dangerous to tell him what they knew and what they were doing. Or was it? Why? He'd expect them to be here now, wouldn't he? Ben shook his head. He couldn't totally follow Freddie's logic, but that was hardly surprising. He often couldn't.

But if Jess was right, and his gut was right, if Marcus was innocent, then Nixon was deadly dangerous. But Marcus was still alive, thankfully. Why? Nixon must surely know Marcus was a double agent. He must have realised that from the moment Ben survived the syringe. He must have told the Chief. But presumably Marcus had told the Chief that Nixon was the double agent. Which would make Nixon hate him even more.

That decided him.

'We'll text him.' He switched on his phone and groaned. 'It's about to die. Can I give his number to you?'

'Sure,' Jess replied.

Ben saw he had a new text, in code, from an unfamiliar phone. A web of tension tightened round his guts. Why wouldn't the Chief leave him alone? He cursed.

'What's up?' Jess asked.

'I've got a new code. I'm sick of codes!'

'I'm not, fortunately,' Freddie said.

'You're nearly out of charge, Ben. Give me Marcus's number and forward it to me,' Jess said.

'Right.' He went to contacts and forwarded Marcus's number, then switched his phone off.

'Why didn't you give me the code?' Jess looked devastated.

Ben had to spell it out. 'It's probably illegal to have them and not tell the police.'

'I don't care.'

'*What*?' Hearing a Winterburn say they didn't care about the police was like seeing a City fan cheering on United.

'They've got Aunt Sue. They've made a terrible mistake. We need to prove that.'

'No, Jess. You mustn't have the code. If you do, I'll tell Mum and Dad,' Freddie said.

Ben couldn't believe it. '*About the codes*?'

'Of course. If it means my little sister breaking the law, I'll tell them everything we know.'

'But they won't believe you without evidence.'

'Those codes are evidence.'

'They're not, Freddie,' Jess said quietly.

'Why not? Aunt Sue can't be sending them when she's in jail, can she?'

'Anyone could be sending them to Ben. You, me, Dad, Mum. Unless the police can trace them, they're not proof of anything.'

'Marcus's are,' Ben said.

'He might have sent us here on purpose. He might be organising a poisoning somewhere else,' Freddie said, eyes darting back and forth.

'No. He wouldn't do that,' Ben said, but the uneasy feeling in the pit of his stomach was impossible to ignore.

'They're coming out!' Jess warned.

They stepped back into the shadows and watched a procession of strangers emerging through the narrow opening, singly or at most in pairs. They were mainly smartly dressed, as if business people or wealthy, except for a few more casually attired students. The first person they recognised was Rufus, tall, brown-haired, with a lean horse-like face, a prominent nose – and, as he spotted them, a scowl.

He marched over. 'Why are you three skulking here?'

'Just waiting to get in. We want to show Ben the pelican in Front Quad,' Jess claimed. Ben gave her a sideways look. She might as well have said they were following an invisible elephant.

'At this time of night? Pull the other one.'

Ben tried another story. 'We're looking for Uncle Henry. We thought he might be at your meeting.' He was pleased he'd remembered that they used to attend OPO together.

'Has he gone missing too? He's not here.' Rufus leaned towards Ben. 'Have you heard from my brother?'

'We saw him earlier. When he came back from the lab.'

Alarm flashed across his face. '*Lab*?'

'He...' Ben broke off as he saw Nixon stomping across the street. His florid face looked furious.

'*Baxter*!'

'What?'

'What the *hell* are you doing here?' Nixon demanded, baring his yellow teeth

'Just talking to Rufus.'

'Only just now. You were hanging about before,' Rufus said. He had no idea how dangerous Nixon was.

'How did you know? Did *he* tell you? Did he?' Nixon ranted. Ben supposed he meant Marcus.

'No. Who? We're looking for Uncle Henry,' he quickly added, before Nixon answered the question he'd been so stupid to ask. Because once Nixon named Marcus as a traitor, it was out in the open. It could be his death warrant.

'If you get in my way...' he began, stabbing his stubby forefinger forward.

'Peter, is there a problem?' someone called. Ben looked across to the college entrance, where Knox was standing. Why had *he* been at the meeting?

'Not at all,' Nixon called to him. He glared at Ben, then turned away, and ambled towards the smaller, slighter figure of Knox.

'Who the hell was he?' Rufus asked. 'What was his problem?'

'He's Nixon. *The one that tried to kill us*,' Ben whispered.

'But my brother saved you?' Rufus said, as if Ben had made the whole thing up.

'No, I don't know,' Ben lied, realising just in time that the last person Marcus would trust with his dangerous secret was his brother.

'You said he was at a lab. What was he doing at a lab?'

'The paternity test.'

Rufus's face contorted into a ball of rage. 'Oh my *god*! How *stupid* is he?'

'*What*?' Ben was taken aback, and deeply offended. How horrible to suggest that Marcus was stupid for wanting to prove that he was his dad.

'That bloody idiot has pushed me into a corner.'

'What's up?' Jess asked.

'I've got a bloody idiot for a brother, that's what's up.'

'Why?'

'But he'll need Sue's DNA too,' he muttered to himself, ignoring Jess's question.

'She gave a swab before…' Ben broke off. He didn't want Rufus to know Mum had been arrested too. Or maybe Daphne had told him?

'Oh, hell!' he cried, clenching his fists and stamping.

'What's up?' Jess asked again.

He rounded on her. 'Will you stop asking that? You're as bad as him!'

'As Ben?'

'He's as bad as Marcus,' Rufus replied, not making any sense at all. 'Well, you'll know soon enough, so I suppose I have to tell you.'

Ben stared at him, holding his breath. Was he about to tell them that he knew Marcus was the Chief?

'I fooled you.'

'Huh?'

'The cotton bud. I never put it in.' Stunned for a second, Ben didn't understand at first. But then he understood all too well. Rufus was referring to Freddie's paternity test. Ben stared at him, hardly able to believe his ears.

But Freddie reacted furiously. '*You lied*!'

'I didn't! I just didn't participate in your puerile test.'

'It was *not* puerile! It was *science*!'

'Yeah. Right,' Rufus responded, rolling his eyes.

'You *lied*!'

'It wasn't a lie. I just didn't dance to your fiddle. You're so like your dad.'

'*Good*!'

'It *was* a lie. It was a cruel deception,' Jess said.

'The only person who deceived everyone was Sue. *That* was the cruel deception,' Rufus retorted.

How *dare* he criticise her? Ben stepped forwards. 'You don't want to be my dad. Mum knew you wouldn't. That's why she never told me. It wasn't cruel, it was *kind*.'

'She didn't know the first thing about me! How would she know how I'd feel?'

Ben stayed put, eyes locked on his, determined not to give way. 'She knew.'

'I think she could probably guess after a few minutes in your presence. I could,' Jess said.

'Rubbish! You're just saying that. You're full of bull, like all teenagers.'

'Jess is not full of bull!' Ben cried.

'Back down, tiger. You're playing with fire,' Rufus warned, using his height to tower over Ben. Ben stepped back. Even taller than Marcus, Rufus was physically menacing.

'You haven't told us. You must know. Are you dominant, or recessive?' Freddie asked. Ben couldn't believe he hadn't thought to ask himself. If Rufus's earwax gene was recessive, there was no problem. But if not…

'Dominant,' he muttered, as if hardly mattered.

'*Dominant*?' Ben echoed, sick to the stomach. 'That means you could be my dad!'

'Yep. Don't look so horrified. How do you think I feel?'

How *he* felt?

'We'll know the truth tomorrow thanks to my moronic brother.'

Ben took a deep breath. 'If you're my dad, I want nothing more to do with you.'

'Same goes for me,' Rufus said, with such a sour look on his face that Ben knew he wouldn't be losing out.

'Fine.'

But it was far from fine. It was heart-breaking and devastating and infuriating in the extreme. If he didn't release some of these whirling emotions, he might well thump him.

Instead, Ben ran.

Chapter 11

The Net Tightens

Ignoring Jess's entreaties to stop, Ben followed the medieval road round to the left and soon found himself racing down High Street. She was chasing him, judging by the clatter of following feet. But he was too furious to talk to her, or anyone. And devastated. Tears were coursing down his cheeks.

He was plagued by so many questions. How could he? What would Mum say? What would Marcus say? He had no answers. He couldn't believe it. Yet he was convinced that Rufus had been telling the truth. His temper was too genuine to be fake.

Why had he lied about the test? What could drive him to behave so horribly to Ben, to Mum and to his brother? They didn't get on, but this wasn't just nasty. It was awful. A betrayal.

'Ben, please, stop!' Jess yelled behind him.

He wiped his eyes before turning to her.

She pulled up, pink-cheeked from the chase.

'I'm so sorry,' she said. 'Want a hug?'

Yes, he did. From Mum. Only she could make sense of his torment. The yearning he felt for her was so strong that tears gushed up again. So he accepted Jess's hug and blinked the tears back whilst she embraced him. Mum would have been his shield against the grenade Rufus had so casually tossed between them. He tried to swallow down the lump in his throat, but it felt like a tennis ball.

'He's horrible,' Jess said, pressing her cheek into his chest. 'He's the most disgusting man I have ever met. He is heartless and wicked and horrible.'

'Yeah.' Ben wiped his eyes again and pulled back, only now aware of the surrounding shops, and across the road the ancient tower of Carfax.

'You shouldn't have run away, Ben. These streets are dangerous.'

'I wasn't running from you. It was *him*. If not, I was so mad, I'd have clattered him.'

'He deserved clattering more than anyone I've ever known. But violence never wins.'

'Sometimes you have to fight.'

'We have to fight together. We have to fight the Chief. And I think we've all been wrong. I think I know who it is, now. In fact, I'm sure I know who it is.'

'Who?'

'Rufus!' Jess looked so triumphant, but Ben felt as deflated as a goalkeeper watching the ball trickle into his net in the ninety-third minute.

'He can't be.'

'He *is*. He is totally devoid of empathy,' Jess began, ticking it off on her thumb.

'Agreed, but—' Jess raised a hand, stopping him, as if to say hear me out.

Okay, he would.

'He's determined to reduce human overpopulation. So is the Chief. He's mad at your mum. So is the Chief. And he's into codes.' She stopped, as if that was enough. But there was one gaping hole in the middle of her argument.

'But he's not SPC. He wouldn't have known about 993.'

'He didn't have to. N did,' Jess said, eyeing passers-by warily. Her voice dropped to a whisper. 'He would have known agrochemicals are mild poisons. He would have just had to ask Nixon if he had a good poison. An unknown poison.'

'But how did he know N?'

'He could have recruited him through the SPC's website.' As if anticipating his next question, Jess added, 'He'd have gone to SPC because of his brother. He knows lots about them. He probably knew Knox.'

'How?'

'OPO? Why was he at the meeting? Nixon wouldn't have invited him. He would have preferred him not to be there. So it was probably Rufus that did.'

'I'm not sure.' Ben paused, to let a group of people pass. But one of them stopped.

'Hello, Ben,' she said. It was Julia, Dr Ashcroft's wife. They had all met at the Warden's reception on Saturday. She reminded Ben of Bellatrix Lestrange from the Harry Potter films in appearance, but, fortunately, not personality. 'And Jess and Freddie too. How lovely.'

Ben turned his head, surprised at the mention of Freddie, but he was marching towards them, glaring. Ben sighed. Whatever petty thing Freddie was annoyed about, he had huge problems to resolve. Who was his dad? And could Jess possibly be right about the Chief?

'Hello, you three,' Dr Ashcroft's deep voice greeted them. She was Mum's favourite tutor, a Chemistry don at St Saviour's. 'We were so shocked to hear about Sue. We understand she's been taken in for questioning?'

Ben was alarmed. Had it reached the media? 'Who told you?'

'Sir Christopher,' replied Dr Ashcroft, meaning the Warden of St Saviour's, who was with Daphne that evening.

'How did he know?'

'He said the Chairman had called him. I assumed he meant Lord Charles.'

Hanbury again, Ben thought. Was that code a double bluff? Could he be the Chief? Though it seemed terribly unlikely, he was surely a more likely candidate than Rufus.

No he isn't, he immediately realised. Hanbury's dumb, but Rufus is smart. And Rufus is nasty.

'The police must have lost.their minds to arrest your mother. Sue is one of the kindest people I know. She would never harm a fly, let alone children,' Dr Ashcroft said, showing how well she knew her. 'And you were poisoned saving them, I believe? She would certainly never hurt you.'

'Exactly!' Jess said.

'Well I hope the tabloids don't hear about your mum. They will have a field day,' Julia said.

Mum's photo on the front page, branded as a mass murderer, was a horrifying prospect. Ben remembered his indiscretion to the students. He wondered if any of them had contacted the media this evening.

'Now, honey,' Dr Ashcroft said, in a tone that meant *Shut up*. 'The media won't know, Ben. We were told in strictest confidence.' She looked at Julia. 'We'd better get back.'

'Perhaps we can walk you back? Where are you staying?' Julia asked.

'In Norham Gardens.'

She goggled. '*Norham Gardens*? I thought they were all private residences.'

'It is. It's Marcus's mum's house.'

'Marcus Wright?'

'Yes.'

'That explains it. Any hotel there would have to charge a small mortgage for a room,' Julia said.

'Why?' Jess asked.

'They are very exclusive and very expensive. They go for millions.'

Jess's eyes widened. 'Gosh. Really?'

Ben was stunned as well. Daphne must be rich. It made him uncomfortable. She must realise that he wasn't. Was he a disappointment as a grandson? She hadn't said that he was, but she might just be being nice.

'Ben, are you okay?' Jess asked.

'He's upset about his mum,' Julia said.

True. But right now, Ben was upset about his dad too. Very upset indeed.

Whilst strolling along High Street, Julia and Freddie dropped behind.

'They very rarely come up for sale, but when they do, bankers and businessmen pounce,' Julia told Freddie.

But Dr Ashcroft seemed keener to understand why Mum had been arrested, so Ben told her about the text Mum seemed to have sent.

'But her phone could easily have been cloned. They'd had it for a week.'

'The police must know that,' Jess said.

'I suppose the key reason is that you keep surviving, Ben. Like that awful man, Mr Ballantyne, said,' Dr Ashcroft said.

'He's probably convinced them,' Ben said.

They halted outside St Saviour's.

'Ben, please do not run into any more danger while your poor mum's being questioned. If anything untoward happens, phone me. Please,' Dr Ashcroft added, handing him her card.

'I will,' Ben promised, grateful for the support of such a distinguished person. But all the academics of Oxford couldn't free Mum unless the police were satisfied that she was innocent.

'Good night. And good luck,' Dr Ashcroft replied.

'Good night.' Ben was grateful for her good wishes. He had the feeling he'd need lots of luck to catch the Chief.

As they went up Parks Road, Jess outlined her new theory to Freddie. Who was arguing, of course.

'He wants to cure overpopulation,' Jess said. 'So does the C. He doesn't like children, but he does like codes. Just like the C.'

'So does Marcus,' retorted Freddie.

Jess stopped. 'Oh, Ben!' Her hand flew to her mouth.

'What?'

'Wouldn't he just love to have Marcus running around in circles after him?'

'Ballantyne would love that too,' Ben replied.

'Even more than B, R would,' Jess said, more carefully.

'Marcus isn't running around in circles for anyone. It *is* Marcus. He keeps protecting Ben,' Freddie insisted.

'But… Oh god. Oh hell. Oh no.' Ben stopped as the awful realisation hit him.

'What?'

'Both my dads could be the Chief.'

'They're not *both* your dad!' Freddie cried, looking really angry.

'I know. I'm tired, right? I just mean possible dads,' Ben explained, through gritted teeth.

'Don't wind Ben up, Freddie. He really doesn't need it.'

'I sure don't.'

Freddie huffed, shaking his head, but kept his mouth shut, wisely.

'We know R is a liar. He lied about the cotton bud,' Jess said.

'He could be lying about his earwax too,' Freddie replied, giving Ben a sudden flash of hope. Yes, he could. If so, Marcus was his dad.

'But why would he do that?' Jess argued. 'He'd be admitting he'd lied when he knew it would never have been discovered, if he had recessive earwax.'

'The earwax isn't recessive, it's the gene that encodes for it that is!' Freddie snapped.

'What the hell does that matter now? Jess is right. It might not be him.'

'Not just that. He's the C,' she said. 'I'm convinced of it.'

'How would he have known about 993?' Freddie said.

'Mum talked about it every night. It was so massive, I'll bet Marcus did too,' Ben said, backing Jess up, even though he was far from sure she was right. But Rufus would love tormenting his brother and was passionate about the environment. The biggest danger to the environment was people, everyone knew that. So he might well want to reduce population growth… but would he really kill?

Even though he was undoubtedly horrible, Ben couldn't believe that of him. But he could hardly believe it of Ballantyne, and certainly not Marcus.

But one of them must be the Chief, unless Hanbury or Knox was.

His cousins were still arguing as they reached Keble.

'Marcus doesn't live with Rufus,' Freddie said.

'He'd have told Daphne, and she'd have told Rufus,' Jess responded, fast as a flash.

'No way. Grown men don't talk to their mums like Ben does with his mum. How often does Dad tell Grandmother about his work?'

Freddie was right. Conversations during those frighteningly formal meals always revolved around family matters, Uncle Henry's mum's theatre trips and the Conservative Party, of which she was a staunch supporter.

'Does Daphne like agrochemicals? I doubt it. Rufus won't, as an environmentalist,' Jess said.

'He might,' Ben said. 'Farmers can feed a lot more people from a lot less land using agrochemicals. They're environmentally friendly, in a way.'

'But they leave pollutants.'

'Less and less as regulations tighten,' Ben replied, well used to Mum's arguments by now.

'They do pollute, though, and they feed more people than the planet can otherwise sustain. He won't like that, will he?' Freddie said.

'No. So you agree with us?' Ben asked. Jess shot him a look. 'I think Rufus might well want to kill the parents of tomorrow, but I can't imagine him doing it. I can't imagine any of them doing it.'

'That's the point. They don't,' Freddie said. 'They get Kashani and Goatee Man, or whoever else poisoned the pool, to do it for them.'

'So it *is* Rufus!' Jess proclaimed triumphantly. 'Oh sorry, R,' she said, noticing a dog-walker look at her.

But it didn't matter, Ben thought. She could have been saying Rufus was anything.

'Could be, if he really did know about... 993,' he added, in a whisper, because the dog-walker had paused nearby. 'There's just one thing. Why would he want to save me?'

'Vanity. He knows you share half, or a quarter, of his genes. He hasn't got children yet. You're the future of his genome,' Freddie added.

'*What?*'

'Your DNA, Ben,' Jess explained. 'The selfish gene, like Richard Dawkins says. Successful genes want to survive.'

'They don't want anything!' Freddie scoffed. 'Genes don't have brains.'

'But they *act* as if they do. If they don't, they don't get passed on to descendants, so they die out. Successful genes have competed for centuries. They're great survivors. They make us want to reproduce. It says so in *The Selfish Gene.*'

'You haven't even read *The Selfish Gene!*' Freddie cried, looking deeply affronted, with his boggling eyes.

'No, but I've talked to Aunt Sue about it,' Jess retorted, going pink.

Ben hadn't. Why not? He felt slightly miffed, but then realised that he'd probably tuned out whenever Mum and Jess had discussed it. He hadn't been interested in genetics until the question of his dad came up. Now it really mattered, he could see that. He would ask Mum about The Selfish Gene one day too, he resolved, as they turned into Norham Gardens. There was a car parked ahead, but it was a Volvo and it was empty. The road was deserted and dark. It would be quiet too, but Freddie was still arguing.

'It's nowhere near as good a reason as Marcus. He believes he's Ben's dad, even if he isn't.'

'It's a better reason than Ballantyne's,' Ben said.

'Agreed.'

'So it's one of my possible dads?'

'Yes,' Freddie said flatly.

'I'm afraid so, Ben,' Jess replied more kindly. 'But R has a much greater motivation for the whole project than M does.'

'It *is* Marcus. I'm almost certain of it. Not quite. It could be Rufus. But it's much more likely to be Marcus,' Freddie said.

Please no. Please don't let Marcus be the Chief. Please don't let Rufus be my dad, Ben implored, though it was far too late for anyone to change that. It was a fifty-fifty chance, like tossing a coin, a coin which had landed fourteen years ago somewhere in Oxford. But which side up? Tomorrow night they would find out.

'Both your parents might play key roles. One is the Chief, but the police don't know it. One isn't the Chief, but the police think she is. Your mum, the Chief's biggest enemy, might be going to prison on your dad's – the Chief's – behalf. For the rest of her life,' Freddie said.

Ben buried his head in his hands. 'No. No! NO!'

'I don't blame you howling. I'd howl too.'

'I'll bet there are times you'd like to throttle my brother, Ben,' Jess said. 'I'll bet that's how Marcus feels about Rufus too. I do hope he's not your dad.'

So did Ben. He hoped he wasn't the Chief either. But he had a growing sensation that Rufus might be both of those men. And he couldn't be more revolted.

Chapter 12

Family Matters

Ben recalled Debs and Aunt Miriam's promise about bringing Mum back with them, but Uncle Henry's car wasn't on Daphne's drive.

'They haven't got Mum then,' Ben said.

'They'd be having dinner.'

'She wouldn't. She'd come to see me.' He knew that however hungry she was, her first impulse would have been to see him. He was longing to see her too.

He found Daphne's keys and started to unlock the door.

'It's worth millions,' Freddie said.

'I don't care.'

'You lucky thing.'

Ben sighed. He didn't feel lucky. He felt wretched. He entered the hall and clicked the light on.

'We've got a code to crack. Shall we do it upstairs?' Jess asked.

'It's safer, I guess,' Ben said, feeling as much like cracking codes as he felt like banging his head repeatedly against the wall.

'We should at least take our bags up,' Jess said.

'Okay.' He led the way upstairs, finding light switches as he did so, listening to his cousins discussing the house. Now he too noticed the mouldings and carvings on the staircase, and the immaculate decoration of the grand house and felt ashamed that he'd treated it like home, dropping his bag when he came in. What must Daphne have thought? Or Marcus? But neither of them had given him any cause to feel discomfort.

Let him be my dad, he pleaded.

'This house is *enormous*,' Jess said. 'Just look at the landing.'

It was certainly long. Ben turned to the second staircase and flicked off the wrong lights, earning a squawk of protest from Freddie, but quickly found the right switch. He led the way up the narrower, steeper staircase.

Jess was delighted with the rooms.

'They've all got bookcases! They're huge! And we've got our own private bathroom.'

Ben was more interested in the computer in the room at the far end, so he asked if could have it. Besides the computer, which was on a large desk with two leather chairs tucked under it, the huge room also contained an armchair, a double bed and a bookcase.

'Sure. I'd prefer the one with the detective books,' Jess said. 'There are loads I haven't read.'

Ben smiled. 'That's perfect for you.'

'I'd like this room too,' Freddie claimed.

Typical! If Ben had said he'd prefer a broom cupboard, Freddie would have fought over it.

'But Ben's missing his mum. Plus, look what I've found,' Jess said, handing him *The Code Book* by Simon Singh.

'That proves they're into codes!' Freddie was almost dancing with excitement.

'We knew that,' Ben said.

'It's more evidence against Rufus,' Jess said.

'Or Marcus. Okay. I'll take the other room if I can have this,' Freddie said, clutching the book to his chest.

'Deal,' Ben agreed, thinking how surprising Freddie could sometimes be. The last time he had backed down so quickly, there was a sabre-toothed tiger in the neighbouring cave.

Jess took his phone to copy out the codes, so Ben clicked the computer on. It opened up impressively quickly. He remembered Marcus telling them the password, tried it out – and it worked. Yet another sign that Marcus wasn't the Chief. But was Rufus?

He searched for Rufus Wright. The first few pages were about an actor. There was nothing about Marcus's brother, so he went onto the OPO website.

'What are you doing?' Jess asked.

'Trying to get inside his mind.'

'Rufus's?'

'Yeah.'

'You'll never get there. You're far too nice.'

There were images of hordes of people around some text, but not Rufus. Ben started reading.

Over Population Oxford abhors the damage caused to Earth's fragile ecosystem by humans.

Worryingly, we have registered one billion more births every thirteen years since Over Population Oxford's foundation in 1974. Global warming, intensive farming practices, environmental pollution, habitat loss, the sixth mass extinction and the consumption of finite natural resources such as arable land, fresh water and fossil fuels, at speeds faster than their rate of regeneration, are just some of the unintended, yet very serious, consequences.

Heavy and boring, Ben thought, yawning.

'Your phone is nearly out of charge, Ben. I've switched it off,' Jess said, handing it back.

The noise of the front door being unlocked startled them.

'Daphne is back early,' Jess said.

Ben shut the computer off. 'Could be Marcus.'

Freddie was reading *The Code Book*, curled up in the armchair. 'It could be the Abominable Snowman. There's no use guessing.'

Ben got up. 'Let's go and look.' Though Freddie ignored him, Jess accompanied him downstairs.

Rufus emerged from the kitchen, looking outraged, whereas Ben felt sick at the sight of him.

'What the *hell* are you doing here?' he demanded.

'Daphne invited us,' Jess said.

'Why would she do that?' Rufus appeared puzzled.

'We've got to stay in Oxford overnight.'

'Why not The Beaumont?'

'It's too expensive.'

'Besides, the pool,' Ben said, testing Jess's theory. 'I never want to go there again.'

But Rufus didn't flinch. 'Where's your mum?'

'She's being questioned by the police.' Surely he knew that?

'Why?'

'The murders in the pool.'

'*Murders*? Your mum?' He looked genuinely incredulous.

'Yeah. It's nuts.'

'They must have something to go on, I guess,' he said, so offhandedly as to be offensive.

'They *haven't*!'

'Okay, okay, they haven't. Where's Mother? My mother?'

'At Oxford Humanists,' Jess said, whilst Ben continued to seethe. But though angry with him, Ben thought Rufus had been genuine. He was either a superb actor, or Jess had got it wrong.

He was going to get a drink, Rufus said, and headed back to the kitchen. They followed him.

'Do you want drinks too?' he asked, looking affronted.

'I'm okay,' Ben said, but Jess requested water.

The doorbell rang. Ben stepped forwards, towards the door.

Rufus moved fast to block him, challenging, nostrils flaring. 'This is *my* house, not yours. *I* will answer the door.'

'Ben just thought it was my parents. We're expecting them,' Jess said.

'Oh, has Mother invited them too?' Rufus huffed.

'No, they've been finding a B and B,' Jess replied. 'Would you please go and let them in? Or do you want Ben to do it?'

'*No!*' He stomped out of the room. Though Daphne and Marcus had made them very welcome indeed, to Rufus they were clearly as welcome as rain at a picnic.

They listened at the door. From the voices, they could tell it was Aunt Miriam, Uncle Henry and Debs – but not Mum, Ben realised, listening to them complaining about the police.

He bowed his head, deeply disappointed.

'You must come in and have a drink,' Rufus boomed, so friendly and cheerful that you'd have thought he was auditioning for Father Christmas.

'Do you still think it's him?' he whispered.

'Yes. I think he's lying. We know he lied about the earwax test,' Jess whispered.

Good point, Ben realised. He was a good liar and he *enjoyed* lying, relished it.

'Are you okay?'

'Fine,' Ben lied.

Was Jess right? He needed to work it out for himself. It was like unravelling a tangled hoover cord. He just needed to work methodically.

Rufus was a good liar, against overpopulation and into codes, so it could easily be him. Ballantyne's motive in seeming to protect him could just have been to incriminate Mum. He hated Mum because she stood up him.

What about Marcus? His concern earlier had seemed so genuine. He was caring, friendly and helpful. Marcus was not the Chief. He was a good guy, not a psychopath. Ben was as convinced of that as Freddie was of the opposite point of view.

'It could be Rufus, it could be Ballantyne, but it's not Marcus. We need to text him.'

'Not from your phone. We need to conserve the charge. I'll do it. Meanwhile, you can crack the code.' Jess handed him the sheet she had put in her bag. 'I'll text him from the loo, so Rufus can't catch me.'

'Great.' Ben was glad Jess agreed with him that they should tell Marcus everything. 'Thanks.'

The adults clearly weren't coming into the kitchen. Reluctant to encounter them in the hall, Ben shut the door. He craved solitude and space and Mum.

But it seemed that the police weren't going to give her back. So he had to get her back. He sat at the table and looked at the code.

laea hb kwturaz
aekx hrf zwysw
dlksax xij etl
axnes etvcri
laea hb hfiorgz
lssm ns qbb
rtl dlksax yalc cym
wybsp ciwyya

The Chief was trying to perplex him, but the Chief didn't know he knew about the Playfair Ciphers. He sat down at the table, found their papers and a pen, and also the COWLEY grid in the drawer where Jess had hidden the codes.

They needed some luck. Maybe, just maybe, this was it.

C	O	W	L	E
Y	A	B	D	F
G	H	I/J	K	M
N	P	Q	R	S
T	U	V	X	Z

So la would be OD and ea would be OF. An overdose of something? Alarmed, Ben continued. Hb would be AI or AJ. Kw was IL or JL – no, it had to be IL. But neither AIIL nor AJIL made sense.

Unless the key was PELICAN? He opened the drawer again, to find that grid.

'What's that?'

Ben gasped. Rufus was standing over him. If he *was* the Chief, he would realise they knew about Nixon's cipher.

He would know Marcus had betrayed him.

He would kill him.

Chapter 13

Caught Red-Handed

'That's a Playfair grid, isn't it?' he said, as if he didn't know.

Ben swallowed. 'Is it?'

'Looks like it. Why's the key Cowley?'

Ben could think of no convincing response. So he said nothing.

'You could have chosen any word. Why Cowley?'

He had to say something. What?

'Mum…'

'What?'

'She lived on the Cowley Road, I think.'

'That's right, she did. That's weird. Are you obsessed with your mum or something?'

'What?'

'I wouldn't remember where my mum lived before she had me. I certainly wouldn't use it for a key to a code.'

'Mum's kind of on my mind right now,' Ben said, as sarcastically as he could manage.

'So why are you messing about with Playfair Ciphers?' Rufus asked, as if he believed Ben.

'Jess had one in her book. She was trying to teach me,' Ben improvised, as casually as he could manage.

'Why?'

'She's always trying to teach me things. They all are.'

Rufus smiled. 'Yes. I noticed that myself.' The smile vanished as suddenly as the sun behind a cloud. 'But why Cowley? Why not her name? Sue Baxter would be a good key.'

Ben blanked briefly, but thankfully not for long. 'No it wouldn't. E's repeated.'

'You can use keys with repeated letters. You just ignore any but the first, so Sue Baxter would be S U E B A X T R.'

'Oh. I didn't know that.'

'No, clearly not,' Rufus said, opening the takeaway menus drawer, which was next to the codes drawer. Ben sat in front of it, blocking it. He mustn't see anything else.

Maybe he was acting. Maybe Ben had got away with the most serious mistake he'd ever made? This wouldn't be a lost mark, a slipped grade, a failed exam. This could be Marcus's death sentence. *You idiot*!

'Your uncle wants food. Do you?'

'No. We've eaten.'

'Right. I'll find out what he wants.' Rufus left the kitchen with the menus. Ben followed him out, and watched him enter a doorway on the right, opposite the study. It closed.

He raced upstairs, meeting Jess on the first floor landing.

'Have you had any luck with the codes?'

'No. Rufus caught me.'

'*What*?'

As they climbed the stairs to the second floor, Ben explained.

'That is suspicious. But Rufus seemed relaxed?'

'Guess so. He was normal.'

'So he mustn't have guessed where you'd got it from.'

'He could have been acting.'

'No, Ben. Think of Hitler in World War Two. There were lots of signs that Bletchley Park had cracked the Enigma code. But because he believed it was impossible to crack, Hitler never realised they had.'

'But Enigma must be miles harder than Playfair.'

'Yes, but it's their complacency I'm comparing. Rufus has no idea Marcus got the codes off Nixon's phone. And he wouldn't dream of Marcus giving the codes to us to crack, so he won't suspect he has. So you're safe. As is Marcus.'

'I hope so,' Ben replied, not entirely convinced. He was still worried he'd made a terrible mistake.

Freddie was still reading in the chair. He looked up.

'This is a great book.'

'Glad you like it,' Ben said. It had secured him a computer, after all.

'It's useful. Not so much on Playfair, but we've got that cracked. There's lots about Vigenère though.'

'What?'

'Vigenère squares. Oh, never mind. They're just a different type of cipher.'

'So is this,' Ben said, showing him.

'Is it from the Chief?'

'Dunno.'

'It might tell us if it's Rufus or it's Marcus.'

There was a knock on the door.

'It's only me,' Marcus called.

'Come in,' Ben said, feeling sick. Had he heard as much as Ballantyne had? Ben would hate him to know that Freddie suspected him.

'Hi,' he said. He looked tired and hassled, but not wounded. Ben guessed he hadn't heard and breathed a sigh of relief.

'Did you get my texts?' Jess asked.

'I haven't had time to check my phone. I've hardly had time to breathe. What did they say?'

Jess told him about the 993.

'I knew about that arriving. In Cowley is it? I'll try and find it, but I'll bet it's very well hidden.'

'Be careful,' Jess urged.

Marcus smiled. 'Don't worry. I am. It's Sue we need to worry about.'

Ben told him about the OPO meeting.

'You shouldn't have gone there! That was dangerous.'

Ben clapped his hand to his mouth. He'd forgotten Marcus didn't know.

'What's up?'

'Rufus lied about the earwax test.' Marcus's eyes widened and his face froze. 'He's dominant too, sorry. He might be my dad.'

'I'll kill him. One of these days I will absolutely swing for him. To get at me is one thing. But to hurt you like that?

Unforgivable! Wait till I see him.' His jaw was tight, his teeth clenched; Ben had never seen Marcus so angry.

'I was furious too,' Freddie said.

'I'm sure it's you, Marcus. You're too much like Ben for it not to be you,' Jess said.

Marcus managed a tight smile. 'Thanks. Sorry I got cross. He makes me so mad sometimes.'

'Brothers are like that. Mine makes me mad sometimes too,' Freddie said, referring to Robert, who was (presumably) still at their house in Didsbury.

'He makes us all mad,' Ben said.

'Especially Dad,' Jess said, as if joking, but Ben knew it was true. Robert was the only Winterburn not to be academically brilliant, and was much more interested in girls than schoolwork, much to his father's frustration.

Now Marcus smiled properly. 'Whatever happens, whether I'm your dad or your uncle, Ben, I'm a very close relative. And proud of it. But I really hope I'm your dad.'

'I hope that too.'

'Great. Tomorrow we'll know for sure. But I will, later, kill him over this.'

Ben exchanged a worried look with Jess. Seeing it, Marcus said, 'Don't worry. I'm only joking. I will talk to him though.'

Ben nodded.

'Marcus, can you help us? Ben's phone is nearly out of charge. Do you have a spare charger?' Jess asked.

'We do have a few. It's worth a try.'

There were cupboards along the back wall. Marcus crouched down to search in the left-hand one.

Ben realised there was another important thing he hadn't told him.

'I'm sorry, Marcus. Rufus caught me with the COWLEY grid.'

Freddie's eyes were as wide as ping-pong balls. 'You *cretin*!'

'Why are you so worried?' Marcus asked, turning around to face them.

He definitely isn't the Chief, Ben decided. He's definitely on our side, and hopefully, my dad. Right, no more secrets.

'We think he might be the Chief,' Ben revealed, expecting Marcus to look devastated.

But disconcertingly, he smiled. 'No. No way. He's a pain, yes. He's a terrible liar, yes. He's obnoxious, yes. But he isn't the Chief.'

'How do you know?' Jess asked.

'No time to explain. But believe me, it's not him.'

Did he really know? Or was he blinded by family loyalty, Ben wondered?

'Doesn't the Chief realise you're double-crossing him by now?' Freddie asked.

'I'm making it look like Nixon's ineptitude, I hope. It's all coming to a head now. We've just got to squeeze in the right place.'

'Ew!'

Marcus grinned. 'Sorry, Jess, aren't we males disgusting? Rats and snails and puppy dogs' tails, that's what we are made of.'

'Mum used to say snips and snails and puppy dogs' tails.'

'What are snips?'

'Single nucleotide polymorphisms. I thought you'd all got that by now,' Freddie snapped, referring to genetics, Ben realised. Marcus, less used to Freddie, looked startled.

'Eels,' Jess said. 'I think.'

'You're probably right. It's a long time since I heard nursery rhymes.' He turned back to the cupboard and rummaged around. 'Will this do?' He held out a charger. It looked good from a distance. Ben hurried over and discovered it was an exact match.

'Perfect!' He plugged it into a socket, switched his mobile on, and showed Marcus the new text, ignoring the sensation that Freddie was glaring at him.

Marcus compared it with his texts. 'It's not from any number I know.'

'Nixon with a new phone?' Jess suggested. 'Or maybe the Chief.'

'It must be. Right, good luck cracking it. I'm glad you're all okay. I'm going to have a chat with my brother.'

'Marcus, can we stop the test? Just in case it's him?'

He checked his watch. 'Sorry, Ben, no. The lab's closed now.'

'Tomorrow?'

'I doubt it. We've signed what I think is a legally binding contract. Besides, we'd need the agreement of all of us to stop it, me, you and your mum.'

This was devastating news. They couldn't ask her. They couldn't talk to her.

'Don't worry, Ben. It'll be me. I'm almost sure.'

'It will be, Ben,' Jess said, as Marcus departed.

But all her good wishes couldn't shift the fear in his gut. His dad might not only be a horrid person, he might also be a murderer. Who in their right mind would want to prove that?

Chapter 14

Tweedledum and Tweedledee

Freddie was glaring at them. Ben didn't care. He had far bigger troubles to worry about than Freddie.

'You shouldn't have told him!' he raged.

'Well we have. So what? My dad might be the Chief!'

'Besides, it was the right thing to do,' Jess added. 'And he might not be, Ben. It could still be Ballantyne.'

'It could be Marcus. So why the hell did you tell him we know?' Freddie demanded, glaring at Jess.

'It was me that told him, not Jess. But it's not him. He wants to be my dad.'

'That's the entire point! He cares about you.'

'So he wouldn't have risked my life.'

'Was that just Goatee Man going rogue?' asked Jess.

'In the Merc, maybe, but not in the pool,' Ben said. To risk breaking into The Beaumont on a whim made no sense at all.

'It doesn't matter. If you're right, Freddie, and he is the Chief, then it's safer for us if we appear to trust him. Now he's confident we don't suspect him, we're *safe*. From his point of view. If he is the Chief,' added Jess.

It was a very good point, and it seemed to calm Freddie.

'Let's get cracking then. The cipher I mean.'

'I've done two copies.' Jess handed Freddie one of her two sheets. 'Why don't you take this whilst Ben and I look at the other at the desk?'

'Okay.' He took a pen and some paper from the desk and installed himself in the armchair, whilst Jess put the other copy between them.

```
laea hb kwturaz
aekx hrf zwysw
dlksax xij etl
axnes etvcri
laea hb hfiorgz
lssm ns qbb
rtl dlksax yalc cym
wybsp ciwyy
```

Jess was trying to crack it. But Ben was thinking again about the pool. Now, perhaps he knew why it had been cyanide in the pool. 993 had just arrived in Britain.

Even if the Chief was his dad, he'd murdered children. He was the opposite of a chief – he was a coward, a sleaze ball, a scumbag. No words were strong enough to convey his loathing, his revulsion, his contempt for the so-called Chief. But what really chilled him was the knowledge that none of the swimmers would be alive now if they had put 993 in the pool.

Dreading Mum being mentioned online, Ben had to check. But, thankfully, she didn't appear, except in the usual places – social networking sites and the SPC website. On the BBC website, the lead story was the pool. There were photos of the victims.

He stared open-mouthed at the image of the red-haired boy, seeing him smiling, conscious and happy for the first time. He would never smile again.

'What's up Ben?'

'He's dead.'

Jess pointed to his image, subtitled, *Alex Goodall, 13, from Headington*, 'Isn't he one of the boys you tried to save?'

'Yeah. Thought I had. Thought he'd be okay. But he's dead. *Dead*!' Ben got up and started pacing the room. 'I *hate* them! They're…' he trailed off, not having the words to convey the horror he felt.

It disgusted, him. It sickened him. It infuriated him.

'Ben, I know you're angry and upset, but unless we stop them, there will a lot more like Alex, Ajay, Charlotte, George, Maisie, Ethan, Salma and Kayla,' Jess said. She shut down the website and turned to him. 'Every single one of them mattered to so many people, their family, their friends and their classmates. We can't let anyone else die.'

'I know!'

'So we've got to crack this code.'

'I'm sick of dancing to their tune!'

Freddie stood up suddenly. He headed for the door, clutching the book and the code.

'Where are you going?' asked Jess.

'To get away from the noise,' he said, glaring at Ben.

Everything had changed now that 993 had arrived. There were antidotes to very dilute cyanide, but not 993. Now hundreds, thousands, millions even, could die.

Freddie returned, rolling his eyes. 'Visitors.'

'Who?'

'Knox and Hanbury, Mum says.'

Ben checked the time: 22:15. Late. 'Why?'

'How should I know?'

'Let's go and see them, Ben. It could still be Knox, remember,' Jess said.

'But you don't believe that.'

'No. Sorry.'

'Neither do I. But it might be.'

'Yes.'

Ben ran downstairs, closely followed by Jess. The two directors were with Uncle Henry and Aunt Miriam in the sitting room. Knox, the small, slight man with a very sharp brain, was standing up. Hanbury, tall, plump and either very homophobic or stupid, Ben had concluded (from the way he'd reacted to learning that Julia was Dr Ashcroft's wife), was sitting down. Brief greetings were exchanged.

'Where's Marcus? And Rufus?' Jess asked.

'Marcus had to go. Rufus has gone too,' Aunt Miriam replied.

Ben gulped. Would Marcus go looking for his brother, intent on vengeance over the paternity test? Would he discover, too late, that Rufus was the Chief?

He realised Knox was addressing him.

'Sorry, what did you say?'

'I haven't time to repeat everything. Pay attention, boy!' Knox snapped, like a tetchy teacher. Ben glowered. 'Marcus and Hazel have been assuring me that your mother is innocent. Lord Charles and I have discussed it, and if you can convince us that she is, we will fund her solicitor and put the might of SPC behind her defence.'

'Not only your mother's defence, but also her career depends on it,' Hanbury said, alarmingly.

'Her *career*?'

'Of course. We can't employ her if she's a murderer.'

Ben was horrified. It hadn't even occurred to him, but of course they couldn't. If Mum was wrongly convicted, she'd lose her liberty and her career – which meant they'd lose their home, as well as each other.

'Hello!' a voice called. Ben thought it was Daphne's, and she soon entered the room, smiling. However, her face dropped when she saw the assembled party. She recovered impressively quickly, though, managing to look delighted.

Introductions were made and drinks were offered. Everyone wanted a glass of wine, apart from Jess and Ben, who requested water.

'Could you please come and help me with the drinks?' Daphne asked, looking at Ben and Jess.

'Sure.'

Once outside, she whispered, 'Why are they here?'

'They'll fund Mum's defence if I can prove she's innocent.'

'Then let's get rid of them. We're funding the defence, we don't need their money.'

'But it's not just the funding. It's Mum's whole career. If I don't convince them she's innocent, she's finished, they said.'

'How dreadful! That's scandalous! I'm tempted to pour them a glass of plonk. However, I usually find a nice drop of Burgundy oils the wheels, so let's give them that. It's in the cellar. Could you get the glasses out, please?' Daphne asked, disappearing behind a door in the far corner.

As they got the glasses out, Jess said, 'Oh, Ben, I'm so sorry you've got to go through this as well.'

'Me too. I could do without it. And the code.'

He broke off as Daphne's footsteps approached. She was carrying two bottles of red wine.

'Would you like a little glass? Does your mother allow it?' she asked Ben.

'I've never asked. I've never wanted it.'

'You're welcome to water, but I got you some coke. I've got a few bottles in the car. Would you mind?' She gave Ben the car keys.

'Are they in the boot?' Ben said, feeling surprised and rather gratified that she trusted him so.

'Yes.'

'Oh, I forgot. Your change,' he said, pulling a still thick wad of notes out of his pocket. 'We really enjoyed the takeaway, thanks.'

Daphne smiled. 'I'm glad.'

Outside the road was quiet. But as he found the coke, a familiar car was drawing up outside.

'Hi Benbo,' called Debs, emerging. 'Is it too late to call?'

Ben was relieved and pleased to have an ally who knew SPC as well as Mum did.

'Come and join the party.' As she drew closer he explained about Mum's job.

'That's scandalous! The old rogues. There is no way Tweedledum and Tweedledee can expect that of you. They're trying to pressure you, that's all,' she said.

'It's worked,' Ben said, picking up the bottles and returning inside, accompanied by Debs. He hoped Daphne didn't mind, but she professed herself – and genuinely seemed – delighted to see Debs again.

There was background music playing in the lounge when they carried the drinks through. Ben recognised the tune.

'Isn't this the guitar concerto?' It was one of the few classical CDs Mum had, so Ben had heard it often, and liked it. But he had never heard it played by a trumpet before. It was haunting, and somehow more poignant.

'It is Rodrigo's *Concierto de Aranjuez*, yes, but it's not him playing, as you'll have noticed,' Daphne replied. 'It's the Chief.'

'Who?' Ben asked, startled.

'Miles Davis, the trumpeter. Geoffrey always called him that,' Daphne said, smiling fondly. 'He was a great jazz fan. Many of its stars were accorded titles of respect by their fellow musicians. Ellington was the Duke, Basie was the Count and Miles Davis was the Chief.'

'Oh.' Relief washed through him.

'And Ella was the First Lady of Song. Did he like Ella? Ella Fitzgerald?' Aunt Miriam, a massive fan, asked.

'Not so much,' Daphne replied. Aunt Miriam's face fell. 'But I do. I *love* her.' They both beamed.

Knox, who had been chatting with Uncle Henry, walked over. 'It's late and I need to talk to Ben. Tell us what you remember of that meeting. When they were threatening to kill you and your mother.'

Knox was staring at him. So was Hanbury. Ben had so many questions but the biggest by far was what *shouldn't* he say?

'Marcus saved Ben and Sue,' Aunt Miriam said.

'Or someone else did,' Ben added quickly, just in case the Chief was present.

'By substituting sedative for 993 in the syringes, wasn't it?' Knox said.

'Yes. And I'm very glad they did,' Aunt Miriam replied.

'That could have been anyone,' Ben lied. 'The syringes were on a table. There were six of them there, the four backers and Marcus and Nixon. Any of them could have done it.'

'It was supposed to be a demonstration of 993's efficacy, wasn't it?' Knox said, increasing Ben's suspicions. How did he know so much?

'That's what they said. But they could have been lying,' Ben replied carefully.

'How did they get you there? Don't you live in Manchester?' Hanbury asked.

How did he think? On a flying carpet?

'They kidnapped me. In a car.'

'*Did* they?' Knox said, as if he knew Ben had voluntarily got into their car. No one else knew that, apart from Freddie,

Jess, Goatee Man and Kashani. Knox was staring at him, his eyes like lasers firing into his brain.

The doorbell rang.

'More company! Maybe it's Marcus,' said Daphne, hopefully.

'Maybe it's Mum,' Ben said, also hopeful.

'Let's hope so,' Debs said, as Daphne left.

'How did they manage to kidnap you?' Knox asked.

'I saw them in the library car park and asked them where Mum was. They said they'd take me to her,' Ben improvised, sensing he'd need a better lie than the version he'd told everyone else (including the police.)

'*Ben*!' Aunt Miriam looked devastated, making Ben feel remorseful. 'They could have killed you!'

'They nearly did. I know. Sorry. But I was so desperate to see Mum.' As he was now. He was straining to hear her voice, but hadn't heard anything yet.

'I know you were, darling. So was I. But to trust those men was silly.'

'Idiotic. Foolhardy. Typical,' Uncle Henry snorted.

'Brave. Ben is brave,' Jess said.

'He certainly is,' said a familiar voice behind Ben. He turned and saw Hazel. 'He's the bravest boy I know. Are you here regarding Sue's defence, Sir John?'

'And continued employment. Exactly. So the million-dollar question is: why have they arrested her?' Knox asked.

'Ballantyne accused Mum at the Warden's party, remember?' Ben said.

'He did. That's right,' Hanbury told Knox, who nodded.

'Someone wanted her to be arrested rather than them,' Aunt Miriam said. 'That could be well be Peter Ballantyne.'

'That's supposition. I need hard facts,' Knox said.

'Mum being arrested *is* a fact.'

'It's a travesty, gentlemen,' Hazel said. 'You must see that, surely? You know Sue. You know she's a good person, and an honourable person. She would *never* commit murder, and she would never endanger Ben.'

'She loves him more than she loves herself,' Debs said.

'She does that,' Aunt Miriam agreed.

'A mother would never do that to her son,' Hanbury told Knox.

'A few have,' Knox replied.

'*Mad* women, yes. But not Susan. She's not mad.'

'No, she's not. In fact, she's been remarkably resilient, considering her kidnap. That's what so suspicious,' Knox said.

'*That's been for Ben*!' Aunt Miriam cried.

Ben stared at her, horrified. It was all his fault?

Aunt Miriam's eyes were wide with fury, but she was glaring at Knox, not him. 'She didn't want to upset him any more than he had been. She *fainted*, did you know that? She wanted to get them both straight home, but that manager of hers, that Peter or Richard Ballantyne, whatever he's calling himself today, he told her she would be sacked if she went home.'

Ben felt horribly guilty and even more worried for Mum now that Aunt Miriam had reminded him of her current frailty.

'He threatened Sue,' Debs said. 'He said that if she went home on Saturday afternoon, she'd be accepting his golden handshake. His bribe to leave.'

'He assured me Sue would want that!' Hazel protested. She looked shocked. Ballantyne had tricked her, like he tricked everyone.

'Really? It seems Peter has been playing his own devious game, again,' Knox said, looking at Hanbury.

'He did accuse Sue of being the Chief,' Hanbury replied. 'Maybe he got her arrested too.'

'Yes, maybe he did,' Knox replied, looking thoughtful.

'The police arresting Sue makes no sense at all. If you ask me, they're crazy. Or corrupt,' Debs said.

'While she's an employee of ours, Sue deserves our support,' Hazel said. 'Just as we are supporting Marcus and Peter Nixon. Until any of them are proved guilty, we should support them.'

'It'd better be sorted out soon,' Knox said. 'It's ridiculous. We're struggling to keep this out of the press.'

'Mum's name mustn't go in the press,' Ben said, alarmed.

'Sue will have to be released tomorrow or charged. And they won't have evidence to charge her,' Hazel said. 'So she'll be free.'

'But who *is* guilty then? Marcus or Peter? Or someone else?' Hanbury blustered.

'We don't know. But it's not Mum,' Ben said.

'It's definitely not Sue,' Aunt Miriam said.

Knox looked at his watch. 'Right. It's late. You've convinced me that there's some doubt, at least. We'll fund her defence for now.'

'And Mum's still got a job?' Ben asked.

'She has. But not if she's a murderer.'

'If she's a murderer, I'm a monkey,' Debs said.

'It's not you that's been the monkey. It's been Peter Ballantyne,' Hanbury said, getting up. 'Again.'

'Tricky Dicky,' Debs said. 'If you ask me, he's a million times more likely to be the Chief than Sue.'

Knox nodded. 'I'd agree. But the police need evidence, not conjecture. And I need sleep. So goodnight.'

As the visitors left, Ben agreed with Knox. To free Mum and convict the Chief, they did need evidence. But how was he going to find it?

Chapter 15

The Weird Warning

When they returned to Ben's room, Freddie was at the desk, his hair more like a drenched sparrow than ever.

'How's it going?'

'I think it's a Vigenère cipher.'

'What's that?' Ben asked.

Freddie opened *The Code Book*. 'This is a Vigenère square.'

	a	b	c	d	e	f	g	h	i	j	k	l	m	n	o	p	q	r	s	t	u	v	w	x	y	z
1	B	C	D	E	F	G	H	I	J	K	L	M	N	O	P	Q	R	S	T	U	V	W	X	Y	Z	A
2	C	D	E	F	G	H	I	J	K	L	M	N	O	P	Q	R	S	T	U	V	W	X	Y	Z	A	B
3	D	E	F	G	H	I	J	K	L	M	N	O	P	Q	R	S	T	U	V	W	X	Y	Z	A	B	C
4	E	F	G	H	I	J	K	L	M	N	O	P	Q	R	S	T	U	V	W	X	Y	Z	A	B	C	D
5	F	G	H	I	J	K	L	M	N	O	P	Q	R	S	T	U	V	W	X	Y	Z	A	B	C	D	E
6	G	H	I	J	K	L	M	N	O	P	Q	R	S	T	U	V	W	X	Y	Z	A	B	C	D	E	F
7	H	I	J	K	L	M	N	O	P	Q	R	S	T	U	V	W	X	Y	Z	A	B	C	D	E	F	G
8	I	J	K	L	M	N	O	P	Q	R	S	T	U	V	W	X	Y	Z	A	B	C	D	E	F	G	H
9	J	K	L	M	N	O	P	Q	R	S	T	U	V	W	X	Y	Z	A	B	C	D	E	F	G	H	I
10	K	L	M	N	O	P	Q	R	S	T	U	V	W	X	Y	Z	A	B	C	D	E	F	G	H	I	J
11	L	M	N	O	P	Q	R	S	T	U	V	W	X	Y	Z	A	B	C	D	E	F	G	H	I	J	K
12	M	N	O	P	Q	R	S	T	U	V	W	X	Y	Z	A	B	C	D	E	F	G	H	I	J	K	L
13	N	O	P	Q	R	S	T	U	V	W	X	Y	Z	A	B	C	D	E	F	G	H	I	J	K	L	M
14	O	P	Q	R	S	T	U	V	W	X	Y	Z	A	B	C	D	E	F	G	H	I	J	K	L	M	N
15	P	Q	R	S	T	U	V	W	X	Y	Z	A	B	C	D	E	F	G	H	I	J	K	L	M	N	O
16	Q	R	S	T	U	V	W	X	Y	Z	A	B	C	D	E	F	G	H	I	J	K	L	M	N	O	P
17	R	S	T	U	V	W	X	Y	Z	A	B	C	D	E	F	G	H	I	J	K	L	M	N	O	P	Q
18	S	T	U	V	W	X	Y	Z	A	B	C	D	E	F	G	H	I	J	K	L	M	N	O	P	Q	R
19	T	U	V	W	X	Y	Z	A	B	C	D	E	F	G	H	I	J	K	L	M	N	O	P	Q	R	S
20	U	V	W	X	Y	Z	A	B	C	D	E	F	G	H	I	J	K	L	M	N	O	P	Q	R	S	T
21	V	W	X	Y	Z	A	B	C	D	E	F	G	H	I	J	K	L	M	N	O	P	Q	R	S	T	U
22	W	X	Y	Z	A	B	C	D	E	F	G	H	I	J	K	L	M	N	O	P	Q	R	S	T	U	V
23	X	Y	Z	A	B	C	D	E	F	G	H	I	J	K	L	M	N	O	P	Q	R	S	T	U	V	W
24	Y	Z	A	B	C	D	E	F	G	H	I	J	K	L	M	N	O	P	Q	R	S	T	U	V	W	Y
25	Z	A	B	C	D	E	F	G	H	I	J	K	L	M	N	O	P	Q	R	S	T	U	V	W	X	Y
26	A	B	C	D	E	F	G	H	I	J	K	L	M	N	O	P	Q	R	S	T	U	V	W	X	Y	Z

Although it was just a list of alphabets, apparently it was a massive breakthrough in coding.

'Because one character could represent up to 26 different letters, making it incredibly difficult to crack without computers,' Freddie explained.

'Oh great.' Ben hadn't the energy for a new cipher and wasn't sure how a computer would help.

'How do you know so much about them?' Jess asked.

'It's all in *The Code Book*. But it's not that difficult, because there's a key.'

'Another key?' Ben was *sick* of keys. But Freddy's claim that Vigenère ciphers weren't that difficult might mean that he was prepared to crack it on his own.

'Yes. Once they'd thought of keys, everyone used them, because they are so easy to remember. Let's use Ben.'

'I do know a few other words,' Ben said, a pathetic joke, but it made Freddie smile, as he'd intended.

'A short key will be easier for you to understand. And spell,' he added, pushing his luck. 'You write your message out and write Ben above it, repeatedly.'

In case that was too hard for Ben's miniscule brain, Freddie demonstrated.

B	E	N	B	E	N	B	E	N	B	E	N
h	e	l	l	o	f	r	e	d	d	i	e

'To put h into code, you go to the B line on the square – that's number 1, the row starting with B.'

'I get it, okay?'

'Don't get snappy. Then you find H on the top row.'

'Okay,' Ben said, making an effort to sound calm.

'Where the two lines intersect is your code letter. So h would be encoded I. It's just a plus one Caesar shift.'

'But e would be I too!' Jess noticed, surprised. 'Oh, that's clever.'

'Yes. And the first l would be Y and the second l would be M. That's why it's so clever. It's a pattern, and a regular pattern, but very hard to crack unless you know the key. If it were a longer message it would be much easier, because we could use letter frequency. But the repetition tells us something. However, it's 48.'

'How do you know?'

'Laea repeats forty-eight letters apart.'

Jess checked the code again.

'Oh yes,' she said.

'The keyword could therefore be 1, 2, 3, 4, 6, 8, 12, 16, 24 or 48 letters long,' Freddie rattled off, without pausing for breath.

'It can't be 48 letters long. Or 24, surely?' Ben said.

'It could if it's a chemical. But it's probably not,' Jess added, as she registered his incredulity.

'It's not 1, 2, 3 or 4. I'd have spotted that already,' Freddie said. 'So it's 6, 8 or 12, I think. But unless we can guess the key, this isn't long enough to crack, really.'

Ben was impressed by Freddie's reasoning. But it would take ages to find the key. Ages they hadn't got.

'Shall we just give up then?' he suggested.

'No! Of course not!' Jess said, wide-eyed with indignation. 'OXFORD has 6 letters and THE CHIEF has 8. We could start with those.'

'We might as well,' Freddie said, shrugging. 'Okay I'll take OXFORD and you and Ben can have THE CHIEF.'

Typical, Ben thought.

'Freddie, could Ben and I sit at the desk?' Jess asked. It had two chairs next to each other, one of which Freddie was currently occupying.

'I need the book,' Freddie said, clutching it like a miser guarding gold.

'I'll copy the square out for us then.'

'I can type that up,' Ben offered, thinking it would be largely a cut and paste job.

'Thanks. I do need the bathroom.'

'Okay.' As she left, Ben opened up a spreadsheet and got cracking. Jess was still in the bathroom when he finished, so Ben started on the first line of the cipher.

laea hb kwturaz

Remembering that their key was THE CHIEF, he found the T line, located L and followed that column to the top, giving S. He checked he'd done it right. He followed the S column down to the T line, saw that S would be encoded L, and realised he'd worked it out. Surprised at himself, he found A on the H line, which was in the T column.

'It starts ST,' he told Jess, as she came into the room

'Hopeful, if we get a vowel next,' she replied.

'Our next is A,' Ben realised. 'Then Y – STAY! We might have cracked it!'

'This isn't,' Freddie. 'It starts XW.'

Jess was keen to take over, as was Freddie, so Ben left his cousins to it, and paced the room, thinking.

Knox had been suspiciously interested in who switched the syringes. But could it have been simply because he was SPC's Chief Executive? Both Marcus and Nixon reported to him. If he was innocent, he'd surely want to know who to sack.

There was no conceivable reason why Knox would want to protect him, or land Mum in it. He was so senior that Mum had hardly ever dealt with him, until the last few days. They hardly knew each other.

It wasn't Knox, Ben concluded.

'Ben, look at this,' Jess said.

He went over to the computer desk and saw what she had written.

STAY AT GRANNY'S
SAFE AND SOUND
WHILST SPC ARE
STILL AROUND.
STAY AT DAPHNE'S
DON'T GO OUT

'Is that the code?'

'It's a cipher! And of course it is. What do you think it is? A blue banana?' Freddie snapped.

Ben rolled his eyes but didn't snap back. He'd heard worse than that in the playground at primary school.

'It's almost playful again,' Jess said. '*Granny* and *Daphne* doesn't sound like Rufus or Marcus talking. Rufus calls her Mother and Marcus calls her Ma.'

'He wouldn't put that in the code, would he? It'd be a dead giveaway. The Chief is far too clever for that. He would disguise himself,' Freddie said.

'But why the hell is he telling me to take care when he's tried again and again to kill me?' Ben cried.

'Oh my giddy aunt!' Jess looked thunderstruck. 'We can prove it.'

'Fantastic, Jess! How?'

'Whoever sent this code must have had *The Code Book*. It's far too specialised for most people,' Jess said. 'They've given themselves away.'

'It is very specialised. So it's Rufus or Marcus,' Freddie said.

'Ballantyne might have it too,' Ben said.

'It can't be him,' Jess said. 'On the Friday this all started, when they were going to kill you and your mum, Rufus and Marcus didn't know you could be their son. Then, the Chief wanted to kill you, but Marcus – or someone,' she quickly added, seeing Freddie's mouth open, 'switched the syringes. The Chief wanted to kill you on Friday.'

'Couldn't Ballantyne have saved me just to incriminate Mum? That's what you said, isn't it?'

'I did think that, yes. But the timing is a very big coincidence in that case. The text was timed precisely at the moment to save you.'

'Which would mean someone had to be watching the pool,' Freddie said.

'Was Goatee Man there? Did you see him?' asked Ben.

135

His cousins answered that they hadn't seen Goatee Man.

'I'd have told you that already, wouldn't I?' Freddie snapped. 'I'd have told the police.'

'But the timing, Ben,' Jess said. 'They didn't need to be watching. They knew what time it started. They knew how tricky the text was to solve. They probably expected lots more people to die before you got involved. They probably expected you not to have time to get into the pool at all. Or even if you would. The rest of us stayed on the side. You might have done that.'

'But I wouldn't have saved anyone then.'

'You wouldn't have endangered yourself.'

Ben bowed his head, ashamed of the worry he had caused her, Aunt Miriam – and even Freddie and Uncle Henry, who had helped him, so were presumably worried too, though he was too fuzzy-headed to notice at the time. And particularly Mum, who had sat by his hospital bed, waiting for him to wake up. Terrified. Worrying. Suffering.

She was still suffering now. She would be scared and worried, both about herself, and probably even about him. She had feared he might be about to die twice in the past few days. She must be worried sick. He had to get her out of jail, somehow.

But his cousins were still debating.

'How would he know Ben was in the pool?' Freddie demanded.

'Because he'd sent him there. With that code,' Jess said.

'The flamingos one?'

'Exactly. He knew Ben had intervened in the ice-cream attack, he knew Ben had tried to fight the six men off to save Aunt Sue,' Jess said, massively exaggerating Ben's efforts, 'so he *knew* he'd get into the pool.'

She was right, Ben realised.

'So would Nixon,' Freddie argued. 'That text could be from Nixon, to get Ben into the pool.'

'Exactly! So Rufus, having found out about it, would want to stop it.'

'Or Marcus would. It could still be Marcus.'

'Exactly,' Jess said. 'We simply need to find out which of her sons owns *The Code Book*, and we've got the Chief!'

'Great. Come on!' Ben said, heading for the door.

'Where are you going?'

'To ask Daphne. She'll know.'

Chapter 16

Daphne Tells All

Daphne was in the kitchen, now wearing slippers and a dressing gown over silk pyjamas.

'I'm getting a nightcap,' she said putting the kettle on. 'Do you want a drink?'

'Hot chocolate?' Jess asked hopefully.

'Sorry, I haven't got any. There's coke in the fridge.'

Ben fetched the bottles. They were lovely and cold now. Daphne offered them glasses, but even Jess was happy to drink from the bottle.

'Freddie loves *The Code Book*. Was it Marcus's?' Jess asked.

'No, that's Rufus's book. He wanted to win the prize.'

Rufus! Then Rufus was the Chief! Ben struggled to keep his cool.

'What prize?' Jess asked, relatively calmly, Ben thought. But her eyes were shining, as if she was excited. She deserved to be. She had worked it all out. What a genius!

'£10,000,' Daphne replied. 'It was a coding competition. A very hard coding competition, just for experts, really.'

'I've seen that. It looks fun,' Freddie said.

'It's been won, I'm afraid. Rufus entered it.' Ben gave Jess a sidelong look. She nodded. 'But he was pipped at the post. The winning team found the book cipher the hardest to crack, he said, much harder than the Enigmas.'

'*What*?' Ben was stunned, and noticed his cousins looked astonished too. 'Enigma? As in Alan Turing?'

'And the rest of the team at Bletchley Park, yes. Now computers can crack Enigma ciphers. But not then. And not book ciphers, unless they are very long with plenty of repetitions,' Daphne replied, getting a mug out of a cupboard.

Book ciphers were even harder than Enigma Ciphers? It hardly seemed credible – but with a race to win a fortune like that, he was sure the contenders would have been busting a gut to crack every single code.

Daphne turned off the kettle, then poured some whisky into the mug. She added hot water and a teaspoonful of honey and stirred it, smiling at them.

'Shocking after wine, but I only had a small glass and I need knockout drops tonight. I'm just so worried about Marcus.'

'Why?'

'Like you, my darling grandson, he's brave. Incredibly brave. And as his mother, it terrifies me. He's putting himself in such terrible danger. If anything happens to him, it would be worse than it happening to me. Far worse.'

Seeing the pain in her face, Ben understood, and was suffused with guilt for the pain he'd put Mum through that morning, waiting for him to recover from the cyanide. She must have been terrified that he wouldn't. And after that morning from hell, she had to endure the humiliation of being marched out of the hospital in handcuffs and then the nightmare of being interrogated about something of which she knew nothing of. Poor, poor Mum.

'That's how you feel when you love someone, isn't it?' Jess said.

Daphne raised her eyebrows. 'You're very sensitive to realise that at your age.'

'You are, Jess. I didn't know it until Mum disappeared,' Ben said. 'I'd have given anything to get her back then, even my life. But I didn't know that until then.'

'Love can break your heart, just as much as it can heal.' Daphne sighed. 'But I truly believe that old saying: *''Tis better to have loved and lost than never to have loved at all.'*

'Shakespeare?' Jess guessed.

'Tennyson, I think. But what dark thoughts! Night always makes everything seem worse, somehow.'

'Yes it does, doesn't it?' Jess replied.

Daphne would suffer terribly, Ben realised. She would be heartbroken to discover that her son was the Chief. Whilst feeling guilty about the pain he was about to cause her, he was also recalling her mentioning Geoffrey's adoration of the Chief, Miles Davis. Rufus would have heard him use the nickname often, which must have given him the idea.

It was yet another piece of evidence to add to the case against him. He hoped he had enough to convince the police.

'What did Marcus read in college?' Freddie asked.

'PPE. That's politics, philosophy and economics.'

'I know. What about Rufus?'

'Biochemistry. What about you? What are you going to study at university?'

Ben's phone bleeped. He ignored it.

'Physics, probably, or maths,' Freddie replied. 'Did either of them like physics?'

'Rufus did it at A-level. He's always been interested in it. That's why he and your father got on so well,' Daphne replied. 'What about you, Ben? Have you plans for university?'

'No. I don't know.'

'When did he get into the environmental campaigning?' Jess asked.

'Let me think.' Daphne took a sip of her drink. 'It would be about seven years ago, because he worked in the City for a few years. Or else he'd never have afforded the house he has, not on third sector wages.'

'Third sector?'

'Charity and voluntary sector jobs. They don't pay as well as the finance sector. Mind you, what does? Apart from football and films.'

'He's not very keen on people, is he?' Jess said.

Daphne looked momentarily confused, then her face cleared. 'Oh, you mean OPO? No, he likes some people, just not those that wilfully damage the Earth. Which, unfortunately, seems to include all of us in one way or another.'

'So he doesn't like anyone, really?'

Daphne looked sad. 'Don't let his curmudgeonly ways give you the wrong impression. He cares passionately about the planet. He'd be happier if we all reduced our carbon footprint.'

'So would Mum,' Ben said.

'Yes, I think most adults would agree with that.' She looked at him. 'He does like some people, you know. Henry for example. And you, I think.'

Unconvinced, Ben said, 'Really?'

'Yes. I'm sure he does. And he liked your mum, very much indeed. But she finished with him.'

'Which made him angry, I suppose,' Jess said.

'You suppose right. You're a very perceptive young lady, aren't you?'

Jess went pink. 'Thank you. I hope so.'

'Does he still feel angry about it after so many years?' Ben asked.

'He hates losing, he always has. He lost her. So I think it does still rankle, to be honest. Don't worry about it,' Daphne said, smiling at him. 'They'll get over it. Your mum and him will work it out. I know he's your uncle, but it won't be as bad as you think.'

Ben was glad that she had misinterpreted the emotion that had obviously flashed across his face. He'd forgotten she didn't know. She should know. He put it as gently as he could.

'I'm sorry to say Rufus tricked us. He didn't use the cotton bud.'

Daphne looked confused. 'I beg your pardon?'

'In my paternity test. You can use cotton buds. It's a single gene,' explained Freddie.

'We think,' added Jess. 'Aunt Sue says the studies are too small to be conclusive.'

'Well it works in our family!' Freddie retorted.

Ben broke into their row, because Daphne still didn't understand. 'We thought Rufus had two recessive genes. He fooled us that he had. But tonight he's told us he's dominant.'

'That his earwax is yellow and sticky,' Freddie interjected.

Understandably, Daphne grimaced. 'Yes, I can confirm that that's true. Why does that matter so much?'

'I'm dominant. Mum's recessive. So my dad must have given me the dominant gene.'

She clasped a hand over her mouth. 'Oh no! So you thought only Marcus had a dominant gene?'

'Yes. Exactly.'

She lowered her hand. 'Do both of them know?'

'Yes. Now. None of us knew beforehand – except Rufus.'

'My boys never tell me anything. Oh, Ben, I'm so sorry. Yet again my sons have behaved disgracefully.'

'Not both of them. Just Rufus.'

'Oh, dear.' She buried her face in her hands.

'It's not your fault.'

She uncovered her face. Her eyes glistened with tears. 'I'm their mother. I brought them up. I feel culpable.'

Though he didn't understand, Ben sensed she was apologising. 'It's not your fault.'

'Isn't it? I think it is. Though your grandfather would have agreed with you. Geoffrey used to say they're grown men now. They make their own choices.'

'Exactly.'

'But how can he behave so appallingly? As if he feels nothing for anyone.'

Like the Chief. Poor Daphne. If she was this upset by his lie, how upset was she going to be?

'It's not that bad. I still think Marcus is my dad. And so does he.'

'So do I,' Daphne agreed.

'I'm really glad about you,' he added quickly. 'Being my gran. You're so kind having us here tonight.'

'Yes, they're lovely rooms. Thank you,' Jess said.

'Did Marcus ever talk to you about 993?' Freddie asked.

Daphne's eyes widened as if startled, but Ben realised that Freddie was still investigating, though he had spoken rather abruptly, as he often did.

'Yes, of course,' she replied.

'Recently? Or when it was being developed?'

'I first heard of it years ago. It was the best prospect for years, I remember, so devastating when it failed. Why?'

'We're just trying to understand how much other families knew of it,' Jess said, smoothing it over. 'Aunt Sue and Ben used to talk about it most nights, didn't you?'

'Yeah. We always chat about school and work over dinner,' Ben said.

'That's nice. I used to talk to my boys every night too. But now they're adults I don't see them so often. Or talk to them much.' Daphne wrinkled her nose. 'I ring them as often as I dare. I dread annoying them.'

'You wouldn't annoy them,' Jess said.

'I do, sometimes. You saw them yesterday in the coffee shop.'

'I can't believe that was only yesterday,' Ben said.

'Yes. You've been through hell and back since then.'

Indeed. But Mum had too.

'I'm fine thanks. It's Mum I'm worried about.'

'Quite right too. You're a good son.' She smiled, her eyes crinkling kindly.

If only. He was a lousy son, who had put his mum through two terrible ordeals when she'd feared he would die, and he'd failed to deduce that Rufus was the Chief in time to stop the police from arresting her.

But now, finally, he knew exactly how to get her free.

Chapter 17

Frustration

Thanking Daphne for the drinks, they returned upstairs. When they reached the top floor, Ben felt safely out of earshot of Daphne.

'We know it's him! *Rufus*,' he whispered. 'You've proved it.'

'We did no such thing,' Freddie argued.

'Not quite,' Jess said.

Ben couldn't believe his cousins didn't see it too. 'Let's go to my room.'

At least he managed to convince them of that.

When they were sitting down, he explained.

'We know he's mad about overpopulation. So is the Chief. We know he loves physics. So does the Chief. We know he loves codes. So does the Chief. And he wanted revenge on Mum. That's why he got her arrested!'

'I'll bet he loves bossing Marcus about. He'll love outwitting him, keeping him guessing, keeping him scared. That's why he recruited Marcus,' Jess said.

'It could still be Marcus,' Freddie maintained.

'It's not Marcus. It's Rufus,' Ben said.

'It was Marcus that kidnapped her. It was him that caught her, when she was trying to escape.'

Freddie was right. When Mum had been spying on their meeting, it had been so dusty in the ancient priest-hole that she had sneezed. She had fled down the secret passages that ran under St Saviour's (built in ancient times for the priests to escape arrest, when being a Catholic could get you killed) but hadn't got far before Marcus caught her.

Clearly, Freddie didn't understand.

'He explained that to her. The American was right behind him,' Ben said, referring to one of the Chief's repellent backers. 'He had to, else they would have known he was on our side, not theirs. You don't think Mum would have been speaking to him otherwise, do you?'

'Isn't he her ultimate boss? Ballantyne's boss?'

'Yeah.'

'Well she'd have to, wouldn't she?'

Ben looked at Jess, worried. 'You do think it's Rufus, don't you?'

'I *think* so. But I don't *know* so. Not for sure. Not enough to convince the police. They need evidence, Ben. Footprints, fingerprints, paperwork.'

Jess had read too much Agatha Christie. 'It's wiretaps now. Electronic evidence. Confessions.'

'Confessions! Like any of that lot would confess,' Freddie scoffed.

Suspecting he was right, Ben switched tack. 'They just need to get Rufus's phones. Then if he's been texting me codes, that's proof.'

'We haven't got proof!' Freddie cried. 'I could have texted you those codes, Jess could, anyone could.'

'Yes, you could. You haven't, have you?' Ben said, getting up.

'No of course I haven't,' Freddie said, hands raised defensively in front of him. 'But the point is that anyone could. Nixon, Marcus, anyone. Even Rufus.'

'He doesn't have your number, Ben,' Jess said, in the tone that said you've made a serious blunder.

But he hadn't. 'Nixon could give it to him,' Ben said.

'But why would he even have thought about you last week? He didn't even know you. Why would he have texted you?' Freddie asked.

'Marcus sent me that first text. He told me. To stop me getting involved.'

'Well that worked brilliantly, didn't it?' Freddie scoffed.

'Nixon might have sent the other two.'

'But they kind of contradicted each other,' Jess pointed out. 'I think one of them was from Nixon and one from the Chief.'

Secretly, Ben agreed with her, but he wasn't going to admit it to Freddie. It was a minor point, but it worried him a little. However, he had an argument.

'He'd have known about me last week because they'd got my mum. They wanted two guinea pigs – that's what they called us, can you believe it?' Ben chose to ignore Freddie nodding and continued. 'They wanted two guinea pigs for their trial. Nixon hated me investigating, so Nixon got me kidnapped, but Rufus, the Chief, wanted me there too. That's why he texted me the other code.'

'Cipher! It was a cipher,' Freddie snapped.

'I know,' Ben replied through gritted teeth.

'Let's vote,' Jess suggested. 'Who thinks it's Rufus?'

Ben shook his head. This wasn't going anywhere near as well as he'd hoped. But he was determined to convince his cousins it was Rufus, because if he couldn't convince them, he couldn't convince the police.

'I think it's Rufus,' Ben said. 'Even though he could be my dad, I still say it's him.'

'I do too. I think. But it could still be Ballantyne,' Jess said.

'I think its Marcus. I think he's getting at his brother, sending Nixon to OPO. I think he meant to catch your mum, and you. I think he's a superb liar, and a psychopath. Lots of business leaders are psychopaths. I think it's him,' Freddie said.

Ben buried his head in his hands.

'What's up, Ben?' Jess sounded concerned.

'I want Mum back. I want to convince the police to let her out. I want to stop them killing people. I thought we could. I thought we had enough.'

'We know its Rufus or Marcus or Ballantyne or possibly, maybe, Knox, but even *we're* not agreed on which. Which proves the evidence is conflicting,' Freddie said.

'We've got to get enough! How *can* we get enough?'

'We simply need more evidence.'

'Great. Why didn't I think of that?'

'Freddie's right, Ben. I'm sorry, but he is.'

'You find it then. You're clever. I'm not. But if it was your mum, you'd be trying to free her too.' Ben was desperate for Freddie's help, but he was just blinking at him. He tried again. 'Can you imagine how it feels? She's accused of killing children. She's accused of being the scumbag who kidnapped her. She's accused of being everything she hates.'

'Can I see that last text you got? The one before the swimming pool?'

Ben was so taken aback that he just stared at Freddie, but naturally Jess asked why.

'I didn't get chance to analyse it. I've a feeling it might tell us something,' Freddie said.

'Great!' Ben scrolled through his Inbox and found it.

mi rw mr ah rr mt mh rw ri ah rh aw mr mh mr
mt aw mr mi ah ri ai rw ag rg mg aw rw mt ar
mt aw mr aw mr rr rg mr aw mg rg
mt mr ag mt aw rw mh mt at

It told him diddly squat. He handed it to Freddie.

'It said…' Ben tailed off. What had it said, exactly?

'I remember that,' Freddie replied, fortunately. 'It's this I need.'

'Do you really think it might give us something?'

'It might.'

'I hope it does.' Ben had so many emotions whirling around inside him that he desperately needed some space. He went into the bathroom.

There was a long shower cubicle along one wall, a window, loo and washbasin opposite and – Jess would be delighted – a bookshelf on the far wall. The multi-coloured books and the red and gold striped handtowels made a fetching contrast to the white walls and fittings. It was a very homely room, but it didn't comfort Ben.

He splashed some water onto his face and dried it, studying himself in the mirror. With his blond hair and blue eyes, he definitely looked more like Marcus. Their faces were broad and square, not long and thin like Rufus's. Plus, both he and Marcus had a dimple when they smiled, but he hadn't noticed one on Rufus – though he had hardly ever seen him smile.

Hopefully, his dad was Marcus. And hopefully, he was innocent. But hope was all he had. And hope felt as useful as a paper umbrella.

He needed help. He needed support. He needed total, unquestioning love. He needed Mum.

There was a knock on the door.

'Are you all right, Ben?'

Reluctantly, he emerged to face Jess. 'Not really. I need Mum. I want her free. I need to know my dad's not the Chief.'

'We want that too, Ben. We want to help you. We're on your side, really.'

'I know.'

Jess handed him his phone. 'I copied out the old text for Freddie. What was that text you got downstairs? I didn't like to look.'

Ben was through with texts, but she was trying to help, so he looked at it. 'It's just a book cipher from Marcus. Two of them. I hope he's okay.'

'I'll crack that for you. And Freddie's analysing that other cipher.'

'Thanks,' Ben said, but he knew it was useless. Still he returned to the room, and sat on the bed and waited, determined not to cry.

Jess knew the book cipher so well that she had cracked most of the message before she got her master sheet out. Soon she had finished.

'Look, Ben.'

He trudged over.

75 46 30 14 5 56 75 39 10 75 95 8 4 86 60 1 75 10 30
6 13 51 1 30 95 11 59 3 46 16 5 56 6   8 5 12 5 39
91 5 64 76 9 8 20 10 75 95

CAN YOU CRACK THIS? I CAN'T. THINK IT'S ABOUT TOMORROW'S ATTACK.

'Tomorrow?' Ben noticed Marcus had sent the message five minutes ago, at 23:58, still yesterday. Did he mean the attack would happen today, Tuesday or tomorrow, Wednesday?

But Jess was showing him the second cipher she had transcribed. 'It's a book cipher. It's not ours. Marcus wants us to crack it.'

'A book cipher? We'll never crack it.' He looked at it blankly.

15 53 41 44 68 57 58 5 22 51 9 76 37 66 75 33 13 11 17 37

'Can I see it?' Freddie asked. Typically, he didn't get up, but waited for Jess to take it over to the armchair. He looked at it. 'That's too short. That's ridiculous. We'll never crack it. You heard Daphne. They're harder than Enigma.'

'Right. Forget it then. It's impossible,' Ben said.

'No, it's not. It's hard. Very hard indeed. Our hardest challenge ever. But it's not impossible,' Jess insisted. 'We simply have to find the right page of the right book.'

'Forget it. *Please*. We have to sleep sometime.'

His cousins bristled with energy, but Ben didn't. He felt like a punch-drunk boxer, reeling with exhaustion, wondering how on earth he could convince them to come to the police station with him. Or knock them out. He yawned, triggering Jess to yawn too.

'She'll be sleeping now,' Jess said.

'Who?'

'Your mum.'

Ben suspected she wouldn't sleep a wink. She must be so tormented.

'Let's go to the police, *please*. Not Inspector Walker, Inspector Cunningham. He'll listen. Let's tell him everything, show him the codes, everything. He'll know it's Rufus or Marcus or Ballantyne, and he'll let Mum go.'

'He won't, Ben,' Jess said, her eyes exuding sympathy. 'We need more. We need rock solid evidence. We've hardly got it straight in our own minds.'

'We haven't got any more evidence. There's nothing else to tell them.'

'It isn't enough.'

'What then? What else can we do to help her? We've got to help her, Jess.'

'I know. I'm trying to, Ben, really, I am,' Jess insisted.

Ben bowed his head. He was being unfair. She was trying. Even Freddie was trying. And he was just complaining.

'Sorry.'

'Don't worry about it. Look, there's the book cipher,' Jess said, as if trying to cheer him up.

'That's even more impossible than Enigma.'

'But maybe we can be lucky, Ben.'

Maybe a magic fairy would wave her wand and make everything better instantly.

'Maybe we have been,' Freddie declared, standing up. 'Look!'

Chapter 18

Freddie's Brainwave

Freddie had prepared a table.

	w	r	i	g	h	t
m	B	E	F	O	R	T
a	H	S	M	N	L	Y
r	I	D	A	G	W	
c						
u						
s						

The letters were a little difficult to decipher in Freddie's scrawl, but to Ben one thing stood out. He frowned.

'What's this? Why are you using Marcus?'

'I'm not using Marcus. *He* did. This is how he constructed the pool code to you. He's so egocentric,' Freddie said, making no sense whatsoever.

'*What?*'

'Using his own name. And so confident we can't unmask him.'

'You think it's Marcus that sent it? To get me in the pool? You're nuts.'

Freddie's eyes flashed with anger. 'I'm not nuts! I'm right. I've worked out how they encrypted it. It's a clue.'

'A real clue?'

He glared. 'It's not imaginary, is it?'

'No. Right, sorry. Tell me what it means. Please,' Ben added, feeling it was needed to get Freddie down from his high horse.

'Okay. I've worked out that it's constructed from another message. That's how he built the code. That message must have begun: BEFORE THE.'

'Really?' Ben was sceptical.

'It starts with B. Yours started with F. But he's used his name.'

'Why?' Ben asked wondering if Freddie meant he, Marcus, or he, the Chief.

'Because he's vain!'

Now Ben understood. He meant that Marcus was the Chief, and was also vain.

'He's not the Chief and he is not vain!'

'Stop fighting, you two. We haven't time,' Jess said, 'Look, Freddie, I think you've spotted a real clue. That's fantastic. And I agree the Chief has used Marcus's name to construct it. It could mean it's Marcus who wrote it – but it's very unlikely.'

'Why?' Freddie demanded frowning at her.

'Well if he is the Chief, he's giving himself away. Even Nixon must have noticed the letters came from Marcus's name. But I think it proves the Chief is someone else.'

'Who?' Ben asked really impressed by her reasoning, and her maturity. She was absolutely right to stop them squabbling. It was an idiotic waste of time when they were under such pressure. In some ways Jess seemed very young still, but in others she seemed more mature than both of them – and she wasn't even a teenager yet.

'Rufus or Ballantyne.'

Ben was delighted. 'Really? This narrows it down to two?'

'I still think it's Marcus,' Freddie muttered, sulking in the armchair.

'It's connected to Marcus, definitely. It tells us that the person who wrote it is taunting Marcus. Either because they suspect Marcus is double-crossing them, or because they just love taunting Marcus.'

'If the Chief suspected Marcus was double-crossing them, wouldn't they kill him?'

'No, Ben. If you were the Chief, imagine for second, then you'd have Nixon working for you or Marcus. Who would you choose?'

'Marcus. Every time. He's smarter, better with people, and faster.'

'Exactly. But the Chief would want to warn him obliquely.'

'What?'

'Not openly. Subtly. So that Marcus understood he was on to him. So I think that points to Ballantyne. But it could also be that the Chief isn't on to Marcus, but just loves taunting him anyway. That's Rufus.'

'That's absolutely brilliant, Jess. And Freddie,' Ben added, because now he knew how important Freddie's deduction had been. 'So please, tell us, how does this code – cipher,' he quickly added before Freddie snapped at him.

'Code!' Freddie snapped.

'Right, code. How does it work? Please.'

'The plaintext letters are in the order they were in a message they sent to each other.'

'Plaintext?'

Freddie rolled his eyes. 'Plaintext is the uncoded message. The code is the code.'

'Thanks. Okay I get it. So after BEFORE THE, what's next?'

'S, or S and M, are in it, maybe. Or maybe not. Maybe it's still the same letters they've used before. THREE for example.'

'Oh, I get it. How many letters?' Ben asked.

'I don't know.'

'*What?*'

'It could be SERMON,' Jess suggested.

Freddie rolled his eyes, huffing.

'I was just giving an example,' Jess protested. 'It's a noun, obviously. *Before the* must be followed by a noun. Or an adjective, I suppose, but they're unlikely to use those in codes.'

Ben sighed. 'So it could be any word in the world?'

'No. It can only contain B, E, F, O, R, T, H and maybe S, and possibly even M,' Freddie said, ruling it down to merely most words in the English language, rather than all of them. Great.

Jess made lots of suggestions, and even Ben managed a few, but none convinced the others, until Jess suggested, 'FOREMEN?'

'What foremen?' Freddie said, looking at her as if she was insane.

But she'd given Ben an idea. 'HORSEMEN! I'll bet it's HORSEMEN.'

'What the hell are you talking about?' Freddie snapped.

He was really getting on Ben's nerves now. But Ben took a deep breath and explained, 'When we were at that meeting with Knox and Hanbury, one of them mentioned the Four Horsemen of the Apocalypse.'

'No they didn't.'

'You weren't there. It was me and Mum. On Saturday. That one where Ballantyne threatened me. Sort of...' He tailed off, remembering. It hadn't been a direct threat, but Ballantyne hinted that he'd sent the Bridge of Sighs text. Possibly it was a coincidence, but it had felt like a threat to Ben.

'Who else was there?' Jess asked.

'Knox and Hanbury and Hazel and Debs. But not Nixon.'

'And Marcus,' Freddie said. 'He was there, wasn't he?'

'No.'

'So what does that prove?'

'Nixon had doodled a horse's head when he was thinking about the 993 meeting. He must have connected horsemen to the backers. There are four of them, aren't there?'

'Plague, Famine, War and Death,' Jess intoned. A chill ran through Ben. He couldn't bear any more deaths. They had to stop them before they used the 993. 'Yes, that would be how those four creeps would like to portray themselves,' Jess continued.

'And the Chief is the Devil that sends them, is he?' Freddie scoffed.

'If anyone's the Devil, he is. Hang on,' Ben added, as an idea struck him. 'Rufus wasn't there. Marcus wasn't there, but Ballantyne *was*. Does this prove it's Ballantyne?'

'It could be coincidence, Ben. Or it could be a genuine clue,' Jess said.

'Or Nixon could just like horses. Or chess. It could have been a knight's head. It proves nothing,' Freddie said.

'It might,' Jess said. 'Can't you remember who said it, or why?'

'No, sorry.' Ben felt so stupid. He knew she would have remembered. He was useless.

'Is one of them religious?'

'Why religious?' Freddie asked, narrowing his eyes. (He looked down on anyone who was religious. And nearly everyone who wasn't.)

'They're from Revelation, the four horsemen of the apocalypse,' Jess explained. 'It's the last book in the Bible. Is any of them a Christian?'

'No idea, sorry. So it's not a clue then?'

'Probably not, sorry.'

Ben sighed. 'Great.' But he felt the exact opposite.

'Let's say you're right about HORSEMEN,' Freddie said. 'BEFORE THE HORSEMEN FLY, what?'

'Why fly?' Ben asked, startled.

'It's a verb. They were going to fly home. Why not?'

'Why that verb, Freddie?' Jess asked.

'We've got LY in the next word.'

'Okay,' Ben said slowly. There was too much guesswork to convince him, let alone the police.

Jess, of course, kept guessing words. And so did Freddie. They were driving him insane and none sounded right.

'Shall we just give up?' Ben suggested, as calmly as he could manage.

'No!' Jess barked, red-faced and furious, but it wasn't with him, he knew that. It was her frustration at not cracking the code.

He took a deep breath. He had been so selfish, just thinking of himself. She was suffering too and trying so hard to outwit the creeps. He had to help her.

'So what do we need then? In the next words?'

'I, D, A, G and W in that order. And any of the letters before.'

'Right. Thanks.'

He tried to shut his cousins out and think. What might the Chief want to do before the four "horsemen" flew out of the country? He would have to prove that 993 worked. Which was what he'd hoped to do on Friday, when he and Mum were supposed to have been murdered in front of them.

At the field trial! That's what SPC called important agrochemical tests. That's how Marcus and Nixon had referred to the attempted murder of Mum and him at St Saviour's.

'It's: BEFORE THE HORSEMEN FLY, THE FIELD TRIAL MUST WORK, or something like that,' he said.

'Can't be MUST. There's no U,' Freddie said.

'Okay, what then?'

'I like FIELD TRIAL, I'll bet that's it. Maybe IS or ARE comes next,' Jess suggested.

'Yeah, IS – THE FIELD TRIAL IS – something.'

'HAPPENING?'

'Can't be HAPPENING. No P,' Freddie said. 'Could be GOING AHEAD.'

'So can this tell us any more than that?' asked Ben.

'Oh yes. It could tell us where. And when.'

'You're joking!'

'No I'm not,' Freddie replied, absolutely deadpan.

Ben beamed at him, deeply impressed. At last! They had got them at last! They could stop the next attack. And it was all down to Freddie.

'You genius. You absolute bloody genius!'

Freddie beamed. 'Thanks.'

'So where is it?'

'Well the next word could be AT.'

'Yes. BEFORE THE HORSEMEN FLY, FIELD TRIAL AT somewhere. That makes sense now,' Jess said, also beaming.

'SAINT SAVIOUR'S?' Ben suggested.

'Can't be. We still need W,' Freddie said. 'WADHAM or WORCESTER, perhaps.'

'Or W might come from another word. Like NOW, for example,' Jess said. 'Or WEDNESDAY.'

'That's the day after tomorrow,' Ben said, alarmed.

'It's tomorrow already. It's gone midnight. It's Tuesday the 11th. Happy birthday, Ben,' Jess said, smiling.

Ben returned her smile. 'Thanks, Jess. If we can crack this code it will be the best birthday ever. And get Mum back of course.'

'Of course. That'll make my day too.'

'So where could it be?'

'Well assuming it's a college, if it needs a W, I can only think of WADHAM, WORCESTER, NEW, WOLFSON and WYCLIFFFE,' Freddie replied.

Ben winced. 'Five?'

'Yes. Of course it might not be a college. If it's hotels or ice-cream carts again, I've got no idea.'

'I think it will be a college,' Jess said. 'But what if it is tomorrow? It could contain other letters too, couldn't it? Not just the ones in Ben's cipher? We wouldn't know about them, would we?'

'Oh yes. But only after G and W. So I suppose it could be any of them,' Freddie replied. 'Or any other public venue.'

Ben could hardly believe it. 'So after all that, it can't tell us anything?'

'Yes it does,' Jess said. 'We've got it down to two. We've ruled Knox and Marcus out.'

'How?' Freddie snapped.

'Psychologically,' Jess replied.

Ben nodded. Her insight had impressed him immensely.

'That's why you haven't,' Freddie argued. 'Because Marcus knows Ben.'

Freddie's comment put Ben on the defensive. 'Huh?'

'He knows you won't have analysed it. You're impulsive. You rush into things. You don't analyse.'

Surprisingly fair. 'True,' Ben admitted.

'He's under such enormous pressure, keeping SPC happy and the Chief happy, or being the Chief as well, that he just used a code he'd created. For convenience.'

Ben looked at Jess, expecting her to argue. But she wasn't. She was looking thoughtful, biting her lip.

'It could have been a code the Chief had created,' Ben argued, 'that he used.'

'No. Proves my point. You don't analyse,' Freddie said. 'If the Chief is Ballantyne or Rufus, he sent you this code assuming you'd be too stupid to work it out.'

Aghast, Ben's jaw dropped.

'You are. You didn't. I did.'

'Freddie, you're being unkind,' Jess said.

'No I'm not. He is. The Chief is an egomaniac, whoever he is. So he would naturally think Ben more stupid than him. He would think everyone is more stupid than him.'

Jess sighed. 'He's right, Ben. Sorry. But he is. It could be Marcus still. Unlikely, but as far as the police are concerned, we might be able to convince them it's Rufus or Ballantyne or Marcus, but we can't get any further than that.'

'We've got to tell the police.'

'We can't, Ben. We'd have to give them your phone. Then if any more clues came in, we wouldn't see them. Marcus is too busy to even crack Playfair ciphers, so he needs us to help him,' Jess said.

'Or to stop us investigating him,' Freddie said. 'And if you give them your phone, that won't help your mum.'

'Why?'

'If Marcus is on our side, he's helping her. If he's not, we need to prove it. Because now the police think it's your mum, they're not searching for anyone else. And all of these texts might rule out Knox and Hanbury, but they don't rule out your mum.'

'Why?'

'Who knows your psychology better than her?' Freddie said.

Ben's jaw dropped, but not from offense this time, but because Freddie was right.

If he went to the police right now, it could get his mother into even worse trouble than she was in.

So what could he do to help her?

As if in answer, his phone pinged.

He checked his messages. A new message from Marcus.

Marcus, their ally. Or Marcus, their enemy. But which?

'It could be another clue, Ben,' Jess said, as if trying to summon up enthusiasm even she could hardly muster at this point.

'Let's face it, whoever that sicko is, whether it's Ballantyne or Marcus or Rufus, they've beaten us. And Mum. And the police. They've won. The Chief has won.'

'That's why they call him the Chief,' Freddie said.

Chapter 19

The Quantum Code

Marcus's text read:

4 68 74 72 52 57 70 10 76 68 66 95

There was a jumble of letters afterwards. Feeling like cursing and kicking something, Ben instead clenched his fists and marched around whilst Jess deciphered it.

'Are you okay?' she asked.

'No.' He was finished with codes. They told them nothing, nada, diddly squat, he thought as he stomped, pumping his fists up and down to dispel some of the inner rage.

'Ben, if you're angry, punch something,' Jess said. 'A teddy or something like that. It helps to relieve anxiety.'

'The only thing that will relieve my anxiety is getting Mum out of prison and the Chief and Nixon and Goatee Man in it. Forever!'

'Me too,' Jess said, so sweetly that he again felt ashamed.

He wasn't the only one suffering. Jess was going through it too. They all were. Even Freddie looked empty, sagging in the armchair, staring into space. He wasn't even bothering with *The Code Book* any more.

'Ben, look!' Jess said, sounding shocked.

He went to the desk.

HELP PLEASE M x

So either it was just the same – Marcus was too hassled to crack the gang's codes, or he was still fooling them.

'Sorry, Jess. And Freddie.'

Freddie shrugged. But Jess said, 'What for?'

'For getting angry.'

'Don't worry. You've every right to be angry. It's just that,' she hesitated, 'it doesn't get us anywhere.'

'Nothing gets us anywhere!'

'We are getting somewhere. We've narrowed it down to Rufus or Ballantyne or Marcus.'

'I hope it isn't, Jess. I hope it isn't one of my dads.'

'You can't have two dads, cretin,' Freddie said.

'Yes you can. Loads of my mates have two dads. There's your real dad and your step dad, there's your…'

'They're not genetic. You meant genetic. Or do you want Rufus to adopt you if Marcus is your dad?'

Ben was shocked. 'No way!'

Freddie smiled nastily. 'Or Marcus to adopt you if Rufus is?'

For a second, Ben wondered if Marcus would be willing to do that. But then he realised he was being stupid.

'I don't need adopting. I've got a mum, a great mum, a wonderful mum. But the police won't let me have her!'

'Ben, try and relax. I think we'll need to work together on this,' Jess said, her tone so kind that Ben attempted to take her advice. He rotated his shoulders and took a few slow breaths before returning to the desk and concentrate on Marcus's message.

HELP PLEASE M x

IVD V IC D IIIA IC IIB IIIA IIB IA IIA IIA IC IC IB IIB

IIA IAIAIBICIBIBIA IIB V IAIAIBICIBIBIA IIIA IIIA IVD IC $\frac{1}{2}$ ID

'What's that? It's not another book cipher, is it?'

'I don't think so. It looks very different to anything I've seen.'

'Oh!' Freddie said, coming over to see, whilst Ben's spirits sank. 'I think it's another code. A proper code. And this time we've no idea of the system behind it.'

'Are they harder or easier?'

'Much harder, usually. It could contain nulls or voids or anything.'

'Oh great,' Ben said, in tone that meant exactly the opposite.

The attack was imminent, they had two impossible codes to crack, and they were no nearer to nailing the Chief.

'We're sunk. We're completely and utterly sunk.'

The Chief had won. They had lost. It was as simple and brutal as that.

If they were getting nowhere, and there really was no way for them to get Mum out of prison, he might as well succumb to the sleep he so badly needed. After a nap he might wake with a recharged brain.

He went and lay on the bed and shut his eyes. The bed was very comfortable. The pillow was delightfully soft.

But ages later, his cousins were still rabbiting on. He got up and went over to the desk, where they were both sitting.

'Give it up, guys, *please*. We all need some rest.'

'Ben, something's happened,' Jess said, so seriously that Ben was anxious.

'What do you mean?'

'They might know we're onto them. Before they used Playfair. I've looked it up and it was our secret cipher in World War I. It was still used in World War II for quick attacks and the like. But by then the Nazis knew about it and could crack it fairly quickly. Nowadays with computers it's easy to crack, apparently.'

'Is it?'

'But this code is unique, we think,' Freddie said. 'We can't find anything like it online.'

'At least you've looked,' Ben replied, impressed that his cousins had turned to technology. 'Thanks for trying, anyway. But we all need some shut-eye.'

'That doesn't mean we can't crack it. We've had lots of ideas. Two things stand out. The half and this string,' Freddie said, pointing to IAIAIBICIBIBIC. 'It repeats.'

'So do you think it's TH?'

'No. Why would we?' Freddie replied, most unfairly, Ben thought, since he had always banged on about TH in Playfair. But this wasn't Playfair.

'Do you think it's digraphs?' he asked, trying to speak Freddie's language.

'Could be. Could be trigraphs or digraphs or a combination of both. There are far too few characters to convey most messages.'

'Or far too many,' Jess replied, confusingly.

Ben shook his head, trying to clear it. 'What do you think the half means then?'

'Half past, half-time, half-brother, a sum,' Jess said. 'It could be lots of things. But none of them seem likely.'

'Okay. Let me think.' Again Ben was forced to retreat to the bathroom to shut his cousins out.

He splashed his face with water to try and wake himself up. He'd slept half the morning. Why should he be so tired now? He desperately needed to stay awake. If the Chief was planning field trials, and they hadn't happened yet, they were bound to happen soon.

And Mum being in prison for being the Chief was so very wrong. Her being suspected of those horrible crimes utterly revolted him, and it would appal her too. He had to get her out, now.

What had the codes tonight taught him? The Chief was arrogant, the Chief was weird and also very clever. He liked quantum physics and knew about the Uncertainty Principle.

Wasn't quantum physics the hardest science? He had heard Freddie and Uncle Henry discussing it, but it had mainly floated over his head. The only thing he had managed to grasp was that when you fired a single particle of light, a photon, at a board in-between two slits, interference fringes build up, as if the particles had been waves.

So light was both a wave and a particle, and so were electrons, and so were protons, apparently. It was nuts, as far as Ben could grasp. To understand it, you had to think of smeared wave functions, believe in multiple worlds or be stark, staring mad, Mum had said.

Though he joked about Uncle Henry and Freddie being so, the Chief genuinely was mad. And evil and ruthless and vain. So maybe this was about quantum mechanics again?

Reluctantly, because he knew it was incredibly difficult, he left the lovely, calm, relaxing bathroom and returned to his bedroom where Jess and Freddie were still jabbering on.

'Could this be a quantum code? Is there a quantum code?'

'No, I didn't think so. Is there?' Jess looked at Freddie, who had his hands curled around his nose, his slim fingertips touching. 'Well?'

He took his hands away. 'I can't believe I didn't think of that.'

'You mean there is?' Ben asked, stunned.

'No. Not exactly. But there's the Standard Model. It'll take me far too long to explain it to you. Can you just google it?' He got up from the chair, vacating his place at the desk.

Ben gratefully accepted. If he'd actually (unbelievably) managed to outwit the Chief, he was going to make sure it counted. He input Standard Model into the search engine and went to a populist site, not a scientific one. There was some blurb saying it referred to elementary particles and quarks but when he got to baryon asymmetry he was out of his depth. He stopped reading and went instead to the colourful diagram.

'What does this mean?' he asked, pointing to an unfamiliar symbol representing a photon, apparently. Jess looked at the diagram with him.

'It's gamma. Ancient Greek for g,' she replied.

'Why don't they just use g?'

'G's for gluon, look,' Jess said, pointing to the top row.

'Oh.'

'But look at the numbers, Ben!' she cried. 'I think you've got it!'

Sure enough, the first three columns, which apparently contained fermions (with very weird names) were numbered simply I, II and III.

'They're Roman numerals, like in the code. If the rows were labelled A to D, it might work,' Jess said.

Ben viewed the code again, and agreed that it might.

IVD V IC D IIIA IC IIB IIIA IIB IA IIA IIA IC IC IB IIB

IIA IAIAIBICIBIBIA IIB V IAIAIBICIBIBIA IIIA IIIA IVD IC $\frac{1}{2}$ ID

He started sketching it out, reflecting that maybe it wasn't as frightening as he'd feared. Freddie came over to see. 'Don't bother with the masses, they're all approximate. The only thing you need to know is the charge and the spin.'

'Do I have to know that?'

'Oh yes. That's the whole point. No two fermions in the same system can occupy the same quantum state. That's Pauli's exclusion principle, one of the foundations of quantum mechanics. And, therefore, life,' Freddie rhapsodised, waving his arms about as he (and his dad) did when excited about physics.

'Really?'

'Oh yes. You're made up of quantum particles, just as much as this desk is.'

'So I'm a plank of wood?'

'Don't be stupid. Everything is. If one has spin up, the other has to have spin down. Hence electron pairs,' he finished, as if that explained everything.

Ben continued drawing the table. Although the online version didn't have columns IV and V, Ben labelled all the columns, because the code contained IV and V, and also labelled the rows A to D.

He recalled Mum being really excited about the discovery of the Higgs boson years ago. To keep Freddie quiet (which was greatly to be desired when it came to quantum mechanics) Ben also copied in the charge and the spin.

'Notice they all have spin of a half, apart from the bosons,' explained Freddie.

'Right. And they all have charges of two thirds, or minus a third…' Realising there were lots of different charges, Ben tailed off.

'Or one or zero, yes. But then they combine to make the particles we know. For example, a proton is two up quarks and a down quark. The charge adds up to one,' Freddie said.

'Right,' Ben said, hardly listening as he finished the table.

	I	II	III	IV	V
A	**u** $2/3$ $1/2$ up	**c** $2/3$ $1/2$ charm	**t** $2/3$ $1/2$ top	**g** 0 1 gluon	**H** 0 0 Higgs
B	**d** $-1/3$ $1/2$ down	**s** $-1/3$ $1/2$ strange	**b** $-1/3$ $1/2$ bottom	**γ** 0 1 photon	
C	**e** -1 $1/2$ electron	**μ** -1 $1/2$ muon	**τ** -1 $1/2$ tau	**Z** 0 1 Z boson	
D	**V$_e$** 0 $1/2$ electron neutrino	**Vμ** 0 $1/2$ muon neutrino	**Vτ** 0 $1/2$ tau neutrino	**W** $+/-$ I 1 W boson	

He checked it against the model on the computer, then noticed the time. He checked his watch, and it agreed. It was 2:55. It couldn't be!

'Is my watch wrong or did I fall asleep?'

'You did. You were snoring.'

'Have you been to sleep?'

Jess yawned. 'No.'

Freddie seemed to stifle a yawn whilst shaking his head. Ben felt guilty. 'Sorry.'

'You couldn't help it. Anyway, it did you good. It refreshed you and enabled you to think,' Jess said.

'I think I need some sleep,' Freddie said. 'I can't think.'

Ben looked at the code.

IVD V IC Df IIIA IC IIB IIIA IIIB IA IIA IIA IC IC IB IIB
IIA IAIAIBICIBIBIC IIB V IAIAIBICIBIBIC IIIA IIIA IVD IC ¹/₂ ID

'I guess IVD would be W, then?' Ben guessed.

'I think you should write it in, Ben. You thought of it,' Jess said.

'Okay,' he agreed, flattered.

'Could I check on something on the computer?' asked Freddie.

'Sure. What?'

'I'm so shattered, I can't remember what a neutron's made of.'

'Okay. Sure.' Ben got up.

'You can have my seat, Ben. I'm going to the bathroom,' Jess said.

So Ben sat down again and carefully started filling in letters, whilst Freddie searched up something online next to him.

IVD	V	IC
W	H	E

He stopped, frowning. There was nothing in the D row that began with F. But surely that word was WHEN?

'Freddie why would Df stand for N?'

Freddie diverted his gaze from the screen to glance at the table. 'Oh, because it's the fermions in row D. The fermions are the first three columns, remember. The D fermions are all neutrinos, which begins with N.'

And patronising begins with P, Ben thought. But he merely said, 'Thanks. Good spot.'

IVD	V	IC	Df	IIIA	IC	IIB	IIIA
W	H	E	N	T	E	S	T
IIB	IA	IIA	IIA	IC	IC	IB	IIB
S	U	C	C	E	E	D	S

He stopped. 'See this? Do you think they mean the 993 test?'

'Almost certainly,' Freddie replied.

The certainty (when, not if) was very, very worrying. Jess came back in. He showed her.

'Oh my goodness. Is that a field trial?' she asked.

'Murder more like,' Ben replied. 'But yeah, I think so.'

'It works then. You cracked it.'

Ben shrugged. 'I just thought of the Chief. And how he likes quantum physics.'

'Rufus likes physics,' Jess said.

'That long string is a proton, a neutron and an electron. So it's an atom,' Freddie said.

'Are you sure?' Jess asked.

'A proton is two up and one down quarks. A neutron is two down and one up. So that's an atom. It probably stands for A.'

'You genius!' Ben cried.

'Not really. Even you know that, don't you?' Freddie sneered.

Though he longed to retaliate, Ben clamped his lips shut. He would have never have worked A out without Freddie. And he had slept, but Freddie was tired and probably grumpy.

IIA	IAIAIBICIBIBIA	IIB	V	IAIAIBICIBIBIA
C	A	S	H	A

IIIA	IIIA	IVD	IC	$1/2$	ID
T	T	W	E		

He halted again. 'What could half mean?'

'It could mean half spin,' Freddie replied. 'Which of the particles have half spin?'

'I dunno!'

'Look at the table. I told you.'

Whilst Ben rolled his eyes, Jess looked at the table.

'All of them. Apart from the bosons,' she said.

'There are six flavours of leptons,' Freddie began.

'*Flavours*?' Ben cut in.

'Yes, flavours, that's what they call them. Electrons, muons, taus and their corresponding neutrinos. Row C and D, columns I, II and III.'

'Oh, right,' Ben said.

'So that probably stands for L,' Freddie said. 'Or Q. Because quarks – up, down, charm, strange, top and bottom – and leptons have half particle spins, whereas bosons have 1, or in the case of Higgs, 0.'

'Well it won't be Q for quark.'

'It's not. It's L. And the electron neutrino's symbol is a V followed by a small e. So ID stands for VE. The last word's twelve,' Freddie said.

Ben filled in the last two characters. It all fitted. To his amazement, his one idea, with a lot of help from Freddie, had worked.

IVD	V	IC	Df	IIIA	IC	IIB	IIIA
W	H	E	N	T	E	S	T
IIB	IA	IIA	IIA	IC	IC	IB	IIB
S	U	C	C	E	E	D	S
IIA	IAIAIBICIBIBIA			IIB	V	IAIAIBICIBIBIA	
C	A			S	H	A	
IIIA	IIIA	IVD	IC	1/2	ID		
T	T	W	E	L	VE		

But the message was very scary indeed: WHEN TEST SUCCEEDS, CASH AT TWELVE.

'They're saying they're going to poison someone somewhere, and if that works, then the four horsemen will pay them at noon,' Jess said. 'Or midnight.'

'Today?'

'Maybe,' Jess said, looking panicky.

Ben checked his watch. It was 3:20. Under nine hours to stop them using 993. *No*! He would *not* let that happen.

'We've got to stop the Chief.'

'This helps, Ben. It really does. It rules out Marcus,' Jess said. But Freddie said nothing. Did he agree?

'How?' Ben demanded.

'He wouldn't be telling us this if he was the Chief,' Jess said.

'Maybe he wouldn't think we'd crack it.' Freddie said.

'He wouldn't risk it, with you and your passion for science,' Jess said.

'You could be right,' Freddie agreed, looking smug.

'The book cipher might tell us more. Where the attack will be. That's what the police needs to know.' Jess yawned.

'You're tired, Jess. I'll try and crack it,' Ben offered. But not for long. If he didn't get anywhere with it, he was going to the police.

She went across to the bookcase. 'I am not going to sleep until we've freed Aunt Sue.'

'I did, Jess. You need sleep.'

'Oh my goodness, look!' Ben swung round. Jess was brandishing a book: *Quantum – A Guide for the Perplexed* by Jim Al-Khalili. 'Inside it reads: *To Marcus, Happy Christmas, from Rufus.* Rufus bought this for Marcus. Rufus knows about quantum theory. It's Rufus!' Jess said, in case he didn't get it.

But he did. It was a horrible present, but a fantastic clue.

'You don't need to know about quantum physics. Any idiot could do what Ben did with a computer,' Freddie said.

'Thanks,' Ben said sarcastically. 'But is this enough? Can we go to the police?'

'You'll lose your phone, Ben,' Jess warned. 'And they'll take you in for questioning.'

'Take me in? Why?'

'You've been concealing evidence from the police for a week and half. Why not? They'll have loads to discuss with you,' Freddie said. 'They'll be furious about the codes and ciphers you've hidden from them.'

'I'm not scared of them,' Ben retorted. But he was. They were all-powerful, extremely formidable opponents. Seeing Mum being arrested was the most shocking, terrifying, humiliating moment of his – and doubtless her – life.

'We've got to stop them somehow. It's today, the attack. This morning.'

'We can't go to them until we've cracked the book cipher,' Jess insisted.

'I need some sleep,' Freddie said. 'But I'll have a stab at cracking that cipher first.' He still had *The Code Book*, but he also grabbed *Quantum* off Jess, because he thought it looked the best bet, probably. Ben agreed that it, or *The Code Book*, was the best bet, and felt sorry Jess didn't have one of them at least. Freddie always got credit for being the smartest child, but Jess was clever too. She just didn't boast about it so often, meaning it didn't get noticed as much. She'd be in every top set at Ben's school.

Freddie made a quick copy of the book cipher and left. But Jess was still searching the bookcase, fruitlessly, Ben was sure.

'Most are popular science books,' she said, adding *The Ancestor's Tale* to the pile.

Popular? Science?

'You've got plenty there, Jess. We haven't got long.'

'Okay.' But she took *A Brief History of Time* as well.

Ben carried most of the books to her bedroom and deposited them on her bedside table. Jess followed him in with the remaining two.

'Thanks, Ben. I know it's unlikely, but it might just work.'

'It might. I hope so. 'Night, Jess.'

'Goodnight and happy birthday,' Jess said, hugging him. 'She'll be back for your birthday. I'm sure she will.'

'You might believe in fairies. But I don't. Sorry, Jess. But unless we can crack this, we can't get any closer, can we?'

'Your mum will win out Ben. She's strong, she's clever and she's lovely. The police will have to realise that soon.'

'They haven't yet, have they?'

'They will, Ben. They will.'

'I'm sorry, Jess. I wish I could believe that, but I can't. And from your face, I don't think you can either.'

Jess blinked at him, momentarily looking just as downcast as he was. But somehow, she rallied.

'Then we've got to crack the book cipher. We have to. We can't let her go to prison for something she didn't do. She'll be vilified in the media, too, Ben. Everyone will hate her. We can't let that happen.'

'Okay. You're right. I'll try and crack it.'

'And so will Freddie, and so will I.'

Ben nodded. He didn't rate his chances, but with his brilliant cousins, any intellectual feat was possible. Unlikely. But definitely possible.

Chapter 20

The Baffling Book Cipher

He looked at the cipher, trying to stay positive.

15 53 41 44 68 57 58 5 22 51 9 76 37 66 75 33 13 11 17 37

The highest number was 78, he noticed – and the other numbers in the seventies made him wonder if it was just a short piece of text.

But what? A song? A poem? He couldn't imagine the Chief using music. Jess and Freddie would know far more poems than he did.

Internet pages also had very few words on them. The internet made more sense the more he considered it. Websites could be accessed anytime you liked, from anywhere, with a smartphone. (One day, perhaps, Mum would entrust him with one). It would be better than carrying books around. Though Marcus and Jess were smart enough to retain vast passages of Shakespeare in their heads, Ben doubted Nixon was.

So many websites. Where to start? St Saviour's seemed the obvious choice. He logged on to it, a surprisingly modern website for such an old place. The impressive green lawn and golden stone of Front Quad was the homepage's static background, but an inset box had various scenes of the college scrolling past. It was annoying, but Ben discovered that by clicking on it, he could freeze it, so he halted it on an image of the dining hall.

He clicked through the site, noticing the pictures of the Warden and his wife, Sir Christopher and Lady Cressida Cockerell, seeing Dr Ashcroft and Julia – and chillingly, the

Old Library, the meeting room in which Mum and he had almost been murdered.

Thinking of Mum made him desperate to get to her. She must be so unhappy, and outraged, and despairing. Despite what his cousins had said about the police, if they couldn't crack this cipher, he would go and tell them everything he knew. How could he make things worse for Mum? They couldn't get any worse than they were right now. And if he showed them everything, all the texts sent whilst Mum was in police custody, which she couldn't possibly have sent, surely that must convince them to free her? Plus it would give them as much warning as possible about the imminent 993 attack.

He got up, padded to the door and looked outside. Though the house was silent, light was streaming under both his cousins' doors.

He felt as restless as a flea-ridden cat but there was still time. It wasn't yet light. Everyone would be asleep, he thought with a yawn, including the police – and even the Chief, hopefully. Everyone except Mum.

He briefly considered leaving immediately. But his cousins would stop him leaving. Or delay him at least. Better to wait until they'd fallen asleep, he decided. They were doubtless working on the cipher. He should be. He printed the homepage out, glad the printer was so quiet.

Welcome! At St Saviour's College we celebrate academic excellence and foster creativity within a progressive and diverse community.

Modern in its outlook, St Saviour's was founded in 1514 by Sir Richard Pole KG and his wife, Lady Margaret, Countess of Salisbury, who continued the building after he died. It has been an acknowledged leader in a range of arts and science subjects ever since.

The college now comprises up to 120 graduate students and 380 undergraduates and offers some of the best accommodation available in Oxford within a welcoming and supportive community.

What were you were supposed to do with numbers and dates? Freddie would know, but Ben had no idea. Maybe 1514 would stand for number 1, or the word ONE or FIFTEEN. He checked online, but couldn't find the answer fast enough. Right, he'd use all three options, if necessary.

He numbered the text, reaching 92 words. Whilst he was doing so, his phone bleeped. He checked it and again it was from an unknown number. He opened it, sighing. But it was exactly the same cipher. He was puzzled initially, but then reasoned that it was probably a reminder from Marcus. He started allocating letters to the numbers.

15	53	41	44
P	A	S	T

Ben was delighted. Could it be he'd cracked it? He continued.

15	53	41	44	68	57	58	5
P	A	S	T	C	R	O	C

Crocus Corner, Ben thought, like the flower bed back home. Was there a Crocus Corner in Oxford? He checked online. Not according to the internet, there wasn't, though Crocus Corner in Heaton Moor was mentioned, which surprised and pleased him. But in Oxford, there were so many important colleges and museums and buildings to boast about, perhaps a flowerbed didn't warrant a mention online.

His cousins' knowledge of Oxford was so comprehensive that they might know of it. If it was right, he would go and ask Jess where it was before she fell asleep. But he needed to prove he'd cracked the code first.

15	53	41	44	68	57	58	5	22	51	9
P	A	S	T	C	R	O	C	O	B	E

Past Croco be careful? Perhaps there was an Oxford shop called Croco? No, he discovered – unless it wasn't listed online, which was about as likely as County winning the Premiership.

But maybe Croco was Oxford-speak for something? A college nickname, or a landmark. Because past Croco the Chief was telling Nixon to be… what?

He continued with his decryption, convinced he was about to uncover a vital clue.

68	57	58	5	22	51	9	76	37	66	75
C	R	O	C	O	B	E	U	L	C	T

He stopped, dismayed. He'd thought at first that they were abbreviations, but as the cipher continued, he realised he simply hadn't cracked it.

But he'd been tantalisingly close. Perhaps he'd just made a simple error, like he so often did in exams? He counted the words again, carefully. He checked the text again. But even if he should have ignored the dates entirely, the message still didn't make sense.

His spirits plummeted. It could be based on a passage from this site, or any other website, a book, a song, a poem or a play. It was pointless even trying to crack the stupid cipher.

It was impossible, a pointless waste of time.

Itching to get out, he went to check at the door. His cousins' bedroom doors were shut and the landing was dark. They had switched off their lights. At last!

He returned to his room and gathered together as many useful papers as he could. Hopefully he'd remember the rest. He folded them up and tucked them into his front pocket. Just as he was about to leave he noticed Daphne's keys sitting on his bedside table, and pocketed them. He left the bedroom, clicking the light off and padded past his cousins' rooms, hardly daring to breathe. Freddie's bed creaked. Ben froze.

But after a few seconds' waiting, and no more noise, he resumed his journey. He went downstairs, glad of the thick carpet muffling his footsteps, and the moonlight filtering through the window, enabling him to see.

He reached the first-floor landing. There was no window at this end, so it was darker, but he daren't switch the light on and alert Daphne. He descended to the ground floor with cat-like caution, clutching the hand-rail as a guide until his night vision enabled him to make out the next few stairs.

He tiptoed down the hall to the front door and removed the chain. As he unlocked it, he heard a thud upstairs. A door closing? A book dropping? He didn't wait to find out but hurried out into the cool night air. Shutting the door as softly as possible, he went down the steps, then ran, down the path, onto the road and around the bend.

There was no one chasing him and no one about. The roads and pavements were deserted. So, having started off far too fast, he slowed to a more sensible pace as he passed Keble College. He rubbed his arms, wishing he'd thought to put on a hoody. Though the days were warm, these early spring nights still had the bite of winter.

A car drove past, a small Fiat. The roads were so devoid of traffic that any engine noise was as noticeable as a siren. He passed the science park, crossed South Parks Road and ran past St Saviour's, considering the best route.

Though there was a glimmer of dawn in the sky, Catte Street opposite looked creepily dark. He took the safer route, Broad Street. He would simply have to turn left at the bottom to reach the police station.

Footsteps pounded towards him from a side road on the left. Rufus emerged. And stopped, right in front of Ben, so Ben had no option but to stop too.

'What are you doing out at this time?'

'I'm just having a run,' Ben said.

His slowly spreading smile was deeply unsettling.

'Were you now?'

Fear snaked into his guts. Ben gulped.

Chapter 21

Jess Gets Cracking

Jess too had noticed the low word count, so discounting whole pages, had gone through the books methodically, first testing the covers, then the acknowledgements, if long enough, followed by the first and last pages of each chapter. But after a few hopeful starts, every decryption had degraded into gibberish.

As the sky started to brighten, and the attack loomed, her mood was downcast and very, very tired indeed. It was unthinkable that another scene of carnage like the pool was going to happen today. She was scared Ben might not be able to stop himself trying to save people again, and with 993, he would die. They would all die.

It was a terrifying prospect. She simply had to stop it. So somehow she had to crack the code.

Ben and Freddie had presumably also failed to do so, or else they would have told her. As she got out of bed she wondered if Ben would still be awake. Though she was scared, he must be going through agony, with the fear for his Mum, and the awful uncertainty about his dad. She went to see him.

His door was shut. She knocked, softly. No reply. She hesitated. Maybe he had nodded off? But she either had to go back and test every page of every book – and checking her watch, she decided there wasn't time – or to get more books from Ben's room, where lots of Rufus and Marcus's old books were stored. (The detective books in her room were Daphne's).

She opened the door softly, but the light from her bedroom didn't filter this far, and since the landing and his bedroom lights were off, she was forced to wait for her eyes to adjust to the gloom. As outlines began emerging, she tiptoed forwards, towards the bookcase, but stopped, noticing the empty bed. Where was he?

Worried, she hurried out to check the bathroom, but as she had thought, it was empty too. Even more anxious now, Jess knocked on Freddie's door.

He didn't answer either. She opened it and went in. He was lying on top of the bed, asleep, with *The Code Book* and *Quantum* beside him. Jess shook him awake. He didn't like it, squawking in protest.

'Freddie, be quiet. Ben is missing. Have you seen him?'

'No. Where is he?'

'I don't know where he is! That's the point.'

'All right, keep your wig on.'

'I'm worried about him.'

'He could just be getting a drink,' Freddie suggested, but Jess doubted that.

Still, she hurried downstairs getting more panicky, as with every step, she heard nothing and saw nothing to indicate Ben was present. She had been very absorbed in the book cipher, but surely she'd have heard him leave?

There were no lights evident on the ground floor, but she opened every door to check. The kitchen was empty. The dining room was empty. Daphne's study was empty. The sitting room was empty. The cloakroom was empty.

What if he'd cracked the cipher and gone to stop the attack?

She ran upstairs to tell Freddie, tormented by horrible visions of Ben in the poisoned pool, begging him to get out, screaming at him to get out, and watching him get feebler and feebler as the poison took hold. She had been terrified that he would die, and was gripped by the same panic now.

She burst into Freddie's room. 'Should we call the police?'

'Try ringing him first.'

'He won't answer,' Jess said, but she went to her room to get her phone and tried his number.

'Hi, Jess.'

Jess was so astonished to hear him that she nearly dropped the phone. 'Where are you?'

'In Oxford. It's okay. I'm with Rufus.'

'*Rufus*? Why?'

'Having breakfast. How have you got on?' Ben asked.

'With the book cipher?' she whispered, in case Rufus was by his side.

'Yeah.'

'No luck yet.'

'It's your favourite book, isn't it?' Ben replied.

'Sorry?'

'What's yours, Rufus?'

Jess clapped her hand to her mouth. Ben was trying to crack the book cipher by going straight to the man who'd written it. He agreed with her that Rufus was the Chief.

Alone with the Chief in a still sleeping city, he was in terrible danger.

'Come home!'

'I'm fine. Haven't you read *The Selfish Gene* as well? Rufus says it's his favourite book.'

Jess heard Rufus say something she couldn't catch. Did he realise Ben suspected him? She bit her lip.

'Jess, have you?'

She realised he was meaning *The Selfish Gene*. It was one of the books she'd checked, but only the starts and ends of chapters.

'I've tried some of it, but not every single page,' she whispered.

'What's your favourite number, Rufus?'

Jess shook her head, despairing. Ben's suspicions must stand out as clearly as a hippo hiding behind a tree. So Rufus would know both that Ben suspected him and that Marcus had betrayed him. She heard his voice again, but not clearly enough to tell what he said.

'Come back, Ben. He knows.'

'No, not everything. It's just that we all have favourite colours and numbers and sports and things,' Ben said.

'What?' Suddenly realising he had been addressing Rufus, she tried again. 'Come back. He *knows*.'

'Kid's fine. People always think I'm older than I am because I'm tall,' Ben told Rufus, ignoring her.

Rufus said something else.

'He likes purple like you, Jess. Blue,' Ben added, telling Rufus his favourite colour, Jess realised. 'Me? 100's nice. Just is. Oh, 16, really? Why? No, mine's the 11th.' Ben was now talking about birthdays, presumably.

But he might have learned something very useful indeed, Jess realised.

'Is 16 his favourite number?' she asked.

'Yeah.'

'Well done. Mission accomplished. Come back right now.'

'I will soon. I'll just have breakfast.'

'No, Ben, *don't*!'

'Gotta go, Jess. See you later.'

'But, *Ben*!'

He rang off, so she rang back, but infuriatingly, he didn't answer. Jess took a few deep breaths, trying to calm down, but it didn't work. She loved her cousin almost as much as her brothers, and possibly even more so (he was certainly nicer), but he sometimes drove her absolutely crazy.

If he thought Rufus was the Chief, why on *earth* would he go to him? Why hadn't he said? What should she do? Jess felt in need of an adult to advise her. Her parents would certainly be asleep, and she didn't even know where they were. It was so unlike them not to have said, she realised, finding Mum in contacts. But before pressing Call, she hesitated. There would be far too much to explain. It would take too long.

Marcus would be a better choice. She found his number, but decided she couldn't phone him, in case he was spying on someone. Better to text him. Her thumb flew over the keys, remembering to group the code into fours, to keep it extra safe: BEN IS WITH RUFUS. She paused. What next? Danger? Rescue him? We know he's the Chief? No, Marcus hadn't believed that. He probably still wouldn't believe it.

So she added: HELP PLEASE, JESS

```
7   68  30   1       19  11   6   4       39  56  89  56
3   4   68   57      52  52   57 70       10  3   68  95
68  3   17
```

Because she had a three-letter group at the end, she added 95, which could stand for J, x or any letter not included in the cipher. She pressed Send, hoping Marcus was awake and free to help.

She went to Freddie's room again. He was checking the cipher against *Quantum*.

'Ben is with Rufus.'

He wrinkled his brow. 'How come?'

'Ben thinks he's the Chief.'

'He wouldn't go to see him then, would he?'

Jess resisted the temptation to roll her eyes. Freddie couldn't help it, he just didn't understand people very well. 'Yes, that's exactly what Ben would do.'

'What an idiot!'

'He's *brave*, not an idiot. And clever. He asked Rufus about his favourite book,' Jess added, to prove her point. 'It's *The Selfish Gene*. And his favourite number is 16.'

Freddie's face was full of scorn. 'If he's not the Chief, that's a waste of time.'

'But he *is*, so it's a clue.'

'He could be,' Freddie admitted. 'But I still think it's Marcus.'

'Let's not start that again. There's no time, Freddie. They're planning an attack. We've got to find it.'

'Okay. So what now?'

'I'll try page 16 of *The Selfish Gene*. And all the other books.'

'Pointless! If he is the Chief, he's not going to give us the page and the book just like that, is he? It's probably a lie.'

'Ben did well to get the clue,' Jess protested, whilst fearing Freddie was right. A wave of fatigue washed over her. She was so worried about Ben that she felt sick.

Freddie was muttering to himself, as he did when he had an idea. He sprang up.

'It needn't be a book! More likely it's a speech, a poem, a website, anything.'

'Website? Good idea. Let's get the computer on,' she said, trying to sound as if she believed him. But a book cipher would be from a book, she believed, or a play perhaps, or a poem maybe, but definitely not a website.

They went to Ben's room and she clicked the light on. Whilst Freddie sat down at the computer, Jess went to retrieve *The Selfish Gene* from her bedroom.

She started on page 16, checking the lower numbers first, and soon realised that it didn't work. Her spirits sank.

'It's not page 16,' she told Freddie. He was on the St Saviour's website. 'And it won't be that website.'

'Why?'

'It's where they met to murder Ben and Aunt Sue. It's too obvious.'

Freddie's eyes flashed fire. 'That's not how they'll see it, is it? Use your logic!'

'Okay then.' Jess folded her arms. 'It won't be a website. It'll be a book.'

'It could be a website. They have short pages. That would explain the numbers.'

'It could just be coincidence.'

'With the Chief nothing is coincidence. He's a control freak,' Freddie said.

'Is he really?' So far the break-in at Ben's, the scuppered assassination attempt, the ice-cream attack and the pool poisoning seemed like random uncoordinated events to Jess, and thankfully most of them had been unsuccessful. Maybe the Chief wasn't the master planner everyone assumed.

Pages were churning out of the printer.

'Can you help me?' Freddie asked.

Ignoring him, Jess checked her phone. Marcus hadn't replied.

'Should I phone Mum?'

'What for?' Freddie asked, picking up the printed sheets.

'To go and get Ben.'

'Where from? We don't even know where Rufus lives.'

'Daphne does. Marcus does.'

'But if he is the Chief, he knows you know Ben is with him. So your call made him safe.'

'I hope so,' Jess said, somewhat reassured.

'Help me on this. He'll call you if he needs help.'

Jess doubted it, but Freddie handed half of the printouts to her. She looked at them.

'What should we do with numbers and dates?'

'Treat them as a written word, I think.'

They quickly ruled every single page out.

'I'll try another site.'

'There are even more websites than books, I should think. Unless…' Jess trailed off, thinking. There was one website that was far more significant to Rufus than any other. 'The OPO website! Try that.'

Huffing, Freddie did as she asked.

Jess looked over his shoulder. 'That looks about the right length.'

'That looks about the right length,' he repeated, in a stupid voice, but Jess refused to be riled.

Her mobile rang. She answered it. 'Ben?'

'It's Marcus. He's not answering his mobile. Neither of them is. Did they say where they were?'

Jess tried to recall Ben's exact words.

'I assumed they were at Rufus's house. They're having breakfast.'

'I'll check it. Unless he's taken Ben into his office.'

'So early?'

'He does start work early. I'll check there too.'

'Thanks, Marcus.' Jess rang off. Marcus would make everything better, she told herself, to try and calm her jitters. She started numbering the sheet.

1	2	3	4	5	6
Over	Population	Oxford	abhors	the	damage
7	8	9	10	11	12
caused	to	earth's	fragile	ecosystem	by
13	14	15	16	17	18
humans.	Worryingly	we	have	registered	one
19	20	21	22	23	24
billion	more	births	every	thirteen	years
25	26	27	28	29	30
since	Over	Population	Oxford's	foundation	in
31	32	33	34	35	36
1974.	Global	warming,	intensive	farming	practices,
37	38	39	40	41	42
environmental	pollution,	habitat	loss,	the	sixth
43	44	45	46	47	48
mass	extinction	and	the	consumption	of
49	50	51	52	53	54
finite	natural	resources	such	as	arable
55	56	57	58	59	60
land,	fresh	water	and	fossil	fuels,
61	62	63	64	65	66
at	speeds	faster	than	their	rate
67	68	69	70	71	72
of	regeneration,	are	just	some	of
73	74	75	76	77	78
the	unintended,	yet	very	serious	consequences.

As she started comparing it to the cipher, her initial triumph was displaced by an icy fear.

15	53	41	44	68
W	A	T	E	R
57	58	5	22	51
W	A	T	E	R
9	76	37	66	75
E	V	E	R	Y
33	13	11	17	37
W	H	E	R	E

With one hand covering her mouth, she double-checked.

'What's up?' asked Freddie.

'Oh gosh! It's terrible.' Recalling the poem from school, Jess recited it.

'Water, water, everywhere,
And all the boards did shrink;
Water, water, everywhere,
Nor any drop to drink.'

'What the hell are you talking about?'

'It's water, water everywhere. 993 in water. Everyone will die!' There was no antidote, no taste, no colour. They wouldn't know.

'But *where*?'

'Maybe everywhere, I've no idea,' Jess said, barely suppressing tears. 'But we do know something. It's from OPO. Rufus's OPO. Rufus must be the Chief.'

'Could be,' Freddie said.

Jess's stomach lurched with anxiety. '*Ben*!'

Chapter 22

The Birthday Breakfast

Given his previous animosity, Ben had been astonished when Rufus suggested breakfasting together.

Suspecting it was a ploy to keep him away from the police, Ben replied, 'No thanks, I'll have breakfast with your mum later.'

'She won't be up for hours. You'll be hungry. I insist. Come and have breakfast with me.'

'I'll be fine.'

'It's too cold to stand here arguing. Come back to mine.' His expression had changed from affability to something darker – anger? Hatred?

Scared, Ben started running. But Rufus started running alongside him. He must know where Ben was heading. How? He hadn't told anyone, not Jess, not Freddie and not even Marcus. But the Chief had seemed to have superhuman mind-reading powers more than once. Ben tried to focus on his running, suspecting Rufus might be a mind reader too.

He turned down Cornmarket – and so did Rufus. Ben stared down at the pavement to hide the emotion that engulfed him. This creep running beside him was responsible for every single death in the swimming pool, the heartbreak their families and friends were now suffering, for Mum being in prison and for the agony she and all the families had endured whilst their children were fighting for their lives in hospital. He had to stop this monster.

They were approaching Carfax, the crossing at the end of Cornmarket.

'To Carfax and back, is it?' asked Rufus.

Ben stopped. Rufus pulled up too.

'What do you want?' Ben demanded.

'What, now? Or ultimately?' The glint in his eye was chilling.

But Ben persisted. 'Now. Why are you running with me?'

'It's my route too. And to keep an eye on you.'

Ben nodded. Most adults would be meaning to keep you safe, but Rufus meant that he wanted to stop Ben. The police station was across the road, but if Rufus stayed with him, he would stop Ben entering it. Or even worse, stay with him. And convince the police that he was innocent, and that Mum was guilty.

The only way to get rid of him seemed to be to play along, for now, and convince him that Ben didn't suspect him.

'Okay. I'd like breakfast at yours. Where is it?'

'Off the Cowley Road. It's cold. Let's keep running,' Rufus said.

That was fine by Ben. The sooner he could get breakfast over with, the sooner he could get to the police.

Under a brightening sky, they ran down High Street. Rufus was fast and fit – and clearly competitive, accelerating to an uncomfortable pace as they approached Catte Street. But Ben was determined to match him.

They got a brief rest at the roundabout, waiting for a supermarket lorry to pass. Then Rufus resumed his fluid run, heading left, down an unfamiliar road with some shops and a few impressive old buildings – but far fewer than in Oxford's centre. Again, Ben fought to keep up. His mouth was as dry as sun-baked soil.

Rufus turned right by what seemed to be a large park, Ben noted, as they pounded past it. A few houses later, Rufus stopped.

'This is it.'

Ben was glad to rest. Rufus's house was an average size, two-storey semi, with a small lawn in front and no drive, though the neighbour's lawn was paved over, with two cars parked on it.

Rufus unlocked the door, deactivated the alarm and switched on the hall light. He pulled off his trainers, so Ben copied him.

'Before I get showered, I always rehydrate,' Rufus said. 'Do you want some water too?'

'Yes please,' Ben replied automatically, then mentally kicked himself for being polite to the scumbag.

The kitchen was at the end of the hall. It was surprisingly old-fashioned with a wooden rack hanging from the ceiling. Noticing Ben eyeing it, Rufus explained that it was a drying rack.

'Can't abide tumble dryers – they waste so much energy – but we get too much rain to use a clothes line.' Rufus handed him a tumbler of tap water. Ben gulped it down. Rufus downed his quickly too. 'Help yourself to a refill. I'm going for a shower.'

He left the kitchen and went upstairs. As Ben refilled his glass he suddenly realised what a great opportunity he had. Alone in the Chief's secret lair!

There must be some evidence hidden somewhere. Ben started exploring. At the end of the kitchen was a dining area, with patio doors overlooking the park. To the right of that was a lounge, but in the grey light Ben could make out a sofa, an armchair, a bookcase and a TV, but no computer. Disappointing, but all he needed was a mobile. Just one. Any of the mobiles from which the Chief had sent him a code would be proof.

He checked all surfaces and the sofa and chair, behind the cushions, under the cushions and the floor. There was no mobile hidden there.

He returned to the kitchen and started opening cupboards and drawers, now frantically rummaging. He found food, crockery and cutlery, but still no phones. Opposite the sink, the wall-mounted unit had biscuit tins on top of it – useful hiding places. He climbed onto the work surface below and got one down. It was empty. He closed and replaced it. But as he reached along the surface, his fingers touched something small and phone-like. He lifted it down. It was smaller than most mobiles, but fatter. The inscription, Digital Voice Recorder, was hopeful. Ben slipped it into his rear pocket and, hearing footsteps descending the stairs, dismounted hurriedly.

Rufus entered the kitchen.

189

'What were you doing?' he demanded, now dressed in a blue checked short-sleeved shirt and navy trousers.

Did he know?

'Just looking around.' Ben shrugged, trying to act casual. But it was hard when feeling so excited. So much could be on a recording unit like that. All their plans. Maybe Nixon used it to record the meetings the Chief wasn't at. Ben's jaw dropped as he realised the recorder could contain a recording of his and Mum's near murder. That would surely convict every single one of the creeps – the investors, Nixon and Rufus.

But if Rufus saw or guessed what he had in his back pocket, he'd be in serious trouble. He leant back against the unit, hoping his hammering heart wasn't visible through his top.

Rufus clapped his hands, making Ben start.

'You're as jumpy as a jack in the box. What's up?'

'I'm worried about Mum.'

Rufus folded his arms, looking at Ben speculatively. Feeling a treacherous heat in his cheeks, Ben tried not to blush.

'You're a very protective son, aren't you?'

'There's just Mum and me,' Ben said, trying to pretend this was a normal adult he was talking to.

Rufus shrugged. 'Suppose you've had to be. Well, I'm starving. What do you fancy? Scrambled eggs?'

The answer to that was much easier. 'Can't stand eggs.'

'Marcus can't. Might be another genetic link between you two.'

'*Genetic?*' Ben was astonished that genes might affect your food likes and dislikes.

'Can you *stop* wrinkling your nose like I do? But yes, genes influence what you like to eat, and what you smell.'

Like asparagus in pee, Ben recalled Freddie saying. Rufus was perhaps telling the truth, in this at least.

His mobile rang, making him jump again. But it was just Jess, he saw on the screen.

'Hi, Jess.'

'Where are you?'

'In Oxford. It's okay. I'm with Rufus.'

'*Rufus*? Why?'

'Having breakfast. How have you got on?'

'With the book cipher?' she whispered.

Typical Jess. If there wasn't an obvious question, she'd invent one. 'Yeah.'

Rufus turned to him. 'Who is it?'

What business of it was his? But he wouldn't suspect Jess of anything but checking up on him.

'Jess,' he mouthed, hearing Jess tell him they hadn't cracked the cipher yet. Right. He was with the Chief. He'd ask him directly.

'It's your favourite book too, isn't it?' he said, into the mobile. He dropped it away from his mouth. 'What's yours, Rufus?'

'Come home!' cried Jess, far too loud. Clamping the phone back to his ear, he was pretty sure Rufus hadn't heard as he assured Jess that he was fine. Rufus continued breaking eggs into a mug, discarding the shells in the green recycling caddy, but was looking up, as if considering.

'It's *The Selfish Gene*, I suppose,' Rufus said. 'What's yours?'

Ben shrugged, whilst conveying the important lead to Jess. 'Haven't you read *The Selfish Gene*? Rufus said it's his favourite book too.'

'Has she read it already?' Rufus said, whisking the eggs with a fork. 'They're well weird, those Winterburn kids.'

'Jess, have you?'

'I've already tried it, but not every single page,' she whispered.

'What's your favourite number, Rufus?'

'Come back, Ben. He knows,' Jess said, whilst Rufus looked at Ben as if he was from another planet.

'Do you want to know everything about me?'

'No, not everything. It's just that we all have favourite colours and numbers and sports and things,' Ben replied, trying to reassure him.

'He *know*s,' Jess insisted.

'You're a weird kid too. Or should I call you a teen or something?'

'Kid is fine. People always think I'm older than I am because I'm tall.'

'Right. Well, I like purple best. What about you?'

'He likes purple like you, Jess. Blue,' Ben added, to Rufus.

'What's your favourite number?' Rufus asked.

'Me? 100's nice.'

'Why?' Rufus asked, using Jess's favourite question. But thankfully, she had quietened down. Ben needed all his brainpower to concentrate on fooling Rufus.

He shrugged, trying to appear relaxed. 'Just is.'

'I'd forgotten what it's like to be a kid. Mine's 16, I suppose, if I have to have one.'

'Oh, 16, really? Why?'

'It's my birthday. Your birthday can't be the 100th though, can it?'

'No, mine's the 11th.'

'Today?'

Ben nodded.

'Is 16 his favourite number?' Jess asked.

'Yeah.'

'Well done. Mission accomplished. Come back right now.'

'I will soon. I'll just have breakfast.'

'No, Ben, *don't*!'

'Got to go, Jess. See you later.'

'But, *Ben*!'

He rang off, and convinced that she would ring back, turned his mobile off.

'Maybe I'll get back to your mum's, thanks. I don't want to worry her.'

'She won't be awake yet, I've told you. She's a night owl. Stays up way too late for me, but she doesn't get up till eight, or even later some days. She's been retired too long,' he added, looking disgusted.

Ben looked at him, aghast. Did he mean *Daphne* should die too? His own *mum*?

'What's up?' Rufus challenged, as if reading his mind.

'Mum,' Ben said, for want of anything better.

'I suppose it's not every day your mum is arrested for mass murder.'

'She didn't do it!'

'All right, back in your box. I know you believe she's innocent. Of course you do. We all do.'

You know it, Ben thought, getting angry now.

Rufus raised his hands defensively. 'Don't look at me like that. I was only kidding. What about muesli then? It's not shop-bought crud, I make my own.'

The last thing he would eat is something the Chief had prepared. But he mustn't give the game away now he'd found such valuable evidence. Everything rested on it.

'Just a piece of toast would be great, thanks.'

'Is that all?'

'Yeah. Thanks.'

'Right. Can you set the table? Cutlery is in the drawer by the sink.'

He knew that already. Ben took out a knife and fork for Rufus and a knife and teaspoon for himself (in case Rufus was as fussy as Uncle Henry about jam) and carried them across to the table.

'So what do you want from me?' Rufus asked, whilst filling the kettle.

'*What*?'

'It's your birthday, isn't it?'

'Oh right, yeah,' Ben said, mightily relieved. 'Nothing thanks. I've never known about you or Marcus, so I'm used to not having a dad.'

Rufus nodded. 'Good. I don't think my mum sees it like that, but at least you won't be stalking me for the rest of my life.'

'No I won't.' *You'll be in jail.*

He put four slices of wholemeal bread in the toaster. Ben watched him carefully. Even a piece of toast could be poisoned.

'I know it's drawing electricity, but it's better than heating up the grill. I've checked,' Rufus said, misinterpreting his interest. Genuinely? Or was he taunting him? Typical Chief, if so.

'I won't eat four slices.'

'Two are for me.'

'Oh,' Ben said, as reassured as he could be in a mass-murderer's house.

'Can you get the drinks? I'll have coffee please.'

Rufus being pleasant was even more unsettling than if he'd been openly antagonistic again.

'Sure,' Ben replied. He refilled his own glass and found a teabag for Rufus's tea, whilst he cooked his scrambled eggs. Ben grimaced at the disgusting smell. The toast popped up. Ben opened the food cupboard.

'That was a good guess,' said Rufus, right behind him, making Ben jump yet again. 'God, you're like a cat on hot bricks!'

'Just looking for jam. This is great,' he said, spotting a jar of honey. Since Rufus was spooning eggs onto his toast, Ben carried his toast and the honey towards the table.

'Couldn't you do that in here?' Rufus said.

'Oh.' Ben was surprised. Uncle Henry hated condiments being applied on worktops, insisting all pots were placed in the middle of the table, on plates with a spoon beside them.

He put his plate on the worktop and spooned the honey onto his toast, disgusted by the pong of the eggs. Thankfully, Rufus took his smelly plate across to the table, so when Ben had spread his honey, he carried his toast across to join Rufus.

'So, you're fourteen now.' He appeared to be weighing Ben up.

'Yep.' Ben bit into his toast, as relaxed as a tightrope walker in a gale.

'Some birthday, eh?'

'Yeah.'

'I expect Mum will have something planned for you.'

Ben nodded, chewing and swallowing as fast as he could.

Rufus smiled again, the creepy smile. 'So have I. You'll have such a surprise later.'

Ben froze. The 993 attack. He was gloating about the attack. He checked the time: 06:45. He dropped his toast and stood. 'I've got to go. My cousins will be worried.' That was true, for sure.

'I'd run you back, but I haven't got a car.'

'I'll be fine running. Or walking,' Ben added, berating himself for having given the urgency away.

Rufus raised his eyebrows. 'Till later then.'

'Yeah. Thanks for breakfast. Bye.'

He couldn't have fled a forest fire faster. He raced out into the sunny morning feeling excited. He had somehow survived and escaped the Chief. Now to finish him, forever.

Chapter 23

Freddie Sees the Light

'It could be as simple as his phone being out of charge,' Freddie pointed out, as yet again Ben refused to answer.

Jess shook her head. Ben was so liable to run directly into trouble when others would run away. If he had worked out where the 993 attack would be, he would be heading there, no question. So they simply had to find it.

'Apart from water, what could that clue possibly mean?' Freddie asked.

'It's from *The Rime of the Ancient Mariner*. We did it in school.'

'We haven't, thank goodness. It's really long, isn't it?' Freddie said. Jess nodded, biting her lip. 'So? Is there a clue in it?'

Jess shrugged, nonplussed. 'It's about a sailor who shot an albatross. It's really unlucky, they believed.'

'There aren't any albatrosses in Oxford. Can't be that. What else happens?'

'It caused fog and mist, then a baking sun and they've nothing to drink and nothing to eat. Eventually they all die, two hundred men. *Two hundred*. Is that what they're planning?' Jess felt sick with worry.

'Who knows?' Freddie replied. 'Maybe even more, unless we stop them.'

Suddenly Jess realised it might be a clue. 'He's talking to a wedding guest!'

'A wedding guest?'

'The ancient mariner is. It could be St Saviour's!' Where their parents had studied and married. And Rufus and Marcus had studied – and Ballantyne too. Every single person they suspected was the Chief.

Freddie checked his watch. 'The porters won't be up yet.'

Jess's eyes fell on the card Ben had put on the desk.

Dr Amina Ashcroft

Senior Fellow and Tutor in Chemistry,

St Saviour's College, Parks Road, Oxon OX1 3PN.

Her mobile number was underneath, so Jess texted her.

Scared of a 993 attack. Wedding St S today?
Thanks, Jess (Sue Baxter's niece)

She read it through. It was vague enough to hide their knowledge of the clue but hopefully would remind her of Aunt Sue's terrible predicament. Dr Ashcroft had seemed very fond of Aunt Sue. Hoping she would be awake, Jess pressed Send.

'Marcus doesn't know yet, does he?' Freddie said.

'No. Good point. Should we tell him?'

'Better had. If it's not him, if it is Rufus, he really is on our side.'

'You think that now, don't you?'

'I'm not sure. OPO almost swings it, but it could be a double-bluff. Even if it is, Marcus will realise we're smarter than he thought, and it will worry him, if he is the Chief.'

Whilst Freddie was talking, Jess was composing a message for Marcus:

Book cipher: Water, water everywhere. Is it a wedding today?

Next to encode it. She got her sheet and, though rattled, remembered to vary the characters when encoding. Shame there were only two Rs and two Es, but that was better than only having one number available, such as for O.

She tapped in the following text:

7 5 5 95	75 1 72 4	68 39 19 9	6 70 91 2
46 71 68 39	70 21 68 91	14 65 15 68	91 70 1 3
11 20 10 2	70 37 22 11	30 36 61 5	35 46 84 95

Since there wasn't a J, she had used 95 again to complete the last foursome, then pressed Send.

Her mobile rang almost instantly. But it wasn't Marcus.

'Hello Jess, it's Amina Ashcroft. There aren't any weddings here today, or in any college, I wouldn't expect. They are usually only held on Saturdays, since all the colleges are Christian chapels, as far as I'm aware.'

'Oh, that's wonderful, thank you.'

'Why are you worried about a 993 attack?'

'We know the gang intended to use 993 as a poison. And the SPC Board are still in Oxford,' Jess added.

'Have you told the police of your fears?'

'No. With Aunt Sue being held…we don't want to complicate things for her.'

'It's ridiculous, isn't it? I can understand your reluctance to go to the police now.'

'We would if we had something concrete to tell them,' Jess said, feeling her face getting hotter and thankful Dr Ashcroft couldn't see her blushing.

'If I can be of any help, please ring me. Or text me. Any time.'

'Thank you so much,' Jess replied, glad of such a powerful ally. She ended the call and added Dr Ashcroft to her Contacts. 'What are you doing?' she asked Freddie, who was on the computer.

'Checking civil marriages, Oxford marriages, anything for April 11th.'

'Good idea. Anything yet?'

'More wedding fairs, whatever they are, than anything else. Oh, this might help. Hotel venues in Oxford.'

'Is The Beaumont there?'

'Of course! It tops the list.' The scornful look he gave her confirmed Jess's suspicion that he was becoming even more snobbish than their father.

'Phone them. The desk will be open. It's nearly seven.'

'Okay.' He picked up the landline.

'That's costing Daphne. Use your mobile.'

'You don't know it's costing her. She might get local calls free. Anyway, it's her grandson we'll be saving if we can stop it before it starts.'

'Freddie!'

Despite her protests, he used the landline. His penny-pinching could be downright embarrassing.

'Hello, is there a wedding there today? Oh right, thanks.' He rang off and turned to Jess. 'No.'

Whilst Freddie continued working his way down the list of hotels, Jess was wondering why Marcus wasn't getting in touch. And Ben. She tried calling him again, but just got silence. His mobile was switched off, out of charge or out of range.

Dare she ring Marcus? No, that was too dangerous. He was right at the heart of the Chief's gang. She would just have to hope he'd found Ben and seen the text.

What else could she do?

Was that the doorbell? It was faint, but certainly sounded like a bell. Jess went to the door and opened it, listening. Daphne wasn't responding to it. She was probably still asleep. It rang again, clearer now. Jess hurried downstairs and managed to reach the front door before the fifth ring.

Two very familiar shapes were visible through the stained glass. Her father had his finger on the bell.

'Sorry I haven't got a key,' Jess told them, in a voice loud enough to penetrate the door but not to wake Daphne, she hoped.

'Find one then!' he snapped.

'Where?'

'Try the top drawers of the dresser, Jess,' her mother suggested, much more helpfully.

Jess went to the walnut dresser and was delighted to find a collection of keys in one drawer. She chose the mortice and Yale and returning to the door, was relieved to discover that they worked.

Her dad was glaring as they entered the house, but her mum looked worried.

'Any news?' she asked.

Jess thought quickly. What could she tell them? They might well hear about the Dr Ashcroft call, so she had better admit to that. There could be a very innocent reason for Ben and Rufus breakfasting together too. So she confessed her ignorance of Ben's current whereabouts.

Her mum looked even more worried now.

'So you can't get in touch with either of them?' she asked.

'No. Marcus went to find them, but I haven't heard from him since he went to Rufus's home or office. He'll be very busy.'

'Not too busy for Ben.'

Jess nodded, agreeing with her.

But whilst her mum looked anxious, her dad looked cross.

'We've not had breakfast yet!' he complained.

'None of us have,' Jess said.

'Except Ben and Rufus,' he huffed.

'Do you have Rufus's number still?'

'No. It's years since we lived together.'

'I have,' a voice said from the stairs. They all turned to see Daphne approaching, wearing a burgundy dressing gown. The adults greeted each other as if it were a social occasion, whilst Jess's stomach churned with agitation.

'We want to get in touch with Rufus because…'

'JESUS! It's Jesus!' Freddie was racing down the stairs faster than Jess had ever seen him move.

'*What?*' Her dad's head swivelled towards him, looking scandalised.

Jess checked she understood. 'The college?'

'Of *course*! I didn't mean the Christian icon, did I? It's breakfast. Schools' visit. 993!'

'Could you drive us there?' Jess asked.

'Dad, trust me. It's 7:05, breakfast starts at 7:30 and no one believes me over the phone. We need to get there now!' Freddie said, at twice his normal rate.

'It's the *police* we need!' he responded.

'Phone them while we're on the way there.'

'And look like idiots? I need more than this,' he objected, ever the scientist, needing peer-reviewed evidence before he'd accept anything.

So Jess was grateful for her mum's intervention.

'It's better to look idiots than let children die,' she said.

'I'll take you. You can all come with me. Anyone that wants to,' Daphne said. 'I'll go and get my keys.' She hurried towards the kitchen, wasting time.

'Henry, it'll be like the swimming pool.'

'*Ben* might be there,' Jess added.

'I hope not. Give *me* the car keys,' her mum demanded, holding out her hand.

'No need. I'll drive you.'

'Fast, Dad please. Now!'

'I could take you,' Daphne called, but they already had the front door open.

'You get ready. We'll phone you,' they promised, rushing out.

It was 7:10 by the time they were pulling out of her drive. Five minutes to Jesus? Ten? Or maybe more?

'Don't phone the police. Please,' Jess begged as they pulled out.

'Why not?'

There was no other way, she had decided. It was time to reveal the truth. Well, some of it, at least. 'Marcus gave us the information. The gang will know that. They'll kill him if you let the police know that we know.'

'Why on *earth* did Marcus involve you?' her mum asked.

'It was a code to crack. He hadn't time.'

'*Code?*'

'Yes. The Chief sends messages in code. Apparently,' Jess added hastily. 'To keep them secret.'

'He should have asked us. Or his brother. He had no business involving you. Wait till I see him.'

'But you won't phone the police?'

'In that case, no.'

'It's probably a wild goose chase anyway,' her father said.

Freddie, who was sitting beside Jess on the back seat, shook his head.

'How sure are you?' Jess asked him quietly.

'It's a cryptic connection at best. But I think I'm right.'

'Typical,' Jess said. But with their parents present, she didn't want to press Freddie to explain. Instead she worried about Ben. Where was he?

As her father drove, and her mother fretted, Jess scoured the passing streets for him. The text to lure him to the swimming pool was evidence that would have satisfied Sherlock Holmes: Ben was still the Chief's number one target. He was in sickening, deadly, danger.

It wasn't cyanide now, it was 993 he'd be swallowing. No taste, no odour and absolutely no cure. But as they turned onto Broad Street from a thankfully traffic-free Parks Road there was still no sign of him.

Where on earth was he?

Chapter 24

Crying Wolf?

Once over the Magdalen roundabout, Ben was sure Rufus wasn't following him, so felt a little safer. But incredulous too. He'd fooled the Chief and escaped! Him. Not Marcus, not Freddie, not Jess, but stupid, careless him.

But maybe that was why, he reflected. Maybe Rufus would have been more guarded with them. Whatever, he was just a few minutes from the police station and the voice recorder in his pocket would hopefully clinch it, before Rufus had time to carry out his chilling threat.

High Street was still quiet, but from a hotel ahead, a familiar figure emerged. The tall, dark-haired, pudgy man had to be Nixon.

Ben stopped and bent down, as if tying a shoe-lace. The look of triumph in Nixon's eyes as he'd plunged the syringe into Ben's arm was unforgettable, and unmistakeable. Nixon hated him and had meant to kill him.

Well, Ben hated Nixon too. And if he headed this way, Ben could surely outpace him. He risked a look. Nixon didn't seem to have spotted him, or if he had, he hadn't bothered, because he was striding away from him.

He didn't usually walk that fast. He was hurrying – as if late for a meeting. Or as if he had a target in mind. Ben abandoned his plan to sprint past Nixon and instead started following him.

He jogged to catch up, but as he got closer, slowed to a walk, keeping about 20 paces behind. As Nixon approached Catte Street, Ben expected him to take it, heading towards St Saviour's, but he continued on.

Nixon turned right, by a small hotel called The Mitre. Ben wondered if he was calling in for breakfast, given that it was 7:15 now. Or was The Mitre their target?

He had to warn them. But as he got closer, and could see through the windows, Ben noticed that it was dark and empty. The road ahead was empty. So where was Nixon?

A girl screamed his name. Jess? He spotted her racing towards him from the top of the Street. Behind her came Freddie and Aunt Miriam, also running – a sight as rare as rainbows.

Nixon emerged from a café between them, looking furious.

'What the *hell* are *you* doing here?' he demanded, glaring at Ben.

'Come here!' Jess yelled, stopping. 'NOW!'

'No you don't Baxter,' Nixon said, lunging for him, but Ben swerved around him.

Jess was vanishing into an opening on the left, so he shot through it after her, surprised to emerge into a college. As he did, he heard a horribly familiar American voice, urging Nixon to cool it. He hadn't heard him speak since he was calmly discussing their murder. He was one of the Chief's backers.

Whilst Jess talked to the porter, Ben ground his teeth, almost overwhelmed by the urge to go and confront them, but reason and Freddie stopped him.

'Not yet,' he warned, holding his arm.

'Why?'

'That book cipher was a poem. It meant here.'

'What? How come?'

'Jesus. This is Jesus College. There's a Northern Schools' Taster Week. Breakfast starts any minute now,' Freddie said, checking his watch.

Aunt Miriam joined them.

'They're going to poison the breakfast?' Ben asked.

'No. The water.'

Jess and the porter emerged from the lodge.

'This way,' the silver-haired porter said. Despite his bowed legs, he led them very briskly indeed through Front Quad, on the path that cut the lawn into four smaller squares.

Ben felt sick with worry. The porter flung open a door and entered it. Dreading what they might see, Ben followed him into the dining hall.

At the far end was a table running across the room. Above it was a huge portrait of Elizabeth I. The tops of the walls were painted white, above wood panelling below, but the walls and ceiling, coupled with the huge windows, made the dining hall brighter than that of St Saviour's.

Chefs in white jackets and hats were at his end of the hall, behind metal serving dishes of hot food. A few students were choosing their food, whilst others were sitting at the long tables running down the hall.

'POISON!' the porter boomed. 'POISON! PLATES DOWN!'

'AND DRINKS!' Jess yelled.

'AND DRINKS!' he echoed.

Plates clattered down. Glasses were thumped on tables. Everyone froze.

But the smell of sizzling bacon made Ben's stomach rumble. Disgusted with his treacherous body, he spotted a tall boy, who looked stunned, pick a glass of water up as if to drink it.

'NO!' Ben yelled springing forward.

He turned his head, startled. Ben managed to knock the glass out of his hands, away from them both and onto the wooden floor.

The glass bounced, but didn't break, amidst a spreading pool of liquid. Poisoned liquid. A lethal pool of liquid, which was spreading towards his shoes. Ben jumped back and pulled the boy back. He looked affronted.

'It's poisoned,' Ben explained.

'*Tap* water? Really?' His voice was even posher than Freddie's. But even though he sounded sceptical he stayed put.

'It's in jugs. Anyone could have added anything,' Jess said.

'It's just water,' the boy said, still looking accusingly at Ben, as if he had assaulted him.

'This poison is tasteless, colourless and extremely deadly,' Freddie said.

'Even if you touch it,' Ben added. Other students had come over to see what was happening. 'Don't even step in it,' he warned. 'Your shoes could spread it around.'

'Or it could soak through to your socks,' Jess said.

'So?' a student inquired.

'That much could kill you,' Jess said, pinching her thumb and finger together, with real authority, Ben thought, though he had no idea, and was pretty sure Jess had no idea, if she was right.

'It's *that* deadly?'

'Yeah. If it is 993,' Ben said.

'You're not sure it's poisoned?'

'Sure enough for you not to touch it,' Ben replied. Though he didn't know Freddie's reasoning, the presence of Nixon and that repulsive creep who had financed the 993 made him very worried indeed that his cousins were right.

The porter had been bustling round talking to staff and students. He had also stationed one chef on each door, to stop anyone else entering; very sensibly, Ben thought.

'Are you that boy from the swimming pool?' a girl asked, staring at him.

'No,' Ben lied, feeling a treacherous heat in his cheeks. He turned away from her and towards Jess, who smiled sympathetically.

'I'll get the police,' the porter said.

'NO! Not yet,' Aunt Miriam cried. She smiled at the startled porter. Ben was startled too. 'We could have made a disastrous mistake. It's only a hint.'

'Is it?' Ben looked at Jess, astounded they'd caused so much fuss for a mere hint.

She shook her head. 'Don't think so. I think Freddie's right. But it is very cryptic if so.'

Uncle Henry entered through the main door.

'Sorry, sir,' the porter began, approaching him, hand raised, but Aunt Miriam explained who he was.

'Oh okay. Could you help guard this door then, please?' the porter asked. Uncle Henry looked delighted to be asked. 'I'm going to get the Principal. Or someone. Whoever's up at this hour,' he added, exiting.

'Principle?' Ben asked Jess.

'Might be the Warden in Jesus. It's principal with an -al, I think,' Jess said.

'Oh. Right,' Ben said, not understanding, but not caring either. One thing bothered him immensely, though. 'Why *not* the police?'

'We might be crying wolf,' Jess said, her wide eyes warning him that she didn't think they were, but to stop asking stupid questions.

'NO PHONES!' Aunt Miriam hollered at the students, who had mostly congregated around the middle of the three long lines of tables running down the hall. Ben watched as she bustled about amongst them, taking charge, commanding them to turn off their phones. He'd never seen her in teacher-mode before, but of course, that was her job. (Aunt Miriam taught History at the University of Manchester, where Uncle Henry was a Physics Professor.)

As a party of college officials arrived, Ben's mobile rang, startling him. He answered it.

'Benbo, good news?' Debs asked.

'Hi Debs. No, not yet,' Ben replied, realising she meant about Mum. 'How do we test for 993?'

'993?' Debs' voice rose about three octaves. 'Where?'

'In water. At Jesus. At breakfast.'

'The college? Oh my giddy aunt! No one's drunk it? Or touched it, have they?'

'No,' Ben said, pleased he'd persuaded them all to avoid the spillage.

'Good. I haven't much time, Benbo, so listen up. PH would tell you if there's anything in the water. We haven't a standard test for 993 yet.'

'Thanks Debs.' Ben rang off.

Aunt Miriam looked as she was apologising to the officials and Uncle Henry and Freddie were schmoozing them.

The porter returned.

'Any luck?' a man (the Principal?) asked him.

The porter shook his head. 'Our new temp has completely disappeared.'

'When?'

'Half an hour ago. Said he was going to the bathroom. Never returned.'

'That's highly suspicious,' the dignitary said. Ben agreed with him.

'What did he look like?' Uncle Henry asked.

'Average height, white, nothing remarkable about him.'

'Did he have any tattoos?' Jess asked, very smartly.

'Yes, two entwined snakes on his neck.'

'It's Goatee Man!' she cried.

'Had he a moustache or beard?' Ben asked.

'No.'

'He's shaved,' he said, looking at Jess.

'Please tell the police he's shaved. They know Goatee Man. We gave them a photo-fit,' Aunt Miriam said.

The official looked startled. 'Don't *you* need to tell the police that?'

'No, we need to go,' said Aunt Miriam. 'They know where we are staying and where we live if they want to talk to us.'

Ben was confused. Why was Aunt Miriam trying to avoid the police? Was she still mad at them for arresting Mum? Probably she was, like him. But he had the feeling there was more to it than that, from the anxious glances Uncle Henry kept darting towards her.

A man from the college clapped his hands and called for everyone's attention. The room fell silent.

'You'll have heard about The Beaumont's swimming pool. The cyanide in the water?'

The nodding heads and murmurs of assent affirmed that they had. Cringing, Ben noticed some girls pointing at him. 'This may be a similar poisoning. The police are on their way. In the meantime, do not eat or drink anything. And please, do not text or phone anyone about this.'

'I'm afraid we may have cried wolf,' said Aunt Miriam.

'Not at all, not a bit of it. If you have saved us from the tragedy that befell The Beaumont, I will be forever in your debt.' The man smiled, seeming as charming as St Saviour's Warden.

'We really need to go,' Aunt Miriam insisted.

Ben's phone bleeped, so turning away from Aunt Miriam, he checked his Inbox.

Marcus had sent Ben a new text, but well over an hour ago.

15 53 41 44 68 57 58 5 22 51 9 76 37 66 75 33 13 11 17 37

It was the other text, sent just a minute earlier that worried him, from an unknown number.

ZKR WROG BRX?

'Any idea?' he murmured, passing the phone to Freddie.

'Jess, question words. Fire them at me,' Freddie demanded as they followed Aunt Miriam and Uncle Henry out of the hall

'Why, who, where, when, which, what. Why?' Jess rattled off.

'You've already said that.'

'No, *why*?' Jess demanded, as she so often did.

But Freddie ignored her. He was moving his lips as if talking to himself, as he so often did when thinking.

'They don't usually use punctuation. That really helps us,' Jess said.

'It's not help,' Freddie said. 'It's a very simple Caesar cipher, the sort anyone could compose on the hoof. Or else it's very easy because they definitely want you to solve it. Or both.'

'What the hell does it say?' Ben demanded to bring his most annoying cousin to the point.

'Oh that? It's: *who told you?*'

'Who told me? You did.'

'But who told us?' Freddie responded. 'Marcus. And they'll know that.'

Ben stared at Freddie, speechless. They would surely kill him now.

Chapter 25

Swapping Suspicions

Ben was trying to get an answer from Marcus. He was expecting to see Nixon again as they emerged from the college onto the road, but there was no sign of him or the American.

But half-way up the road, just as he rang off, Marcus phoned him.

'Happy birthday.'

'Thanks. Are you okay?'

'Fine. What's up? Where are you?'

'Leaving Jesus College.' He lowered his voice. 'We think there was 993 in the water jugs. Goatee Man was a temp. Nixon and the American were watching.'

'Oh my god! But you stopped it?'

'Freddie and Jess did.'

'That's superb! Tell them well done from me.'

'They'll know you told us.'

'No, they won't. It's fine. Don't worry. I've got it all in hand.'

'Really?' Ben said, whilst thinking, but you didn't stop this attack.

'Yes. By tonight it will all be over.'

'Mum will be back?'

'Definitely.'

'That's great!'

'I know. Got to go, sorry.' Marcus rang off as they turned into Broad Street. Ben wondered why he had sounded so confident, but the fact that he had calmed him.

'Is Marcus okay?' Jess asked.

'Yeah. Sounds fine. Says Mum will be back soon.'

'I should think so! If they think my sister could have ordered that attack from jail, they have better imaginations than Agatha Christie. But I'd rather we didn't have to face them. Whilst I can obfuscate in front of college officials,' Aunt Miriam's voice dropped to a whisper, 'I cannot lie to the police.'

'*Lie*?' Ben couldn't have been more shocked if she had announced that she was invisible.

'As long as they believe our story of how Freddie guessed,' Uncle Henry responded.

'I didn't *guess*. I deduced!' Freddie's eyes were wide with indignation.

'Deduced what, exactly?' Ben asked.

'It's difficult out here,' Aunt Miriam replied, eyes darting left and right. 'But this could be good news, in a way. They will need crystal clear evidence linking Sue to the crime scene, and they won't have that, will they?'

'They can't send fake texts from her phone, because the police will have it,' Jess said.

'Yeah! This might actually free her. If they see my phone, it's proof,' Ben said.

'You can't give them that!' Freddie looked scandalised.

'Why?' Ben asked as they arrived at the car. But Freddie didn't answer. Police sirens were wailing, and Aunt Miriam was urging them to get in. Jess climbed into the middle of the back seat and Freddie sat behind his dad, so Ben got in behind Aunt Miriam.

'Drive fast, Henry,' she urged, as if it was a getaway car.

'Why not give them my phone? They'll know Mum couldn't have texted Marcus that book cipher. All the timings will stack up,' Ben murmured.

'But if they've got your phone, if the Chief texts you again, we won't know what they're saying,' Freddie objected, as if Ben was hard of hearing.

'Again?' Aunt Miriam said. Ben wasn't surprised she'd heard. He wouldn't have been surprised if everyone in Oxfordshire had heard Freddie's objection.

'Yeah. I've had a few texts from the Chief,' he admitted.

'Saying *what*?' Unsurprisingly, Aunt Miriam sounded horrified.

'In code. Just taunting me really, yeah?' Ben glared at Freddie, willing him to agree.

'Pretty much, yes,' he said, nodding.

'You mean you *knew*?' Aunt Miriam sounded angry with him too.

But Freddie didn't look as if he cared. He never did.

'Oh yes. How could he have cracked them otherwise?'

'Jess got lots of them too!' Ben protested, aghast that he'd claimed all the credit for himself.

'And you did,' Jess replied. 'Sorry we didn't tell you, Mum.'

'What about the police? You've not told the police about the codes?' Uncle Henry sounded hopeful, not angry, as Ben would have expected.

'No. Why?' Ben said. 'You do realise they're evidence?'

'We think the police might be corrupt. Or some of them are.'

'*What*?' Ben was stunned. Jess looked astonished as well. But Freddie nodded.

'We discussed it last night. What's happening at our alma mater?' Aunt Miriam added, noticing the crowd of people – and cars dropping them off – outside St Saviour's. Uncle Henry was forced to pull up.

'Not a wedding,' Freddie replied confusingly. But Ben was still bothered by a foreign phrase or at least he suspected it was.

'What's alma mater?' he asked Jess.

'Your old school or college. Latin,' she explained.

'Oh right. Do you think the police are corrupt too?'

'I can't believe they would be. Can you?' Jess said.

Ben grimaced. It hadn't occurred to him, but now he thought about it, it would certainly explain a few mysteries.

'It first crossed my mind, and your Mum's too, Ben, when they released them all. Though we hoped they were releasing the sprats to catch the mackerel,' Aunt Miriam said.

'The Chief, you mean?' Jess asked, whilst Ben felt hurt that Mum hadn't also shared these thoughts with him.

'Exactly. Then I thought back to their lack of activity when Sue was kidnapped.'

'Lots of people go missing,' Freddie said.

'Yes, but it was totally out of character. They should have investigated.'

'They should,' Ben agreed.

'If the Chief texts you again, you bring your phone to me, Ben. Promise? Or I'll confiscate it. Sorry, but your mother would do the same.'

'I know. I will. I promise,' Ben said, hoping he wasn't lying. If Marcus managed to get the Chief and Nixon arrested, then hopefully he wouldn't have to worry about any more codes.

'We had a visit from an Inspector Cunningham. He didn't seem to agree with Inspector Walker about Aunt Sue. Maybe she's corrupt,' Jess said.

'And that's why she arrested Mum!' Ben replied, getting angry now.

'Maybe. If so, I'll kill her. And the so-called Chief. Is there any clue at all in these codes as to who that is?' Aunt Miriam asked.

'Not really,' Ben said. 'Except that they text me, not Freddie and Jess.'

'Which is suspicious in itself.'

'No, it isn't,' Freddie retorted. He turned to Ben. 'You gave them your number, remember, when you went into SPC? Marcus's secretary asked for it. They didn't have ours. They had yours.'

'Oh yeah.'

'So it wouldn't help the police?' Aunt Miriam asked. 'If we can get to the honest police.'

'I don't think so,' Ben replied. 'He never texts me except in code. And some of them are from Nixon, we think.'

'But the police could probably trace the numbers,' Uncle Henry said.

'They use pay-as-you-go phones and change them often. Marcus has used about five different numbers for codes,' Ben replied.

'So it wouldn't tell them anything, except that Marcus is on our side,' Aunt Miriam said to her husband.

'If there is a corrupt officer, you definitely shouldn't take it to them,' Uncle Henry replied.

Thanks for that. I was thinking of handing it all over to her, Ben thought, but he didn't say it. However, he had some very important news for Jess. 'I've nicked a digital recorder from his house,' he whispered, showing it to her.

'Oh, Ben. What if he finds out?' Jess exclaimed.

'Who? Finds out what?' Aunt Miriam demanded from the front seat, whilst Ben pressed Play. Nothing happened. He tried sliding the Hold switch down, then pressed Play again. There was a sickening lack of response.

'What's happening? What if who finds out?' Aunt Miriam persisted.

Ben sighed. 'I found a digital recorder at Rufus's. We need some batteries to get it working.'

'He's given it you?'

'No, he doesn't know.'

'You stole it?' Uncle Henry sounded horrified.

'No, I took it for the police. I'm hoping it gives us the evidence we need to free Mum.'

'You don't think he's the Chief, do you?' Aunt Miriam said, cottoning on fast.

'That's exactly what I think,' Ben answered. 'He hates people, he hates his brother and he keeps trying to kill me.'

'*Kill you*? In what way?' Uncle Henry asked.

Ben hesitated. So many secrets – but he'd be in less trouble if he took them into his confidence now, rather than landing the bombshells on them when he finally told the police, he calculated. So he started bringing them up to date, partly at least.

'They nearly knocked me down last night.'

'When?' Aunt Miriam sounded horrified.

'Early evening.'

'What were you doing, Ben? Why were you out?' Aunt Miriam said.

Ben couldn't tell her he was going out to stop Ballantyne. He came up with an alternative reason that was also true.

'I wanted to see Mum.'

'Oh, Ben. You didn't think they'd let you, did you?'

'Not really. But I wanted them to.'

'Of course you did. And they nearly knocked you down you say?'

'Yeah. On South Parks Road. The lights were on green, but their Merc started up and headed straight for me. I only just made it to the pavement.'

'You reported that to the police?'

'Yeah. That's when Inspector Cunningham came round.'

'I see. So you didn't get to the station?'

'No, I went back to Daphne's.'

'Good. That was sensible. And when else has he tried to kill you? You said, "he keeps trying to kill me",' Aunt Miriam unfortunately remembered.

'In the pool.'

'They were trying to kill everybody, not just you,' Uncle Henry said.

'No. The Chief texted Ben to tell him the pool would be poisoned a few minutes before it opened. He knew Ben would go straight there and get in,' Jess said.

'You thought it was poisoned with 993, yet you dived into it?' Again, poor Aunt Miriam sounded horrified.

Ben could only nod. He'd been an idiot, a thoughtless, senseless idiot.

'To save lives,' Jess said admiringly.

'Sorry. I was stupid. I just wanted to get them out. As many as possible. I didn't want any of them to die.'

'It wasn't Rufus who texted you. He didn't know you're reckless,' Uncle Henry said.

'Brave!' Jess protested.

Ben shook his head. Uncle Henry was right.

'But Marcus does,' Freddie said.

'And so does that swine Ballantyne,' Aunt Miriam said. 'I can't believe it's Marcus. He's just too good. It's palpable.'

'What's that?' Ben asked.

'It shines out of him so strongly that you can almost touch it.'

'Oh.'

'Or he's a brilliant conman,' Freddie said. 'We know he is. Remember how he conned us all he had no idea where Aunt Sue was?'

'He was trying to protect us. It's not Marcus,' Ben maintained, confident he was in the clear. But not Ballantyne. Once again, he had a sneaking suspicion that Ballantyne, the sneaky, mean, but highly intelligent creep could be the Chief. But it was almost certainly Rufus. Hopefully, the voice recorder would tell them.

'It's not Rufus,' Uncle Henry said, as if reading Ben's mind. 'He's far too intelligent to have used his own website for a book cipher.'

'His own website?' Ben echoed.

'OPO,' Jess explained. 'It could easily be a double bluff, though, Dad.'

'He couldn't expect us to crack that book cipher. It's almost impossible,' Freddie said.

'Not for you, though, son,' Uncle Henry said proudly.

'If he couldn't expect you to crack it, then he would feel safe to use his own website,' Aunt Miriam said.

'That's exactly like the Chief, Mum. Arrogant and vain,' Jess agreed. Ben nodded too.

They were turning into Norham Gardens. Ben hoped to see Marcus's car parked there, but it wasn't.

'For now, say nothing at *all* about Rufus,' Aunt Miriam warned. 'You might be right about him, Jess, but personally I think it's that swine Ballantyne. There's far too much doubt to worry Daphne.'

'Unless this voice recorder works,' Ben said.

'True.'

'But that's prying,' Uncle Henry protested.

'If it exonerates him, we're doing him a favour,' Aunt Miriam replied. 'We'll ask Daphne for the batteries.'

'Good.' Ben recalled Marcus's text. He found it and it looked suspiciously familiar. 'Is this the OPO cipher?' he asked, handing his phone to Jess.

'Yes, I think that's it. Water, water everywhere. Yes, it is,' she confirmed.

'Is that what it said? That's why you knew it was in the water?'

'Yes.'

'But how did you know where it was?'

'That poem was written by Coleridge, who went to Jesus College, Cambridge,' Freddie said.

'You mean there's one there too?'

'Not as good, obviously,' Freddie joked.

'They have lots of colleges with the same names. Lots of different ones too,' Jess said.

'But they're all in Oxford, so I deduced it would be here. And the poem told us it would be in the water. But I didn't want to tell them that, because that might give away what Marcus did,' Freddie said.

'Thanks,' Ben said.

'Saving *hundreds* of lives,' boasted Freddie, but for once he was right to boast.

'If you get Mum free as well as saving them, it's the most important thinking you'll ever have done. Both of you,' Ben added, careful to give Jess the credit she so deserved.

Jess beamed.

'So far,' Freddie agreed, nodding.

'Now why does that terrify me?' Ben quipped.

They shared a smile.

'Not just ingenious, but a life-saver too. That's my boy!' Uncle Henry said, switching off the engine.

Chapter 26

The Second Birthday Breakfast

Daphne emerged from the house onto the steps, immaculately dressed and smiling brightly. Poor Daphne. She wouldn't be smiling soon. The news would surely devastate her.

'Give me the voice recorder please, Ben. We'll say it's mine, from work,' Aunt Miriam said.

He was reluctant to lose possession of it, but unable to think of a reasonable excuse, he passed it to her.

'No one say anything about Rufus, remember,' Aunt Miriam warned, opening her door. 'All fine!' she called.

'Oh!' Daphne looked surprised – and disappointed, Ben noticed with a stab of alarm. *Surely* she didn't know? *Surely* his seemingly lovely Grandma wasn't in on it? 'Sue's not with you?'

'Not yet, no.'

'I wish she was here for Ben,' she said, explaining her disappointment. Ben felt terrible for his flicker of suspicion. Daphne was far too kind to be involved with murder. She'd be horrified about Rufus.

'So it was a false alarm?'

'No it wasn't,' Aunt Miriam said.

'But you stopped it in time?'

'Just in time, thankfully.'

'Oh, how wonderful! Have you all had breakfast?'

'No. *We* haven't!' Uncle Henry grumped, glaring at Ben.

'I didn't have much,' Ben said.

'Excellent.' Daphne beamed. 'Please, come in.'

He followed Daphne down the hall, entered the kitchen, then stopped. Balloons, banners, a stack of presents and an amazing feast awaited them. It was the most extraordinary birthday breakfast he'd ever seen.

Daphne beamed at him. 'Happy birthday, Ben darling. May I give you a hug?'

'Of course,' he said, submitting to a sophisticated-scented cuddle. What a lovely new grandma he had – and how wretched he felt at the news he would have to break soon.

'I've been longing to spoil a grandchild. Now at last I can,' she said. 'Eat! Enjoy! You all deserve it after this morning's wonderful work. And I'm sure we'll have Sue back very, very soon.'

No one hoped so more than Ben. He tried his best to hide his trepidation as they feasted on fruit, yoghurt and warm pastries, including the most delicious almond croissants he'd ever tasted (from the coffee shop they'd visited on Sunday).

'Before I forget, Daphne, I've got a memo I simply must get to work, but it's on a voice recorder and I need some batteries,' Aunt Miriam cleverly lied. 'Do you have any, please?'

'Plenty. Do you need them now?'

'Yes please. I'm *so* sorry. 9:00 a.m. deadline.'

Daphne got up to get the batteries, which were in her study. Ben checked his watch. It was 08:15. Why wasn't Mum back yet? He so wished she was sharing this amazing breakfast. She'd love it. It felt wrong to have a birthday breakfast without her. Although her job involved lots of international travel, Mum had never missed his birthday before.

Were the police really corrupt? Would they keep Mum, whatever evidence they got?

'What's up?' Jess asked.

'What if they never release Mum? What if they're *all* corrupt?'

'They won't all be. She'll be back with us any minute, you'll see.'

'I hope you're right.'

When Daphne returned to the kitchen with her battery box, it quickly became apparent that she had every size of battery they could possibly need. Aunt Miriam selected two.

'Thank you so much. I could do with doing this in private. It's a bore, I know. It's just work,' she added, grimacing to show what a nightmare they were.

'Of course,' said Daphne. 'Use my study.'

Watching them leave, Ben admired his aunt's ingenuity. Maybe he should have confided in her earlier. He yearned to be with her, to listen to the recordings with her, but couldn't think of a plausible excuse.

The doorbell rang, startling them. *Mum*? Thrilled, Ben raced to the front door, meeting Daphne, who opened the door.

It was Marcus, dressed in a smart navy suit and carrying a beautifully wrapped present and card.

'Happy birthday,' he said, handing them over to Ben.

'Thanks. But you've already given me an amazing gift,' Ben said, referring to the DNA test. The package was large, square and light.

'It's only a little something to make you smile. I know you won't be entirely happy until we get your mum back.'

'No, but your mum made me an amazing breakfast,' Ben said, smiling at her.

Marcus grinned at Daphne, looking enormously proud of her. 'I'll bet she has.'

'Come and join us,' she said. 'There's plenty.'

'Good. I'm famished.'

'Is this a flying visit?'

'Unfortunately, yes. I've got ten minutes, no more.'

'Come and have some coffee then. I'll bet Miriam would love some too.' She knocked on the study door. 'Have you finished, Miriam?'

'I have, yes,' she said, emerging from the study. Her expression was blank, telling Ben nothing, except that she too was pleased to see Marcus, because she smiled.

Ben hung back to give her an enquiring look. Aunt Miriam shook her head telling him she'd found no evidence. Ben tried to conceal his deep disappointment as he entered the kitchen.

Marcus was sitting at the table enjoying an almond croissant. He urged Ben to unwrap the present. As Ben tore off the paper, he saw the name of his favourite designer on the box. Astonished Marcus had realised this – or even more amazingly, guessed – he opened the box. It contained three gorgeous shirts, in pale blue, light green and lilac.

'Wow! They're awesome. Thank you so much. It's my favourite label.'

Marcus nodded, beaming. 'I hoped so. Debs tipped me off.'

'Good old Debs.'

'Indeed. Of course, I would have asked your mum if...' He looked embarrassed.

Ben smiled at him to put him out of his misery. It wasn't his fault that Mum had been arrested.

'I'm sorry we haven't got ours, Ben. They're at home. You'll get them later, hopefully,' Aunt Miriam said.

'Thanks. Don't worry about it.' The only present he wanted was getting Mum back. And for Marcus to be his dad, Ben added quickly. Two immense wishes, but he had a real chance of both coming true.

'While I'm here would you mind opening Ma's presents too?' Marcus said.

'Sure. If that's okay?' Ben added, looking at Daphne.

She smiled. 'Of course it is, sweetheart.'

The first gift was a beautifully wrapped box from the same designer, containing a blue jumper.

'Thank you so much,' Ben said, checking how soft it was. 'It's silky smooth.'

'Yes, cashmere's lovely, isn't it? It's a lambswool blend, so machine washable, but tell your mum not to put it in the drier.'

'Sure,' Ben agreed, opening the next parcel, a long, thin box. Inside it was a silk tie.

'I haven't got a tie, except for my school tie,' Ben said, stroking it. It was so smooth, and a gorgeous swirl of green, blue and lilac, which would match his new shirts beautifully. 'This is gorgeous. Thank you so much.'

'You need a good tie. You're a young man now,' Daphne said and, unexpectedly, it made Ben feel proud. Fourteen was well on the way to being an adult, and for him, a landmark age. When Mum was entertaining clients after work in Wilmslow, they had agreed that he could stay at home, rather than being ferried to the Winterburns', when he was at last 14.

And finally, he was. YES!

'These are amazing presents. Thank you so much.'

'It's the least we could do,' Daphne said.

'You've already given me an amazing present, the paternity test,' Ben told Marcus, who was gulping a coffee.

He put his mug down. 'That was for me. Entirely selfish. You're either my nephew or my son. Either way, I'm very, very proud of you, and I want to prove it.'

'I'm nothing special,' Ben said, aware of the heat in his cheeks.

'Every child is special,' Daphne replied, making Ben feel so guilty about Rufus again. He was her child. But he was the Chief. Children didn't always turn out how you hoped. Had he, for Mum?

'I couldn't be more proud of you two, averting such a tragedy this morning,' Aunt Miriam told Jess and Freddie.

The doorbell rang again.

Mum? Again Ben tore to open it, leaving Daphne in his wake.

But it was Hazel in a bright red suit, with lipstick and shoes to match. She was beaming and her green eyes were shining with excitement.

'Your mum wants to see you. I'm to be your taxi.'

'Fantastic!' He turned to Daphne. 'Mum's free!'

'Oh, Ben, that's wonderful.'

'Hazel's taking me to see her.' He stepped outside. 'Let's go!'

Chapter 27

At Last

'So she's totally cleared of all charges?' Ben asked, as Hazel started her bright red convertible. It was a beautiful morning, so she had the hood down.

'Totally. Apparently, there was an attempted attack this morning, which finally convinced them of her innocence.'

'Great!' Ben grinned, delighted.

Hazel smiled. 'Thought you'd be pleased.'

'I am. It's the best birthday present ever. *Yes!*' Ben pumped his fist. He could hardly wait to see her. So when Hazel turned right, leading out of Oxford, rather than towards the town centre, he asked, 'Where is she?'

'Well away from prying eyes.'

'Why?'

'The media. Oxford centre is overrun.'

'Oh yeah, sure. Thanks, Hazel.'

'It was your mum's idea, not mine. She wants some quiet time with her boy, well away from everyone else,' Hazel said. Ben beamed. 'The last thing she needs is more questions after being interrogated all night by the police.'

'You're joking! That's awful.' Ben felt so sorry for his poor mum, and understood why she want to avoid the Winterburns for a while.

Hazel grinned. 'She can't wait to see you.'

'I can't wait to see her.' Ben settled back in his seat and reflected on how lucky his birthday had already been. They had stopped the attack, Mum was free, he was about to be reunited with her and his new dad (or uncle, he reminded himself, trying to prepare himself should the crashing disappointment arise) and Grandma had bought him amazingly generous birthday presents.

He wished he'd put his new clothes on. Having been up all night, he was still in yesterday's clothes. But Mum wouldn't mind. She would be so happy to be free. He was so happy she was free. He was ecstatic. Yes!

They were moving faster now, on a dual carriageway. Ben's eyes were watering with the force of the wind. He could understand why Hazel had donned sunglasses at the last lights. Her bright auburn hair was streaming behind her. She had turned a CD on, a cool trumpet solo.

'Who's this?'

'Miles Davis.'

'I heard him playing at Daphne's, I think. Rodrigo's guitar concerto, but on trumpet.'

'That's right. He did record that. But this is his best album ever: Kind of Blue.'

The trumpet was haunting and expressive, floating away into the clear blue sky.

'It's often rated as the best ever jazz album, and it's perfect for a day like today, don't you think?'

'It's good. I like it,' Ben said, tapping his foot in time to the music. 'How far are we going?'

'Not far. A lovely little hotel, well away from the media but only a few minutes from Oxford, when you're ready to face the family together. The room's on SPC, of course.'

'Thanks Hazel.'

'My pleasure. It's the fault of two of my colleagues that she got arrested.'

'Who?' asked Ben, wondering if they'd got him at last.

'Peter Nixon and Marcus Wright. They were the men that attacked you, weren't they?'

'Yes, but Marcus says he's innocent,' Ben said carefully, wondering how much Hazel knew.

'They both say that.'

'Right. So they haven't arrested them yet?'

'Not yet. Not as far as I know. Soon, I hope.'

'Me too,' agreed Ben, thinking not Marcus, but Rufus. Marcus had said he was close to nailing the Chief, so hopefully he would have plenty of evidence to prove it.

'I thought she might want a nap whilst I picked you up.'

'That's kind of you.' Of course, after being questioned all night, Mum would not only want sleep, she would *need* sleep before driving them home later. The effects of just a couple of hours' sleep might tell on him later too. But for now, he was fine, buzzing with excitement. Mum was free!

They crossed a couple of roundabouts and were soon in sunlit countryside, but on a single-track road were forced to drive much slower.

'Is it much further?' Ben asked, practically bouncing with excitement.

Hazel smiled at him. 'Not much, promise.'

They were entering Yarnton, a sign said. There was a pub on the right, but Hazel didn't stop. Understandably, Ben reflected, because it wasn't a hotel.

'Where is she?'

'Ben, cool it. You're fourteen now, not four. Happy birthday, by the way.'

'Sorry. Thanks.'

'Have you had a good day?'

'It started out rubbish, but it's turning into a fantastic birthday, thanks.'

'It's one you'll never forget.'

'That's true.'

He settled back, shut his eyes against the whipping wind and, listening to the music, imagining how exciting the reunion with Mum would be. It would be like when she returned from those horrible week-long trips to the Far East or America. They had rushed into each other's arms when he was younger. But not nowadays, in front of the Winterburns (since that was where he stayed). They hugged, of course, but in private.

It was him that had changed. Mum still wanted to cuddle him just as much as she used to, she made that clear. He wondered if she minded. He would give her a great big hug,

226

he resolved, when he saw her, whether Hazel thought him babyish or not.

The car turned right, towards Oxford Airport.

'I didn't know Oxford had an airport.'

'It's hardly Ringway,' Hazel said, using the local name for Manchester Airport. 'We're very nearly there now.'

'Great.' Ben spotted a few planes. As they approached a roundabout, he saw a modern complex ahead on the left, that could well be a hotel, but he couldn't see the sign.

'Is that it?'

'No, that's Thames Valley police's HQ.'

'Is that where she's been?' he asked, as they continued straight on, rather than turning left towards the airport.

'Last night, yes. You didn't think they'd keep her at St. Aldgate's, did you?' Hazel looked at him with a wry smile.

'Yeah, I did,' he admitted. This station looked far more modern, and hopefully more comfortable than the old police station in the town centre. 'So that's why we've come so far.'

'It's not far from Oxford. Six or seven miles. It just seems far because you're desperate to see her.'

Ben smiled. 'True.'

They came to a T-junction. Hazel turned right.

'It's just off here.' Turning a sharp right, she drove into the car park of The Highwayman, a former coaching inn, apparently. 'It's over three hundred years old.'

'That's modern, by Oxford's standards.'

Hazel grinned. 'You're getting the hang of this place, I can see.' Like Marcus, she was so unstuffy, considering she was a director, and very kind too.

She led him into reception, which was like a pub.

'The rooms are in the old barn.'

'Oh. Mum's there?'

'She is.'

'She'll let us in then.'

'I think she'll be asleep.'

'Oh right, yeah,' Ben replied, feeling stupid. Of course she would be asleep, after being questioned all night.

Hazel smiled. 'You can wait outside whilst I get the key.'

'Thanks.' He headed outside as Hazel had kindly suggested, and waited in the sunny car park. He noticed that the garden led down to the canal. It was a much smaller hotel than he had expected, but more charming. It was the best hotel in the world right now. He could hardly stop smiling. Mum was inside and at last she was free!

Hazel came out, carrying a key.

'Thanks for bringing her here, Hazel. And for bringing me here too.' Only two minutes in a car from Thames Valley Police HQ, it was perfectly situated for Mum. She hadn't had to endure a long drive, or face the media.

'It's my pleasure. Follow me.'

He followed Hazel into the annex and up the stairs.

'It's this one. She'll want to see you, not me,' Hazel said, standing aside to let him get to the door.

He knocked and waited, fizzing with excitement. But Mum didn't respond.

'She'll be fast asleep. But she won't mind being woken by you. Excuse me.' Hazel edged past him with the key. She inserted it and turned it, then stood back to let Ben in first, a thoughtful and kind gesture, he thought.

It was a double bedroom, with a double bed, a wardrobe, a couple of armchairs and a central table – but no Mum.

He turned to Hazel, confused. 'Is this the right room?'

'I think so. She's probably in the bathroom. I wonder if she's all right.'

Ben ran towards the door, suddenly scared. Mum had been frail over the weekend. Being questioned all night must have been terribly hard on her.

He knocked. No answer. He rushed in. It was empty.

Worried, he turned to leave, but Hazel had followed him in. With the shower cubicle, washbasin and toilet there was hardly enough room for both of them.

'She's not here.'

'I can see that. But never mind, *we* are. And we're going to set her free, get you home and put the horrible baddies in jail. But first you have two things to do for me.'

'*What*?'

'Why don't you come out here so that we can talk?'

'What's happening, Hazel?' Ben asked, baffled.

'Well, I'm awaiting my fortune, Richard's determined to get his fortune and Peter is after your father. Or uncle. But I'm pretty sure he's your father, you're both so alike. So incorruptible. So palpably honest. And so very, very easy to manipulate.' She pursed her lips. 'You look confused. Don't be. Richard's Ballantyne. Peter's Nixon. And I'm usually called Hazel nowadays. But you probably know me as the Chief.'

Chapter 28

The Chief

'In case you have any stupid thoughts, this is a gun,' Hazel said, pulling what looked like a phone out of her bag. 'It's *meant* to look like a phone. Picked it up in the States for less than the price of a real phone, can you believe it?'

No, Ben couldn't. His mind was reeling like a punch-drunk heavyweight's. Was she serious? Was this some kind of cruel, insane and very, very sick joke?

'It's only got two shots, but I'm good. Very good, actually. A practised shooter. But I hate that word. So inelegant. The official word is marks*man,* like policeman, postman, bin-man, and fireman. Don't you just hate that? Because any sharpshooter obviously has to be male,' she said, her green eyes flaring to emphasise her sarcasm. 'Any big hitter obviously has to be male. And any big chief certainly has to be male. Well, not any more. I'm the boss. I'm the Chief. And I've run rings round the lot of them for years.'

Ben had by now realised that the top hole at the end of the phone she was pointing at him was far too big for a charger socket. It was built for bullets. She was serious.

'Sit down.' She gestured to one of a pair of armchairs. He sat. She sat opposite, about four feet away. Even a rookie would hit him from there.

He took a deep breath, to try to calm his pounding heart

'I want Mum back.'

'I know, and you'll get her back as long as you do what I say. But if you try to escape, I'll kill you.'

'I won't.'

'There's a lot to say, and we haven't got long. But very briefly,' she said, kicking off her killer heels, 'your Mum and Jess were right. Women again, you see?'

'About what?'   •

'It is a con.'

Mum and Jess had certainly believed it might be a con before the ice-cream poisonings had occurred. But not now.

'People died in the pool. Teenagers, children. It's no con.'

Anger flashed across her face. 'Well it was, until Nixon screwed up.'

'What?'

'No one was meant to die. But those dear investors, who should be winging the money over right now, insisted they wanted to see 993 working. Hence Marcus.'

'*What*?' She was making less sense than Uncle Henry ranting about physics.

'Marcus would save you, so it was him and Peter, not Richard and Peter.'

Ben was struggling to keep up. 'In St Saviour's, do you mean?'

'Exactly. We had enough for a sample, but not the bulk 993 that Peter had promised. And failed.' She grinned. 'Peter had no idea Marcus had switched the syringes, did he?'

'How do you know?'

'I was spying on them. I always am. On all of them. Then we had to wait for over a week for Peter to ship the 993 here. It didn't arrive until yesterday.'

'Right.' The fact that Hazel was confirming what he already knew was disturbing. It might mean she was telling the truth.

'It was Peter's fault that it was late, so he got jittery. You see he, our investors and everyone else believes that the Chief is a homicidal maniac who wants to kill children.' Hazel laughed. 'If I was, I'd have killed you by now, wouldn't I? But that's the con,' she said, pulling at her hair.

Pulling *off* her hair! Her glossy auburn hair was a wig, Ben realised, astonished. Underneath her hair was completely different – short, cropped and mousy brown. She stood to toss the wig onto a bag on the bed and looked much smaller than

Ben had realised without her heels. She kept the gun aimed at him.

He was sweating. He wiped his forehead, saying, 'What do you want me to do?'

'Just listen, for now. So Peter tried to fob off our investors and fob me off too. I ask you?' She smiled, as if he would agree how ludicrous that was. 'By killing children.'

Ben shuddered. 'He's evil.'

'Isn't he? But luckily, he's not very bright. He thought of the ice-cream cart. Pathetic, wasn't it? So Richard, realising it was a dumb idea, suggested azalea nectar. Very mild indeed,' she added, unbuttoning her jacket with one hand whilst keeping the gun aimed at him.

'Those little girls nearly died.'

She waved a hand as if wafting away a wasp. 'Nixon's fault. He used too much. Then there was the Warden's party, and Richard saw his chance. He decided to divert the police onto your mum,' she said, smiling as she pulled off her jacket. Underneath was a plain white T shirt.

'It *was* him!' Ben was angry with Ballantyne now. Really angry.

She got up. He tensed. She smiled and walked to the wardrobe, facing away. He looked at the door. Should he run? But, before he'd decided, she swung round and aimed the gun at him again.

'Don't try and escape, Ben. I don't want to have to kill you.'

He swallowed. 'I won't.'

She took a pair of jeans off a hanger.

'Look away. At the window.'

Ben did so. There was nothing out there but a cloud-studded bright blue sky. His throat was so tight. He swallowed again, but he couldn't clear the constriction, as if her fingers were squeezing the life out of him.

'Right, you can look again now.'

She was wearing the jeans and had removed her bright lipstick. She looked totally different from the sassy company director she had been. She walked towards him, with the gun trained on him. She sat opposite him again. He swallowed, but the lump in his throat wouldn't shift.

'Richard had the clever idea of the swimming pool. He organised the cyanide, made sure it was weak, and told Peter to send you a cryptic clue. What was it? Something about flamingos and hedgehogs? He wouldn't know cryptic if it slapped him in the face.'

'The cyanide *wasn't* weak. People died.'

Hazel shrugged. 'A few. Not many.'

Ben gasped at her callousness.

Her eyes flared as if angry. Ben gulped. He'd gone too far.

'I didn't kill them. They did.' She exhaled. 'Anyway, that text from your mum's phone was enough. It took the heat off us until the 993 arrived.'

'That was why Mum was arrested?'

'Sorry about that.' Stunned, Ben gawped. 'I *am*. I like her. It didn't suit me either. He should have landed it on Marcus, not your mum.'

'Who? Ballantyne?'

'Yes.'

So Mum's arrest was Ballantyne's fault. He'd get him for that, Ben resolved. One day, he'd get him.

'Despite her meddling, I've done my best to look after your mum. Didn't you notice how well she looked when you got her back?'

'After you'd kidna...' Seeing her eyes narrow ominously, Ben broke off.

'She looked well, didn't she?'

She wanted him to agree, but Ben absolutely refused. 'She was thin.'

'Thin because we kept her asleep. She wasn't awake to eat. I didn't want her to be frightened, see? I didn't want her to be hurt. I like her and I like you,' she claimed, with the gun still trained on him. She was absolutely insane. He had no idea what to say or how to respond. His only aim was to somehow escape this madwoman without losing his life.

'Until Peter came up with his sick plan to murder you both, and I couldn't see a way to stop him.'

'But you're the Chief!'

'Yes. You didn't even notice the clues, did you?'

'Notice what?'

'The four horsemen, Miles Davis, the quantum code. Telling you to stay safe while they are still around – who could *they* be? The men, of course!'

'Right,' Ben said, whilst reminding himself that she meant the quantum cipher, not the quantum code, the code based on the Standard Model, which she had no idea they had seen, or cracked. That told him the deadline was noon. He carefully checked his watch. It was 10:55.

'I played fair. I'm not a murderer. I haven't murdered anyone – yet. But I will be forced to kill you if you try anything.'

'I won't,' Ben assured her.

She crossed her legs. 'I'm simply a hustler and they're my marks. They had to believe I was ruthless, that I would happily kill anyone. But I'm not. I don't even want to kill you. So don't make me.'

'I'm just listening to you,' Ben said raising his hands in a gesture of surrender. Anything to placate her and get out alive.

Hazel smiled again. 'I like you. I've protected you.'

'*What*? How?'

'The cyanide text. And last night. The quantum code, to keep you busy. To keep you out of trouble.'

Ben said nothing. She was pointing a gun at him, and she thought she was protecting him? She was nuts.

'That's why I'm giving you this chance,' she continued.

'*What* chance?'

'The chance to win, again.'

'Again?'

'When I sent you the book cipher, I thought you hadn't a snowball's chance in hell of solving it, but you did. And stopped the massacre at Jesus. I was so pleased. It would have been terrible.'

Sickened by her hypocrisy, Ben blurted out, 'I didn't. It was Freddie and Jess.' Immediately followed by guilt. *Why did I tell her that*? Had he put them in danger too?

Hazel smiled. 'Pity. It's not them I like, it's you. Well I quite like Jess, but Freddie's just like the rest of them. Too up his own masculine tree to even notice us women. Though I think he might be gay.'

Ben had no idea whether he was or not. He couldn't care less. 'So what? He's all right.'

'You see? You're so nice. Defending your cousin, but you can't stand him, can you?'

Wrong. He's alright, Ben thought, but he said nothing.

'They did well, your cousins. Peter couldn't crack that book cipher. Richard has to copy him in, I insist, but it was far too cryptic for him to solve.'

'He was there this morning, outside Jesus.'

'Because Richard had told him to meet him there for breakfast, with the investors.'

'The American one was there.'

'Only one? Pathetic Peter again. Shambolic,' she said crossly, looking at her watch, a thick black plastic timepiece she hadn't been wearing before. 'Never mind, I'm depending on Richard pulling off an attack and getting me the rest of the money.'

'*Another* attack?'

'Meanwhile Peter is after revenge on your dad. So you have to save him, save the children and save your mum. Right up your street, eh, Ben?'

Was she serious? Was Nixon really after Marcus? And Ballantyne determined to kill children?

'Don't move.' She got up and walked over to the dressing table.

He quickly checked his pockets for his phone, hoping to send a surreptitious text, but it wasn't there.

She turned back. Her striking green eyes were now brown. She had applied a transfer to her cheek, a worker bee of Manchester. Everyone would remember that, not what she looked like. Clever.

'Tinted contacts,' she explained, noticing his double take. 'Right, here's your chance. Richard sent Peter a second code this morning. I haven't had chance to share it with you yet. Or crack it. But I will, if you can't.'

'Thanks.'

'Now, don't get sulky. You didn't get the point of the quantum code, did you?'

'What?'

'For every particle, there's an antiparticle, for every up spin there's a down spin, for every Pete there are two. That's why he changed his name. They've been calling him Tricky Dicky for years,' she said. '*He* wants to get off scot-free and land it all in Peter's lap. I must say it's tempting. But I merely need to remember one of the five hundred times that Richard has patronized me, and I get mad. So mad. Mad with the lot of them, the whole sexist, incompetent lot of them,' she said, her lips tightening with anger again.

His whole body was screaming at him to run. But with that gun trained on him, he daren't.

'But you're not sexist, yet. Show me, Ben. Show me there's a decent man in the world.'

'Marcus is decent.'

'Yes he is. But he's not here. You are.' She handed him a piece of paper. On it was typed:

RGRUEZ'F SGEFJ'F TGYC XZJIUE

'It's one of Richard's. So there's punctuation!' She laughed as if she'd cracked a great joke. She was absolutely nuts. 'You have a code to crack. You haven't long. Good luck. Though I don't rate your chances. You don't do cryptic, do you? Far too straightforward for that.'

'I can't crack this.'

'Shame. It's your last chance to be a hero, Ben.'

'I don't want to be a hero. I don't want anyone to die.'

'Well, it's your choice. If you can solve it, and get there and stop it, we lose. If you can't, people die, but I win. If you decide to save your dad instead of the victims, I win. Your call.'

Ben stared at her aghast. 'If I save Marcus, people will die?'

'Probably. Unless they mess it up again, but it's Richard this time. It'll be better planned. And with 993 it's hard to see how he can go wrong, isn't it?'

Ben gulped. It was a chilling prospect.

'But you're not going anywhere or saving anyone until you've cracked this. To escape, you have to crack it.'

'You're not giving me a choice at all.'

Hazel pouted. 'Oh, am I not playing fair? I'm sorry. You men have been so fair to us for so long, haven't you?'

'No, but that's not my fault.'

'Yes it is. It's all your fault. I'll bet Jess won't be on the news tonight. You were all over the news, yet it was your cousins who cracked the code. No mention of Jess there, was there?' She was angry again. He was handling this so badly.

Ben changed tack. 'Let me go, please.'

'No! You've spoiled this morning already. We're on to the backup plan. But I am giving you a chance. Crack the code.'

What would she do then? She was utterly insane. The urge to run was almost overwhelming, but he had absolutely no doubt that she'd shoot him if he did.

Marcus would die. Lots of people would die.

'Please, Hazel, let me go.'

'Not until you crack it, no.'

'And if I can't?'

She tilted her head, raising her eyebrows, and smiled. Her meaning was as clear and chilling as ice. She'd kill him.

Chapter 29

Ben vs the Chief

He was panting. He was sweating. He felt sick. He could hardly even think, let alone code crack. Yet somehow, he had to.

'Can I have a pen?'

'No. Haven't you heard? The pen is mightier than the sword. If you're as amazing as they say, you'll solve it in your head.'

Ben shook his head in disbelief.

'Do your best,' he heard Mum say, as if she were there. 'That's all you can do.'

A pleasant warmth, like sunlight, spread within him.

Calmer, he viewed the code.

RGRUEZ'F SGEFJ'F TGYC XZJIUE

The apostrophes meant *F* was the code for S. The ending of the second word implied *J* was H or maybe T.

A phone rang. Ben looked up, startled. It was Hazel's mobile.

'Hi, Jess,' she said, smiling brightly.

Ben gasped. Was this his chance? Should he yell for help?

As if she'd read his mind, she shook her head. He daren't. She'd shoot.

'Yes, he is. He's so excited. We're waiting for Sue to wake up. Yes, she's shattered. But delighted to be free, of course.'

Ben sat shaking his head, utterly disgusted by her lies. But she seemed to be fooling Jess. Of course she was. He had believed Hazel was taking him to Mum. She was clever, she was convincing and utterly, utterly ruthless. She was playing a game with the lives of hundreds of people.

He longed to yell to Jess, but the gun was still trained on him, and even if Jess heard a shot, she would have no idea of where they were. Or of where Ballantyne's attack would be.

Hazel rang off. 'She's so excited.'

Ben swallowed down the sourness this caused and continued to stare at the code. He simply had to crack it.

But it was useless. He couldn't even picture an alphabet, let alone a pattern. Hazel must be loving watching him fail, and would be exultant at having fooled Jess.

It was worth another try.

'If I can't have a pen, could you write out an alphabet for me, please?'

Hazel smiled. 'You've asked so nicely that I will.' She got up and crouched at the central table, where there was a pen and some paper. She put the gun on the table, between them. He had about six feet to cover to get it. Could he? Dare he?

He was being reckless again. She'd surely snatch it before he got there.

She looked up at him, and a little smile played about her lips, which was unnerving. It felt as if she could read his mind. He tried to make it blank, watching her.

She stopped writing. With the paper and pen in her left hand, she picked up the gun in her right and, aiming it at him again, walked towards him.

And kept coming. Ben shrank back. She smiled. She was too close. She smelled of something cloying and sickly and choking.

She put the gun against his chest.

He held his breath. This was it. She was about to kill him.

But she laughed. Laughed as if she would lose control. Would she? Would she accidentally fire? Ben braced himself, but she stopped laughing, so suddenly; as if someone had flicked a switch.

'Remember. Be good,' she whispered in his ear. He could feel her breath on his cheek. He recoiled, as he would from a snake.

With a light in her eyes – anger? Or amusement? – she handed him the paper and a pen.

'Stop cringing and crack it, if you want to escape,' she said in a much harder tone.

Escape? Yes please. Ben focused on her alphabet, trying to calm his ragged breathing. Her handwriting was as neat as Jess's. Jess. If only he could have communicated with her, somehow.

But there was no time for if-onlys. Think! *F* stood for S. Was *J* H or T? Though Freddie would probably choose H, he thought it more likely to be T, at the end of a word.

For a few precious seconds, he dithered over whether to enter the *F* under the S or the S under the *F* in her table. But then he remembered something about plaintext. What had Freddie said? The plaintext was the pre-coded, or decoded message, conventionally written in small letters.

Hazel was an expert in codes, so she presumably used the same system.

He thanked Freddie fervently.

'You're smiling. Why?'

He glanced at Hazel and the gun and his smile vanished.

People were about to die. How could he be so callous? And relaxed? Urgently, he entered the letters under the plaintext – if it was – hoping he'd guessed right.

a	b	c	d	e	f	g	h	i	j	k	l	m
n	o	p	q	r	s	t	u	v	w	x	y	z
					F	J						

He checked his watch. Fifty-two minutes to the deadline. He hadn't enough time to crack it.

Unless… F and J were close together in the alphabet. Could it be a substitution cipher with a key? That implied G, H and I were in the key!

G, H and I were in WRIGHT.

Ballantyne would find it funny to make Marcus the key to a cipher about him. It would suit his twisted personality perfectly. So Ben tried it out, careful to remember to delete the second R, as Rufus had instructed him, and to omit all duplicated letters.

He'd wrongly suspected Rufus. He owed him such a huge apology, he thought as he concluded.

a	b	c	d	e	f	g	h	i	j	k	l	m
M	A	R	C	U	S	W	I	G	H	T	V	X
n	o	p	q	r	s	t	u	v	w	x	y	z
Y	Z	B	D	E	F	J	K	L	N	O	P	Q

Hoping it would work, under *R* he wrote C, and beneath *G* he wrote I, then continued. Soon he had a puzzling message written out.

CICERO'S FIRST'S KIND MOTHER

Ben stared at it, desperate for inspiration. If only he had Jess here, or Aunt Miriam. They would know who or what Cicero was. He looked at Hazel and attempted a smile.

'I've cracked the code, I think. It's: *Cicero's first's kind mother*.'

'Well done. I am impressed. What now, big man?'

Recognising the danger, knowing bullies love to dominate and hate to be threatened, Ben grovelled.

'This is way out of my league. Please help. Who or what is Cicero?'

'A Roman orator. A politician. Friend of Caesar's, rival of Pompey's,' Hazel replied, waving her hand holding the gun. How easy was it to accidentally fire? 'What else do you want to know?'

'Did he come to Oxford?'

Again, the manic laugh. You'd have thought he'd cracked the funniest joke ever.

'Oxford wasn't even a gleam in the establishment's eye then,' she said, wiping her eyes with her left hand, clutching the gun in her right. 'But you might be interested in his name: Marcus Tullius Cicero.'

So Cicero's first name was Marcus! Maybe that's what Ballantyne meant: *Cicero's first* meant Cicero's first name.

'Marcus? Marcus's kind mother? That's Daphne!'

'Benny–Ben–Ben–Ben, calm down.'

What the *hell* had she just called him?

'I am calm.' As calm as he could be with a homicidal maniac about four feet away.

'You're being far too literal. Not cryptic at all. What language would Cicero speak?'

'I dunno. Latin?'

'Exactly. So what's kind mother in Latin?'

'I don't do Latin. Freddie and Jess do.'

'I'll be kind. I am kind, see,' Hazel said, looking at him as if she expected him to agree. Kind? The Chief? But with that gun pointing at him, he wasn't going to argue. So Ben sat, taut as a tightrope, as she continued. 'I'll tell you. It's alma mater.'

'Alma mater?' he echoed, perplexed.

'Now, now, Ben,' she said, with such a smug smile that he knew the Dumb Ben routine was working. Unfortunately, it had stopped being an act a few seconds ago.

Hazel's smile vanished. Her mouth was a thin, hard line. 'No more clues. You've had enough. If you can't solve it, I win. People die, but that's not my fault. It's their fault, the men. They want people to die. I don't.'

'Neither do I.' Ben leaned forward, looking as beseeching as possible. 'Let's save them together, *please*.'

She was looking at him as if he were mad, her pale brown eyebrows halfway up her forehead. 'Save them? Why would I want to save them? I want my money. That's what I want. To get my money, *they* say – the men say – that people must die. Typical men, all tough and ruthless.'

'But you're not,' Ben said, going along with the image she wanted to have of herself. 'Just tell me what it means, please.'

'No. Enough talking,' Hazel snapped. 'You have one minute. Work it out yourself, or that's it.'

'That's it?'

'Fifty-nine seconds, fifty-eight…'

Ben racked his mind. Alma mater seemed vaguely familiar. Where had he heard that before? Aunt Miriam had said it recently – when? Oh yes! Aunt Miriam, you star!

'It's your old school or college.' As Jess had explained. And Freddie had taught him about plaintext. He would never, ever ignore a Winterburn trying to teach him something again.

Cicero's first name was Marcus. Marcus's alma mater was St Saviour's. It was a poncey, show-off clue, exactly fitting Ballantyne. He stood up.

'It's St Saviour's!'

She checked her watch. 'Forty-nine seconds. Well done. You might even be on time. Or it might be too late. But wait!' Wasting precious seconds, Hazel returned to the dresser and took out a small box. She opened it up to show him. Inside were four USB sticks of different colours. 'Silver is Richard and black is Peter, to match their hair. Red is both Nev, that's Goatee Man to you, and Walker, and blue is Marcus.'

'Marcus? He's innocent.'

'This proves it. And proves your mum is too.'

'Do you mean Inspector Walker?'

Hazel raised her eyebrows. 'Yes. Well done. I needed a competent insider in the police. That's why I picked a woman.'

'What about the investors?' Ben was careful to use her word. He didn't want to rile her again.

'There's plenty there for the courts to convict them, if the police are inclined to prosecute.'

They would be.

'Can I go then?'

'Yes. There's a bike outside. You can have that.'

Clutching the precious box, he raced out, hoping she won't shoot him in the back.

He sped down the stairs so fast that he almost fell, but somehow managed to keep his balance. He reached the car park, amazed he was still alive, and spotted the bike. It looked new and of decent quality.

'Wait!' Hazel called, as he mounted it. Still holding the gun, she walked over and handed him a rucksack. 'For the box.'

'Thanks,' he said, wondering if it would contain a bomb. But it was empty. He put the USB box inside it and slipped the bag over his shoulders.

'Turn right and head down the Banbury Road. It's a quieter route, and not past the police station.' Hazel smiled, knowing she'd read his mind. 'I'll be watching you all the way.'

'Huh?'

'You're carrying a tracker. If you go anywhere else at all, Marcus dies.' She waved the gun at him.

'But if not, he lives?'

She shrugged. 'Maybe.'

As he cycled out of the car park he looked back. She was watching him right enough, but he wouldn't have known it was Hazel, if he hadn't seen the transformation. Before, she turned heads. Now she wouldn't, she would be ignored.

But not by him. She was nuts, scary and exceedingly dangerous.

Was she lying about the tracker? And, perhaps, killing Marcus? Was it another con?

But she had told the truth about so many things. He daren't risk it.

Okay, Oxford it was. He only hoped he'd arrive in time.

Chapter 30

The Race for Life

The wind was with him, whipping him along. It was a single lane road through the countryside, a good route for a bike, with fewer lorries and less traffic than the bypass Hazel had driven on. As he passed house after house, Ben pumped his legs as fast as possible, still amazed that she had let him go.

He came to a small town or village called Kidlington. Traffic was busier, but he was allowed plenty of space by the cars going past. He saw some lights ahead, accelerating as they turned green, and just made it through before they turned red.

The sign saying Oxford 6 miles was a relief, a thrill and an incentive to keep his legs pumping as fast as possible. There were tree-planted grass verges in the middle of the road now, separating traffic approaching Oxford from that leaving the city. He passed a few shops, but then the fairly quiet road joined a major road, past an out of town superstore.

Ben was nervous, never having ridden in such busy traffic before, and even more so when he reached a major roundabout. He waited for two huge articulated lorries to pass, and then a couple of cars, conscious that precious seconds were passing.

He couldn't afford to stop. Hoping it was allowed, he entered the roundabout and rode alongside the cars. Nobody beeped their horns or knocked him off and suddenly, a cycle lane appeared, in the middle of the roundabout, as unexpected and welcome as rainbows. Ben entered it, and was able to stay in the sanctuary of the cycle lane as he left the roundabout. It then became a bus lane too, but there weren't any buses about, so he was able to zip along despite the busy traffic.

On the next stretch of road, he saw a reassuring sign: Welcome to Oxford. As the houses and shops started to appear, the cycle lane vanished again, so he was forced to slow down. The outskirts of Oxford seemed never-ending, but at last he spotted Martyr's Memorial, as the road split ahead.

On familiar territory now, Ben headed left up Broad Street, past the Caesars' heads of the Sheldonian and turned left onto Parks Road. He passed Trinity on his left and Wadham on his right, and at last reached St Saviour's.

He dismounted, dropping the bike to the ground behind him and raced into the lodge.

But it was empty, alarming him. He ran through to Front Quad, which was also empty, and raced round the huge lawn towards the dining hall. He bounded up the steps to tug on the ancient wooden doors, but they were locked. He ran down the steps, heart thudding, having horrifying thoughts. Had Ballantyne already succeeded? Was everyone inside the college dead?

'Ben! Are you all right?' someone called. Across the immaculate quad he saw Dr Ashcroft. Mightily relieved to find anyone alive, let alone a trusted ally, he raced towards her.

'Attack. Here. Now!' he gasped.

Her jaw dropped. 'Where? The Warden's reception?'

'Dunno.'

She checked her watch. 'It's already started.'

They ran towards the ivy-framed wooden door of the Warden's lodgings. He rapped on it without stopping. Sir Christopher Cockerell, the tall, imposing Warden, opened it himself.

'Amina and Ben! Is something wrong?'

'Ben believes we're being attacked.'

'993,' Ben added.

Rather than asking the thousands of questions Ben was expecting, the Warden turned away.

'Come in!' he called, striding back into his apartment. 'Stop eating! Stop drinking! Poison!' he bellowed.

Following him in, Ben understood the extent of the attack they had been planning. The enormous room and the vast garden beyond were packed with people – men, women and lots of children, plus legions of waiters bearing trays of food and drink. The adults and older children had frozen, staring at Sir Christopher.

'We may have been attacked by the terrorists that have been plaguing our beautiful city,' he announced, his voice loud and authoritative. 'Our refreshments may be poisoned.' He turned to Ben. 'You arrived in the nick of time. We had only just begun.'

They were all looking frightened, but as he surveyed the anxious faces, he saw no agony, no signs of pain or distress, other than the fear he'd caused. Lots of people were holding drinks.

'They poisoned water in Jesus.'

'They're just the welcome drinks. They must be fine. No one's been ill, yet.'

'I've got a sore throat,' a little girl complained.

Lady Cressida, the Warden's wife, beamed at her. 'Poor you. I believe gargling with salt, followed by lots of ice-cream, works very well for that.'

'Can I have an ice-cream?'

'*Please*!' her mum hissed, but Cressida, as she had urged everyone to call her, continued smiling as she bent towards the girl.

'Not yet, darling,' she said. 'Not until we've checked if it's safe.' She straightened up, looking distressed. 'It's shocking. This is the staff party.'

Ben was starting to feel uncomfortable. 'I could have been conned. She's a con artist. I thought it was a real threat though. It seemed real.'

'We're very glad indeed that you warned us. It could well be true. Who is this woman?' asked Sir Christopher.

'Hazel Finch from SPC.'

'*Hazel*?' Their astonishment reassured him that he hadn't been a complete idiot not to have suspected her. Clearly none of them had. But the notion that she might have fooled him again, that he might have ruined a lovely party needlessly, was sickening.

'We need to stop anyone leaving. Just in case. Could you call the police please, darling?' Sir Christopher asked Lady Cressida. 'Nigel, would you join us?'

'Certainly, sir,' a waiter answered, depositing his tray on a side table. 'Would you make sure no one touches that? Or anything?' he asked a colleague, who nodded.

'Ben, would you kindly accompany us to our kitchen?'

'Sure,' Ben replied, impressed by the Warden's courtesy and the respect with which he was treating him. Sir Christopher and Nigel looked immaculate, whereas Ben was all too aware that he was still in yesterday's crumpled (and very sweaty, after the bike ride) clothes.

He followed them into the hall and through a door on the right, which led straight into a very large kitchen. It was very bright and surprisingly modern. There were four chefs working, two women, one man and another male, who was turned away from them, but that didn't hide the unmistakeable snake tattoo on his neck.

'Can you identify anyone?' Sir Christopher asked him.

'That's Goatee Man,' Ben said, pointing at him. 'He'll have the poison.'

He reacted fast. Grabbing a cleaver he shot towards the door. Nigel tried to stop him, but he swerved, so Ben stuck his foot out. The oldest, simplest and most effective stop he knew.

It worked. Goatee Man crashed to the ground, still clutching the cleaver. Before he could rise, Nigel threw himself across his body, so Ben dropped to his knees and grabbed his legs, pinning them down.

'Gerroff!'

'Hand over your weapon,' Sir Christopher ordered.

But Goatee Man clutched it even tighter.

'You're not going to escape. There are many more of us here than there are of you. Now release that cleaver!' Sir Christopher boomed, in a voice so commanding that Ben wasn't surprised to see Goatee Man obey him.

Sir Christopher crouched to get hold of the cleaver (bravely, Ben thought, since Goatee Man could have grabbed it again and attacked him). He rose and placed it on a surface.

Someone tried to enter the kitchen, smashing the door into Goatee Man's head. He cursed.

Ben grinned, not just at that, but also mightily relieved that they had caught him at last.

'We mustn't let him escape. Have we any rope?' Sir Christopher asked one of the chefs.

'I'll go and see,' she offered.

'Marvellous, thank you. Could you be sure what the scoundrel has prepared?'

'The fruit salad. That's all,' the senior chef replied.

'He helped out on the salads too,' the youngest chef said.

'Well we certainly must scrap those,' said Sir Christopher. 'What about the cold meats and sandwiches?'

'He hasn't been near them. We did those,' said the head chef.

'The puddings?'

'I made those,' the young man replied.

'The drinks?'

'All clear. I mixed the punch,' the head chef said. 'He's not been near the bottles.'

The other chef returned with a coil of rope as Goatee Man informed them in extremely fruity language that he had only managed to poison the fruit salad, which seemed to frustrate him mightily, since no – he used other words, but Ben knew he meant children – would touch it unless their – he probably meant parents, Ben supposed – forced them to.

'We'll ask Dr Ashcroft to check every salad, savoury and fruit, just in case,' said Sir Christopher. 'That's the trouble with the staff party. So many temps. We try to vet them, but evidently it's possible to slip through our safety net.' He heaved a sigh. 'Could we pop in a few pizzas, do you think?'

'Good idea, Sir Christopher,' said the senior chef. 'They'll be ready in ten minutes. The oven's hot.'

'Marvellous. Well get those in, then help us tie up this vagabond, eh, Ben?'

'Sure. I think pizzas will go down even better than salad.'

'So do I,' Sir Christopher responded, smiling. 'But you haven't just improved the party, you have again saved lives, young man, and I'm sure your poor mother will be delighted to know that this time you did it without endangering your own.'

'Yeah.' Ben bowed his head, realising how much he'd put Mum through. If *only* he'd realised it was Hazel before. If only they all had.

The streets were a lot safer now, Ben reflected as he helped Nigel and the Warden bind the creep.

'What's your name?' Sir Christopher asked.

Goatee Man cursed.

'No wonder you've turned out bad if your parents called you that,' Sir Christopher responded, eyes twinkling.

Ben grinned. 'Never met anyone with the surname Off before.'

'It suits him though, doesn't it?' joked Sir Christopher.

'Sure does. Make sure his hands can't loosen the knot,' Ben advised, recalling how he'd escaped Nixon's binds. Or had they been Marcus's? Maybe that's how he'd escaped them. So many questions, so much to understand but first…

Suddenly, he remembered. She had been telling the truth about the code. She had even helped him solve it. She had been telling the truth the whole time. Which meant that, whilst Ballantyne had been organising this, Nixon wanted revenge on Marcus.

Where were they? Where was Marcus?

Chapter 31

Where's Marcus?

With all the college staff being at the Warden's party, no one had much of a clue what was going on in college. The porters, gardeners and scouts were usually the best sources of information, Doctor Ashcroft said.

'*Scouts*?' Ben was confused initially, but in Oxford scouts looked after the students' rooms, she explained, so were a cross between a cleaner and a parent.

'College staff, however, does *not* include academic staff. We're not staff at all,' she added, seemingly contradicting herself, but Ben had no time nor the inclination to understand. He was totally focused on finding Marcus. 'So I could help you look for him, if that helps.'

'Yes please.'

'SPC usually meet in the new conference suite, the Norrington Suite. Or the Barrington Room sometimes,' she said. 'But of course, there's the Bellingham Suite too.'

'Which is nearest?' asked Ben, trying to quell the unease in his stomach. Marcus would be unaware of Ballantyne's attack, so wouldn't know it had failed, whereas Nixon and Ballantyne would be furious, if they found out. If he was in a meeting with them both right now, they would realise he had won and they had lost. He was in terrible danger.

Regrets. Guilt. Bad decisions. If he had found Marcus first, he would still have got to the party before they started on the puddings. He could have saved him – but maybe not them, all those children and adults at the party.

So many of them could have died.

And so could Marcus. Would he already be dead?

'He's in terrible danger. Can I phone him, please? I haven't got my mobile.'

'I haven't got his number, sorry. It's probably quicker to find him,' said Doctor Ashcroft. 'Come on.'

They hurried into Back Quad. It was surrounded by the old college on their left and behind them, but to their right and ahead were newer buildings, covered in climbing plants. They took the steps to the left of the JCR, the Junior Common Room. He had to wait for her at the top.

'I'm sorry Ben, I can't run like you.'

'Sorry.'

'I know you're scared for him. I understand your fear. They are very dangerous. Shouldn't you leave this to the police?'

'I need to warn him *now*.'

'Your mother would never forgive me if I got you hurt.'

'It's not you. It's them. We've got to stop them hurting Marcus.'

They went past the old Senior Common Room.

'What's in the rucksack?' asked Dr Ashcroft. Ben had forgotten he was wearing it.

'Hopefully, the evidence to free Mum and convict them,' Ben said, again wondering if Hazel had been telling the truth. She was the most contradictory character he'd ever encountered: eye-catching one minute, non-descript the next; a kind assassin, a considerate murderer and a control freak who gambled.

According to her, now that he had prevented the mass poisoning, she didn't get paid – and hadn't she said that was her whole aim? To make money out of the threat of 993? Yet she had given him the chance to beat her and provided him with the means to do so. Without that bike, he'd have been sunk.

She was confusing. An enigma. Or perhaps simply nuts.

Nixon wasn't nuts. He was sickening. He had tried to murder again and again and again – and Ballantyne had murdered, or commanded Goatee Man to murder, all those children in the pool. He was responsible for their deaths, just as much as Goatee Man was. He was a murderer who hated Marcus and they could be together right now.

They passed the Domestic Bursar's office and approached the Norrington Suite. It was locked. Ben pulled on the handle, hammered on the door and yelled, but no one answered.

'Why don't we check the other meeting rooms?' suggested Dr Ashcroft.

Ben stared at her. Her face was impassive. She was being far too calm.

'No! No time.' In his moment of desperation, he was rewarded with an idea. 'Jess. We could phone Jess. Or any Winterburn. Do you have any of their numbers? Aunt Miriam, Uncle Henry, Freddie?'

'I have Jess's number,' Doctor Ashcroft said. 'Under J,' she added, handing over her phone. Ben was so delighted that he could have hugged her.

'You genius! Thanks,' he said, retrieving the number and dialling.

Jess answered immediately.

'Hi, it's Ben.'

'Hi, Ben. I've been asleep. How is she? We've been dying to hear.'

'Who?'

'Your mum!'

'Oh right, yeah,' he said, realising Jess was several eventful hours behind. 'Mum's still in jail and…' He broke off at the sound of approaching sirens.

'*What*? Why?'

'Long story. I need to see Marcus.'

'You got a text from him a few minutes ago. *In code*,' she whispered. '*I cracked it. Hope that's okay*?'

'That's great! What's it say?'

'He asked what's happening. We all want to know that.'

'I'll tell you soon. I need to see him first. One second.' The sirens were getting louder. He removed the phone from his mouth and said to Dr Ashcroft, 'I need to keep away from the police and see Marcus.'

'I see. The Turf would be best,' Dr Ashcroft said.

253

'Jess, text Marcus and ask him to meet me A.S.A.P at the Turf. In code. But fast.'

'Of course. You mean The Turf Tavern, don't you?'

He asked Dr Ashcroft, who nodded.

'Yeah I do, Jess. Tell him it's urgent.'

'Sure.'

He rang off and handed the mobile back. 'Thanks.'

'If it's urgent, we need to go now,' said Dr Ashcroft. With frequent glances over her shoulder, she led him down the steps into a much smaller quadrangle at the rear of the college. 'We have a secret entrance here in Clarence Quad.'

The gate was so successfully concealed behind an accommodation block that he hadn't noticed it.

'It's for night use. Or at times like these. We all have a key,' Dr Ashcroft said, rummaging in her bag. She produced a keyring and started to unlock the door.

Ben had another idea. He removed the rucksack. 'Could you give this to the police, please? But *not* Inspector Walker.'

'Your enemy?'

'On their side, Hazel said. She arrested Mum.'

Her eyebrows rose. 'Oh. I will certainly give it to someone, but not Inspector Walker, I'll make sure of that.' She stepped through the gate. He followed. There were no police cars on this narrow, old-fashioned street. Dr Ashcroft pointed up it, away from Parks Road. 'Turn right at the top, then right again. On the left there's a narrow lane called Bath Place. Go down that and you will come to the Turf.'

'Okay. Thanks, Dr Ashcroft.'

'Glad to help. Good luck.'

He sprinted away and soon found Bath Place. It was like something out of the Harry Potter films, a cobbled lane between tall medieval houses, which were smartly painted in pastel shades. It contained a 17th century hotel, a sign proclaimed. Ben expected that to be The Turf Tavern. But the hotel was relatively modern. The Turf was a 13th century inn, another sign said – the oldest pub in the world, surely?

There was a beer garden at the back, but Marcus wasn't there, so Ben went through the open doorway into the tiny pub. It looked exactly like the bars Ben had seen on Oxford detective shows, with low beams, a curved bar and low wooden tables – but no Marcus.

'Can I help you?' the barman asked.

'No thanks. Looking for someone,' Ben replied.

He returned outside to the deserted beer garden, sat down on a bench and waited, fretting, tapping his fingers on the wooden tabletop.

Running footsteps clattering on cobbles brought him to his feet. His spirits soared as Marcus entered the courtyard, unharmed.

'Marcus!' I've found the Chief! It's *H*,' he said, remembering the need for initials.

'*H*?' Marcus looked puzzled.

'Hazel,' Ben whispered.

His jaw dropped. 'You're *kidding*?'

'No. She told me. It's a con. We caught Goatee Man too. We stopped them poisoning…' Ben broke off. Someone else was running along the cobbles, very fast indeed.

They wheeled round and saw Ballantyne pounding into the courtyard, his eyes wild with fury. He was carrying a gun, which he aimed it at Ben.

'You *fool*!' he cried and fired.

Ben ducked, but Marcus launched himself forwards, between them.

As the gunshot echoed around the courtyard Marcus fell back, eyes shut. There was a red patch on his shirt, expanding at a terrifying rate, like spilled red paint.

Devastated, Ben fell to his knees and pressed his hands on the wound, trying to stem the gushing flow. His mouth was filled with an unpleasant metallic tang, but Marcus seemed unaware of anything. Ben put a hand over his mouth to test for breathing. There was a faint flutter of breath, but he was fading fast.

'HELP!' Ben yelled, tears streaming down his face, pressing both hands to the wound. But blood was welling up between his fingers. Marcus's life force was pumping out of him and there was nothing he could do to prevent it.

'Don't die, Marcus. Please don't die.'

But brave, selfless Marcus didn't seem to hear.

Chapter 32

The Endless Wait

They were all waiting at Daphne's; except Daphne, who was the only person allowed to be at Marcus's bedside. Ben had begged to accompany her to the hospital, but she had insisted he stayed at her house.

'You've had a terrible time. You need to recover in comfort.'

'But I want to be with him! I want to be with you!'

'I know, darling and I feel the same,' she'd said. 'But Marcus won't even know you're there whilst they operate. There's someone else that needs you even more than I do. Wait at my house for her.'

She meant Mum. They knew the police would release her very, very soon. At last Ben would get her back. But he was scared that he would lose Marcus, before he could even call him Dad...

He'd so wanted to prove that Marcus was his dad, as had Marcus. The test would arrive back tonight – but Marcus might never know it.

Sadness hung over him like a heavy blanket. He had a headache and a full throat, but in front of Uncle Henry and Freddie he was determined not to cry. What good would it do, anyway? (Apart from release his pent-up torrent of grief.)

They were in the lounge. Jess and Aunt Miriam were cuddling on the sofa, whilst Ben paced around. Freddie and Uncle Henry were making them drinks. Ben didn't want a drink. He didn't want anything, except for Marcus to survive.

He kept replaying those terrible moments. The uselessness of his hands in staunching the gushing blood, the precious seconds wasted before people had dared to emerge from the pub to help and Marcus's face, seemingly asleep, turning paler and paler as the seconds passed.

He never recovered consciousness. The paramedics arrived impressively quickly, people said, but to Ben it had seemed like a terrifying eternity.

It was an awful location to be shot in. There was no room for ambulance access, so they had to lift Marcus onto a trolley and push it through the passage onto the street. Ballantyne must have known that. He'd picked the perfect place to cause maximum harm. He was evil, repulsive and disgusting.

Apparently, he fled immediately, which was why he hadn't shot at Ben again, but Ben hadn't even noticed. He had been totally focused on Marcus. Trying to keep him alive. Trying to bring him back. But he'd failed.

The police had got Ballantyne now. They'd got them all, even Inspector Walker. Except Hazel. But that didn't matter to Ben right now. Nothing did, unless Marcus was safe.

Jess, who hadn't seen his washed-out face, thought he might recover. She was desperate for the phone to ring with good news. But Ben was dreading the phone ringing. It would be to tell them that Marcus had died.

The last time he'd seen Marcus was as he watched them pushing him into the ambulance. As they shut the doors, he had a terrible premonition that it would be the last time he'd ever see him. He'd known then.

What made it even more painful, even more agonising, was that he needn't have died. Ben should have died. He was Ballantyne's intended victim.

'He was saving me,' he'd told Daphne. 'It's my fault. I'm so sorry.'

They'd all shouted him down, assuring him that it wasn't his fault, that it was Ballantyne's fault, but they hadn't been there. They hadn't seen.

Ballantyne had meant to kill him.

Inspector Cunningham had questioned him for ages. They had needed an appropriate adult, but they hadn't yet freed Mum, so Ben had insisted on Aunt Miriam, and she had kindly insisted on Daphne's house.

He felt terrible for Daphne. She was as kind to him as Marcus – and to Jess and Freddie and everyone else too. But particularly to him. Although she could have been en route to the hospital, she had waited to see Ben and assure him that it wasn't his fault (wrong, but very, very kind).

He wondered if she'd like him to call her Grandma. He would like to do so, if she didn't mind. She was going to be a lovely grandma. At least he'd have her, he reflected, blinking the tears back fast, because Uncle Henry and Freddie were coming down the hall. Marcus would have been a wonderful father. But he'd never had the chance.

'You were right about Ballantyne from the start, Ben. Sorry I led you astray,' Jess apologised, over their hot drinks.

'But it wasn't Ballantyne who was the Chief. That was Hazel,' Freddie said. 'And even I didn't suspect her.'

'Ballantyne murdered Marcus. Or tried to,' Ben added, seeing mouths open to protest. 'And he set up the swimming pool.' Ben burned with anger whenever he thought of Ballantyne. It was the only emotion that could cut through the grief.

'But Hazel's just as bad,' Aunt Miriam said. 'She had Ben at gunpoint! She nearly killed him. Drink your tea, darling,' she added, to Ben. 'Sweet tea helps after a shock.'

Knowing she believed it fervently, he took a sip of the sugary, milky, drink. He didn't like it, but what did that matter? It comforted her a little, to believe she was helping him.

Towards Hazel, who had lured them all in, seduced them with promise of money and power, and stitched them all up apparently, he had mixed emotions. For ensuring the charges would stick against them, and for giving him the chance to prevent the mass murder at St Saviour's that Ballantyne had planned, he was grateful to her. But for getting the creeps involved in the first place, for temping them with money and for failing to protect Marcus and Mum and all the children who had died, he loathed her and feared her.

It appeared that she had left Oxford airfield on a privately chartered helicopter under the name of Sue Barker ('Outrageous!' Aunt Miriam had protested) but she hadn't been seen since. She had also got all the money, apparently, which was £20 million in total, £5 million from each of her backers.

'She's changed her appearance yet again, we think,' Inspector Cunningham had announced wearily, after taking another call. 'And probably her name. Looks like we've lost her.'

He had left to continue leading the search for her, busy now that there was a vacancy at the station. Besides Inspector Walker being arrested, a senior member of Greater Manchester police had been too, apparently as a result of Hazel's evidence.

'She was responsible for this. She planned it, she recruited them, and she pushed Nixon and Ballantyne to worse and worse offences, all for the sake of money. Just money. That's why those children died. That's why you nearly died. Just money,' Aunt Miriam had raged.

Good to know the rest were in jail, and that even the backers had been punished a bit – although he believed they deserved much more than losing a few million to Hazel.

Now that Inspector Walker was out of the way, the police wanted the backers too. They were trying to keep them from fleeing the country, but it would be hard to stop them, and even harder to convict them. They all had enormous wealth, powerful political connections – and apparently one was an almost unassailable minor royal.

Before they had finished their drinks, there was a key in the door.

'Daphne?' said Aunt Miriam looking stricken, putting her drink down and rising.

Would she come home if Marcus had died? Ben exchanged an anguished look with Jess, then went into the hall with her and her mum.

But it wasn't Daphne, it was Rufus. His face was ashen, his shirt stained, his expression distressed.

'How is he? Have you heard?' he asked.

'Marcus?' Ben asked, confused. Rufus had never exhibited anything other than animosity towards his younger brother. But his nod confirmed that it was Marcus he was worried about. He seemed to be on the verge of tears.

'We've not heard yet,' Aunt Miriam replied. 'Daphne – your mother – said she would call as soon as he was out of surgery.'

Rufus screwed up his face, as if bracing himself for a blow. 'How bad is it?'

'He was breathing, but unconscious, I think.'

'Ballantyne hit him from about four feet away. He was aiming for me. Marcus jumped between us. He saved my life. It's my fault he's hurt.'

'It's not your fault! It's that swine Ballantyne's. It's not your fault in any way, Ben,' Aunt Miriam said, again.

'You're both alike. You're both altruists,' Jess said. 'You'd have saved him. But he saved you.'

'He's a hero,' Rufus said. 'I knew he was. I wish I'd told him when I could.'

'I'm sorry. I'm really, really sorry,' Ben apologised, head hanging.

'I know. So am I. Heroes are hard to live with,' Rufus replied, 'But I agree with your aunt. It's not your fault.'

By now Uncle Henry had joined them and they led Rufus into the kitchen to make him a drink.

'Sweet tea's good for shock,' Aunt Miriam said.

But Rufus told them he hated tea, so she made him a coffee instead, and Freddie decided to have a refill of his.

'I'm still brewing tea. Do you want another, Ben?' Aunt Miriam asked, looking at him.

'No thanks.'

'Shall I get you some water?' Jess offered.

'Thanks. Yeah.'

The phone rang. Rufus jumped up. 'That might be Mother.'

Ben held his breath, watching Rufus's reaction, listening to his words.

'Oh, I see.' His voice was terribly flat.

Ben bit his lip.

'Okay, thanks.' He rang off.

'He's made it through the operation.'

'Oh good,' Aunt Miriam said.

Ben exhaled, realising he'd been holding his breath.

'He needed a lot of blood. They're waiting for him to wake up.'

Or not. Though the words were unspoken, they hung heavily between them. The others sipped their drinks in silence. Ben shut his eyes and tried to hope. But it was no good. He knew Marcus was going to die.

The doorbell rang again.

'It could be your mum, Ben. Come on,' Aunt Miriam said. So he and Jess trudged to the door with her.

He was dreading breaking the news to Mum.

But it wasn't Mum, it was Debs.

'Come and have a cup of tea,' Aunt Miriam said. 'I've just brewed one.'

'I'd love one, thanks. Work is as pointless as an avocado today. Without Marcus and Tricky the whole damn caboodle has come tumbling down.'

'Sorry?' Jess said.

Debs explained that the negotiations couldn't continue without Marcus, SPC's Commercial Director, and Ballantyne, the Head of Strategy.

'And without Nutcase to oil the wheels, there's just Laurel and Hardy left. And Curtis the Comatose Camel.'

'Do you mean Lord Charles and Sir John by Laurel and Hardy, Deborah?' Uncle Henry asked, eyebrows raised.

'I do that. JRK's alright, but Lord Charles is as useful as a perfume in a piggery.'

Despite everything, Aunt Miriam smiled. Debs often had that effect on others.

'I've not heard that one before.'

'You won't 'ave,' Debs replied, reverting to her childhood Yorkshire accent, as she often did when joking. 'Mine are as fresh as a baker's bap.'

Uncle Henry spluttered out his tea.

'They're what you Mancs call barm cakes, baps. Not breasts, Henry,' Debs said, causing Uncle Henry to choke.

'I didn't think so for a moment,' he eventually claimed.

They had finished their drinks and lapsed into a tense silence by the time that the phone rang again. Again, Rufus sprang for it.

'Ma, that's quick,' he said. 'Right. Oh. Good. Oh yes, that's wonderful. Oh Mother, that's marvellous. I'm so glad. Tell him, won't you?'

He rang off.

'He's awake. He's talking. He's fine!'

Chapter 33

At Last

They were all celebrating as if they'd just won the cup.

'He's going to be okay!' Rufus exulted.

'That's wonderful!' Aunt Miriam cried.

'It's amazing!' Jess said.

But Ben said nothing. He was fighting tears again. Tears of delight and relief and exhaustion. He couldn't believe it.

'It completely missed his vital organs. He was very lucky indeed.'

'Golden Boy is always lucky,' Debs said.

The doorbell rang again.

'This surely must be Sue,' Aunt Miriam said.

They rushed to the door. Even Freddie was sauntering down the hall, Ben noticed, as he pulled open the door and saw two women, both tall, both slim, but only one with the smile Ben adored.

'Mum!' he cried, throwing his arms around her, relishing the hug. It was as warm and delightful as a comfort blanket.

'Thank you so much for all your help,' the police officer said to Mum.

'I'd rather have done it voluntarily.'

'I can imagine. I can only apologise again on behalf of myself and all my colleagues, except Inspector Walker, of course.'

'It's hard to spot corruption in colleagues, as I know, only too well.'

'Thank you for your understanding. I'll leave you in peace for the rest of today,' the officer said. 'Happy birthday, Ben. You deserve an amazing evening after what you've achieved today. You too, Freddie and Jess. You can be very proud indeed of your children.'

'Oh, we are,' Mum replied.

'She's not met Robert,' Aunt Miriam said, as they closed the door. Everyone laughed.

Typically, Mum made light of her arrest and wouldn't talk much about it. Rather she wanted to hear of all the events of the day.

If they hadn't saved so many lives, Ben was sure they would have been in far worse trouble over the codes they had hidden from the adults (and the police), but as it was, they got a mild remonstration, which was quickly interrupted by Debs.

'Good job you hadn't given your phone to the police, Benbo. You'd never have known how to crack that final code unless they'd given you so much practice.'

'At gunpoint! Wait till I get my hands on her,' Mum fumed.

'Thankfully, I don't think the police will give you the chance,' Aunt Miriam said. 'Or you'd be in prison for murder too.'

'How you held your nerve, Benbo!'

'Do you think she genuinely believed she was merely a con artist? That she didn't bear any responsibility for the murders?' Mum asked.

'Yeah, I think so,' Ben replied. 'I think in her mind it was the men who'd wronged her, the men who wanted to murder and the men she wanted to rip off.'

'She was getting her revenge on the patriarchy,' Debs said.

'But she is as guilty of murder as they are,' Mum said. 'The fact that they paid Goatee Man – don't we know his proper name now?'

Ben shook his head. 'Unless he's called Beep Off. His first name was a swear word I'm sure Uncle Henry wouldn't like me to repeat,' Ben said. He had a feeling Hazel had said something about his name, but he'd forgotten.

'And neither would I,' Mum said, giving him a warning look. 'I hope they lock Nixon and Ballantyne up for life. The fact that they paid that monster to carry the attacks out doesn't make them any less guilty of the murders. They wanted them, they planned them, and they paid for them to happen.'

'Yes, they are equally culpable,' Aunt Miriam agreed.

'They'll be questioning *them* all night tonight,' Mum said.

'Did they question you *all* night?' Jess asked, looking distressed.

'No. They let me sleep,' Mum claimed, but Ben knew her better than that.

'Sure. And the Birthday Fairy brought my presents.'

'She did a pretty rubbish job, then,' Mum replied. 'She left mine at home.'

Debs grinned at her. 'I don't know. The fairies of today, eh, Sue?'

'I wish I *had* got your present. I haven't given you much of a birthday, have I?' Mum said, looking ashamed.

'It's been the most exciting birthday anyone ever had.'

'I'll bet. It's still your birthday now. Shall we go out?' Mum asked, feigning enthusiasm. But Ben knew she was exhausted.

'No thanks. I'm shattered. And filthy.'

'We've noticed,' Freddie shot back.

'I'd like a shower and to put on clean clothes. I know! I'll wear one of Marcus's shirts.'

Rufus looked confused. 'Why? Haven't you got your own?'

'He bought me some shirts for my birthday.'

'Oh, right. Just shirts?' he said, back to sneering about his brother. But Ben knew the truth now. Rufus loved his brother. 'He's always been far more interested in fashion than ecology.'

'You're both lifesavers, Rufus. You save animals' lives and he saves people,' Debs said.

'True,' he said, looking flattered.

Mum flashed Debs a curious look. Debs returned a bland smile. Teasing each other. Ben left them to it and went upstairs to get freshened up.

The shower reinvigorated him. He felt much better afterwards, particularly when he put on his new shirt. He selected the blue, his favourite colour, and also because it matched Daphne's tie best. If she came back, he'd put it on, he decided, but for now an open collar was more comfortable and the night was far too warm for the jumper. He put on the socks she had given him. They were so soft; the most comfortable and stylish socks he had ever owned.

He felt fantastic going downstairs.

'Wow!' Mum said. 'My little boy, so grown up. We've ordered in a takeaway, by the way. I hope you don't mind?'

'No, that's great,' Ben replied, remembering that he hadn't eaten since breakfast.

'We ordered lots of your favourites,' said Mum. 'That blue suits you perfectly.'

Ben brandished an ankle at her. 'Check out these socks!'

'They're gorgeous, aren't they? You look so grown up.'

It seemed she'd never stop saying it. Ben smiled. 'I feel more grown up.'

'After the last fortnight, you've had to grow up,' said Aunt Miriam. 'You faced down the Chief. And won! I'm so proud of my nephew. And my children. You've saved hundreds of lives.'

'Thank goodness,' Jess said.

But someone was missing.

'Where's Rufus?' Ben asked.

'He'd forgotten something. He's coming back.'

There was then a discussion about how surprising his reaction to Marcus's injury was and how he must love him.

'Blood's thicker than water, after all,' Aunt Miriam said.

'It's about 3–4 centipoise in adults,' Uncle Henry replied, looking surprised when they all laughed.

Rufus soon returned carrying a very large parcel.

'It's for you,' he said, handing it to Ben. 'Happy birthday.' It was wrapped in brown paper and was much heavier than the shirts.

'Thanks. You didn't need to.'

'You're my son, or my nephew. Yes, I did.'

'It's lovely of you to be so generous to Ben,' Mum said, as he unwrapped it, trying to suppress the ungrateful thought that he still hoped his dad was Marcus.

Rufus' present was amazing. A red box with Oxbridge Chess on the front contained handmade chess pieces, Oxford in dark brown and Cambridge in cream.

The figurines represented important figures in the history of each university town: the king and queen were King Henry VIII and Lady Margaret Beaufort for Cambridge and William Herbert, 3rd Earl of Pembroke and Queen Caroline of Ansbach (who?) for Oxford. Uncle Henry and Freddie were fascinated by the set too, but were miffed at first that Henry VIII didn't represent Oxford, until Aunt Miriam reminded them that he became a murderous monster, whereas William Herbert was such an important Elizabethan that Shakespeare dedicated his First Folio to him.

'And he founded Pembroke, of course.'

'Who's that?' Jess asked about a Cambridge bishop.

'Isaac Newton,' Ben murmured, knowing that Newton was a superstar to Uncle Henry and Freddie, and that whoever he was, John Locke couldn't possibly compete. He turned the page of the guide book. 'That's Carfax tower,' he said, pointing at the rook. The pieces were amazingly detailed. 'This is awesome, Rufus. Thanks so much. I'll love playing Naz on this.'

'I'll give you a game now, if you like,' he said. 'I'll even be Cambridge.'

'You *can't* be Cambridge!' Uncle Henry couldn't have looked more affronted if Rufus had grabbed Aunt Miriam and kissed her.

'Ben can't be Cambridge on his birthday, now, can he?' Rufus teased.

'True. We couldn't do that to him,' Freddie replied, enjoying the old joke that Cambridge was rubbish.

'I suppose not,' Uncle Henry conceded.

They hadn't even got the pieces set up before the takeaway arrived.

'That was quick. They said thirty minutes, but it was only twenty-five,' Uncle Henry said.

'They must have been on Oxford time,' Rufus said.

'What's that?' Freddie and Jess chorused.

267

Ben couldn't resist a dig. 'You mean there's something about Oxford you two don't know?'

'I'll explain over supper,' Rufus promised.

The food was from Daphne's favourite Chinese, and Mum had made sure all Ben's favourites were there: barbecued spare ribs, crispy aromatic duck, prawn dumplings and chicken satay skewers.

Over the meal, Rufus did explain Oxford time. (If he hadn't, Jess and Freddie would have had him on the rack). In olden times, he claimed, every town and city had its own time, with noon being when the sun was highest in the sky.

'Really?' Jess flashed a sceptical look at her mum.

'Yes. He's quite right,' she confirmed.

'It was only when the railways were introduced that they needed to coordinate the clocks, and GMT arrived,' Rufus explained. 'So Oxford time is five minutes earlier than GMT.'

'At 9:05 each night, you can still hear Tom Tower being rung a hundred and ten times,' Uncle Henry said.

'Why?' Jess asked (of course).

'There were a hundred and ten Christ Church scholars originally, in the time of Henry VIII. It's to call each of them in for the night before the gates are locked at 9 pm. Which is 9:05 by GMT, but 9 pm Oxford time,' he explained.

'It has its own language, its own customs and even its own time. It's another world,' Ben said. 'No wonder Lewis Carroll wrote about *Wonderland* here. He had plenty of inspiration.'

'Now you've got a grandma here, you might get to know it much better,' Mum said.

'And an uncle. Or dad,' Rufus said – and this time, he wasn't scowling or spitting it out. In fact he almost looked hopeful. Ben and Mum exchanged a look. Evidently, she had noticed too.

Though everyone had feasted, there was still plenty left in the end.

'We can heat it up for Daphne when she gets home,' Aunt Miriam said.

After dinner Ben enjoyed two games of chess with Rufus. The first time he got slaughtered by a new opening – high risk but foolproof, apparently, unless you defended correctly – but the second time he was prepared and managed to counterattack and win.

'You're not bad,' Rufus said.

'Thanks. You too.'

Next Jess and Freddie wanted a game, so Ben let them play and went and sat with Mum. She was in the sitting room with Aunt Miriam, Debs and Uncle Henry (though he was looking at his phone).

'Shame we've got to stay tomorrow,' Mum said, because the police wanted to interview them both again. 'I can't get a room at Henry and Miriam's B and B.'

'I'll bet Daphne will let you stay here. She's really kind.'

'I wouldn't like to intrude. She'll have a heck of a lot of bedding to wash already.'

'I don't think she'll worry about that,' Aunt Miriam said.

Suddenly, Ben had a terrifying thought.

'Do you think she'll mind Marcus saving me?' he asked. Now she was over the shock, she'd have time to think. 'He's her son, after all. He's half of her. I'm only a quarter.'

'Of course not. She'll be delighted that he did,' Mum responded.

'Can you imagine how heartbroken we'd have all been if that awful man had succeeded?' Aunt Miriam said.

'He nearly did. He nearly murdered Marcus.'

'But thanks to the wonderful medics, he didn't succeed.'

When Daphne at last returned, at 21:35, she revealed that it had been a much closer call than anyone thought.

'He'd lost so much blood. A couple of minutes longer and we'd have lost him. But thankfully we didn't and he's fine. In fact, he wants to speak to someone.'

'Do you want a cup of tea?' said Mum.

'I'd rather have a glass of wine. Could you ask Rufus to open a bottle, please? I've got to call the hospital.'

'Certainly.' Mum left the lounge.

Daphne rang the hospital on her mobile and spoke to a nurse.

'Is he still awake? Oh good. Yes, please.' Daphne looked at Ben. 'He wants to speak to you.'

Ben was thrilled. He felt a bit shy as he accepted the receiver and said hello.

'Ben, is that you?' Marcus sounded exactly the same.

'Yeah. How are you?'

'Fine. I was very lucky.'

'So was I. I was so scared for you. Thanks for saving my life.' The words sounded so trivial for such a gargantuan gift, but Ben couldn't think of anything better.

'I'm very glad I did. I'll bet your mum is too.'

'She is, yeah. I'm wearing your shirt. The blue one. And your mum's socks,' he added, lifting a trouser leg to show her. Daphne beamed. 'You were awesome to save my life like that. So kind.'

'It was self-interest, that's all. You're carrying half my genes around.'

For a second Ben looked down at his jeans, confused, but then the fog cleared.

'What?' he said, the thrill in his stomach rippling up his body as he grasped the implications of Marcus's words. 'That means…'

'Yes, it does,' Marcus cut in. 'I'm officially your dad!'

'That's awesome!'

'I couldn't be happier either.'

'Can I tell everyone?'

'Definitely. I'd be shouting it from the rooftops if I wasn't stuck in here. I hope your mum doesn't mind?'

'She doesn't,' Ben was happy to tell him. She had grasped what was going on and had run over to hug him.

'Can I have the phone?' she asked.

Ben handed it to her.

'Marcus, thank you for saving my son. Our son. Your bravery was amazing. I'm delighted for you both. And for myself. I'd hoped it was you.'

Ben couldn't hear what Marcus said. But from Mum's reaction – startled, then pleased – he knew it was good.

'I'd have to think about that. It's early days, but maybe, yes.' Mum handed the phone back to Daphne.

'Was he asking you out?' Debs asked.

Mum shook her head. 'Asking me about work. Apparently, Lord Charles is about to retire, and of course Nixon's gone and so has Ballantyne. With so many vacancies upstairs, he thinks they might be prepared to promote me. Or us.'

'About blinkin' time! But never mind that. Congratulations, Benbo,' Debs said, slapping his back. 'What a wonderful dad you've got. Delighted for you.'

Everyone came over to congratulate him. Even Uncle Henry patted him on the back. Ben was pleased that Daphne was delighted.

The only person who seemed disappointed was Rufus.

'But you didn't want to be Ben's dad,' Mum pointed out.

'I was getting used to the idea. But I suppose I'll have to be his uncle.'

'I'm his uncle,' Uncle Henry said.

'Well, so am I, it seems. Brothers in arms again, eh, Henry?' Rufus said.

'You can have him to stay whenever his mother's on business,' Uncle Henry replied.

'*Dad!*' Jess protested.

'No he can't, and your father knows it. Ben's got to be in South Manchester to be able to get to school,' Aunt Miriam said.

'He might be able to stay with Marcus,' Daphne said.

'Great!' Ben declared, delighted.

'Well, we'll have to see what he says,' Mum said.

'I know exactly what he'll say: *how soon?*' Daphne said.

'Cool! Where does he live?' Ben asked excitedly.

'Hale village,' Daphne replied. 'There's a station.'

'It'll go to Heaton Chapel,' Mum said.

Uncle Henry checked on his mobile. 'It does. There's a direct train, but some change at Stockport.' He looked as pleased as Ben.

'You'll still come and stay with us, though, Ben, won't you?' Aunt Miriam said, looking so hurt that Ben went and hugged her.

'If that's okay, yes please.'

'Of course, it's okay.'

271

'It's obligatory,' Jess said, looking stern.

'But if I get promoted, there might not be as much travel,' Mum said.

'A lot of things will change,' said Daphne.

Mum smiled, her eyes shining with happiness.

With one arm encircling her, Ben looked around the room. Uncle Henry and Rufus were chatting together on the far sofa, enjoying bonding as uncles, Debs and Aunt Miriam were chatting and laughing on the biggest sofa, and Daphne and Jess were getting to know each other on the nearest sofa, whilst Freddie was setting up a new game of chess.

Apart from Marcus (and Robert) his entire family was present, and he couldn't be happier about it.

His head was starting to swim with tiredness, but he was determined to stay awake until midnight.

'Happy birthday, my darling.'

'It's the best birthday ever, now that I've got you back.'

It was lovely cuddling her. It had been the weirdest birthday ever, and it been a more terrifying, exhilarating and heart-breaking Easter break than he could ever have possibly anticipated.

But right now, it was just about perfect. Birthdays couldn't possibly get better than this.